*Dedicated to my wonderful husband Shaun
who makes all things possible.*

For Humanity

SURVIVAL INSTINCT

FORCES OF CHANGE

SANDI GAMBLE

SURVIVAL INSTINCT – FORCES OF CHANGE

Published by Ambitions Publishing 2018

Original cover concept by Karen Baumanis
Book cover design and formatting by Book Cover Cafe

ISBN:
978-0-9922846-3-3 (pbk)
978-0-9922846-5-7 (hbk)
978-0-9922846-9-5 (ebk)

Visit: http://www.sandigambleauthor.com

CONTENTS

CHAPTER ONE
THE EVENT

Even now, all these years later, I can still feel the sensation just as I felt it that day. The terror is buried deep in the marrow of my bones, though to show fear would be weak, even after all that has happened, I still find myself reaching out for Jace's hand and not finding it. You'd think that time would have tempered these things, these memories and feelings. Perhaps it has. But coming back here… has brought it all back to me. Confusion sets in as I try to sculpt two worlds into one. It is so strange, to be sitting here now, in this place. This very place. For all this time, I had considered this place to be a sacred place. A holy place. A once innocent sanctuary where many times Jace and

I had spent time together. Often, I had considered making a pilgrimage here, but I never found the... the what? The courage? The will? Only heartache.

Whatever had been lacking in me simply remained lacking... until now.

So strange. My memory of that day still seems so fresh, yet the day itself seems distant and unreal.

With mixed feelings, I entered this place with trepidation. I had longed to return each and every day that had passed. In so many ways, I considered it my spiritual "home". And yet I could not feel "settled" here. I paced back and forth like an animal. I was edgy. Skittish. I felt a cloud of uncertainty and threat all around me. Every noise made me tense. Every movement made me shift my attention. Everything put me on edge. But slowly, my body began to relax. I could feel myself become more accustomed. Not safe. No, I would not say I felt safe, but I felt comfortable enough to settle myself down and sit cross-legged on the ground in the warm sand, to breathe slowly and steadily; to rest my hand protectively across my belly and to allow my thoughts to return to that day and the days that followed.

* * *

If I was still that girl, the girl that I was before my world was turned upside down, then perhaps I would weep. But that girl is as much a stranger to me as this place has become, as the world that I knew has also become. Recognizable and fresh to me in memory but not in reality. So my eyes remain dry as they dart back and forth, watching, watching, watching.

"Watching for what?" I wonder as I let my gaze fall to my hands that now rest in my lap. I grip my hands into fists and study them closely. These hands… they are not the hands of a young girl; they are the hands of a warrior, calloused, torn, rough. They are scarred from the battle, and too much blood. I release my hands from tight fists and study my palms. The lines crisscrossed there tell me no secrets. Shaking my head, as if in disbelief of what had happened, I hang my hands down at my sides and comb the soft white sand next to me. The sand's rough texture and warmth against my stiff fingers both pleases and surprises me.

I remember the feel of this sand. So true. So real. Like every other aspect of that day. But one. There is only one piece of that day's puzzle I struggle to find. A missing piece lost somewhere in my emotions and heart. No matter how hard I try, I cannot seem to conjure up Jace's face.

So much is crystal clear to me. The battles I've fought. The battles yet to be fought. Why can't I see him? Why can I remember him only by his absence and not by his presence? Why does his name remain such a talisman to me and yet his face eludes me? My memory of him is wistful. I have only myself to blame, Jace had warned me. If only I were not so tempestuous. I can only remember the remembering of his face, not his face itself.

As my body continues to relax, my weariness takes over. I am so tired. My head feels as if it weighs a hundred pounds. Keeping my eyes open is an effort. Thinking is an effort. Even relaxing is a greater effort than I have the energy for! I am beyond weary and yet I cannot rest. My body aches in every muscle and joint. Even so, that ache is dwarfed by the ache in my heart. My longings and memories torment me.

I can hardly stand the burden I carry and yet I know I will not be free of it, not as long as my days stretch forward into the future.

Look at my legs! Scarred and bruised, covered in dried mud, my skinny legs might still be mistaken for the legs of a young girl. But they will never again belong to a young, innocent girl. And the bruises and still open wounds will take time to heal, perhaps more time than I have left. Who knows what the future now holds for me?

The snap of a limb above me gains my attention. Although I cannot see anything there, my body is once again on high alert. I cannot stay here any longer. I cannot stay in any one place long. Not if I am to survive. And survive, I must. For I am not the only one who has suffered. I am not the only one who has lost. I am however the one who has broken every sacred law that I am obligated to uphold as a global citizen.

I am not the only one for whom innocence is a distant, mocking memory.

For we have all lost and sacrificed much in the pursuit of our goal, our goal together as a global community.

I am also not the only one who has lost the man that I loved. I am simply one of the very last who might be able to still act.

* * *

We have not properly met. My name is Arianna, Arianna Vay. But I go by Ari. Six years ago, when the world changed, I had just turned twenty-one. I felt then no different than a child. Now, at twenty-seven, six long years since, there are moments when I feel like I might be a hundred and twenty. But it has been only six years. Only!

When I am able to rest and think back, it is astonishing to think of the girl I was. I remember hurrying excitedly to the door at the sound of his familiar arrival. Jace had arrived to pick me up so that we could "paint the world fantastic" as he'd so cheerily said; so we could celebrate.

Five years before that, we had both entered Military and Further Education Studies at the Pandec Military Academy. Both graduating with honors after our thorough education, we were set to start work at the Ministry on the following Monday.

I swung the door open with a big smile on my face. My smile widened even more when I looked over Jace's shoulder and saw his brand new vehicle. "Oh my, Jace..." I said, my eyes widening. "It's amazing..."

He grinned then turned and looked behind him. "Oh that?" he said with exaggerated weariness. Then he laughed. "My parents gave it to me for graduation," he said, clearly more than a little pleased by his gift. "So, m'lady, shall we?" he asked, extending his arm to me. "Your carriage awaits!"

Jace was never one to boast about himself, but I understood how proud he must have been. The gift that his parents gave him would have required many credits. It was not something to be done lightly. However, it demonstrated how much he meant to them and how proud they were of his success. Jace respected his parents for their thoughtfulness.

I giggled as I extended my arm into his. He could be so charming and silly when he wanted to be. Despite his absolute seriousness about his studies, and his determination to be the best he could be, Jace was absolutely fun.

"Where to?" I asked when I was seated in the cabin.

He glanced over at me and smiled. "I thought we might begin with a quick walk along our favorite beach."

And romantic. Did I mention, romantic? We had both looked forward to this day for the longest time. Our course of studies and the examination period were harrowing. There were days when we had barely enough time to glance at one another across a classroom, or a lab, or in the library where we spent our downtime hours. We would simply smile at each other and once again place our attention back on our studies.

But we had done it! We had graduated with the highest of honors and were ready to take on the bright future ahead of us both. And the future before us did seem bright indeed. Our positions at the Ministry would allow us to accomplish all we were trained to do. We would have real responsibility and autonomy. We would no longer be interns or students.

Jace input the destination and before long we were pushing away from the curb.

What I did not know as Jace pulled away from the front of my house was that, in addition to the things he was carrying in his pack, he had tucked into his pocket something else, something special. He carried with him a small box that contained a wedlock ring.

How could I have known that in his mind and heart, our celebration that day would include a proposal? Had I known, I would have understood the reason he glanced over at me the way he did, the sly smile he gave me as we headed towards our beach, and the reason why his eyes glittered with happiness and joy.

He had such wonderful plans for that day. But his plans, like so many plans at the time, were destined not to come to fruition.

As we walked along the shoreline, with the sea lapping at our feet, we talked about how we had come to this very beach hundreds of times since we were children. For us, it was a place of happiness and sanctuary. A place where memory returned us to when we were just children and splashing through the waves together was innocent fun. As we walked, he bent down and teasingly splashed some sea water my way.

I laughed easily as I danced out of the way of the water.

Everything was always so effortless when I was with Jace. So comfortable and safe. But, even in that safety, I knew something had changed. In the past months, our time together had taken on another aspect; an edge. I could not deny that when I saw him now, I no longer saw just a dear friend but someone who awakened deeper feelings in me. Sometimes, I was surprised to find myself feeling awkward around him. Other times, I felt shy and coltish. There were times I wanted nothing more than to have his hand in mine and yet other times when I shocked myself as I imagined what it might be like to kiss him!

And then there was the evening when we did kiss for the first time.

All these moments and hundreds of others played in my thoughts as I skipped away from him; he scooped up more of the tide as it gently rolled to the shore, laughing as he chased me and showered me in the white froth.

"Enough!" I cried, giggling from the game. "I surrender!"

His eyebrows arched. "Surrender?" he asked, his eyes glittering with mirth. "And what terms shall I demand?"

I stopped giggling and, feeling suddenly serious, said, "Any that you care to make!" And I meant it. His face suddenly became serious, and then he smiled again. His perfect smile!

If only that day could have remained as perfect as it had begun! We continued to play along the shore, laughing and talking, making plans, thinking of the future, sharing thoughts about our classes and our professors as well as what our fellow graduates would soon be doing. In short, we were imagining the world that we would inherit.

We had learned enough to know that it would be far from perfect, but with the training we'd received we were confident that we would be able to do what was required of us to make it what we needed it to be. Our training had made it clear that the dangers were real and close by, but manageable. With vigilance and skill, we would be able to place our mark on the world that would be handed to us.

Little did we know how foolish and short-lived that confidence would prove to be? The sun shone down on us as we continued to walk along the familiar shoreline. But then, in a turn that will forever cause a chill to form in my soul, the sky suddenly clouded over.

This then was the day, the day the earth – our world – changed; the day that the world as we knew it was taken away.

"Was there a change in the forecast?" I asked Jace lightly, hearing in my own voice a hint of fear. "I thought it was to be sunny all day."

Jace pressed his hand against his eyes, shielding them from the sharp shafts of sun glare showing between the rapidly gathering clouds. "No," he said. "I checked just before I left my house. There was no suggestion of clouds…"

His voice trailed off as if we both understood that, forecast or no, these were not ordinary clouds.

"What is happening?" I cried out. "Jace!"

He turned to me. "What is it, Ari?" he asked, as he gripped my hand tighter.

"Look!" I shouted, staring out toward the ocean.

I don't know if he started to speak, but if he did, what presented itself to us at that moment choked back whatever he might have said. Not ten minutes earlier, we had been frolicking in the gentle surf. The sea-blue waters struck the soft sand and turned to foaming white bubbles. But now, as the sky above us darkened, the color of the sea did as well. Far from the beautiful sea-blue it had been, the ocean became an angry blood red.

"What is happening? What does it mean?" I asked Jace.

It would not be the last time I would cry out those questions, nor the last time my questions were met with dumbfounded silence.

Neither of us knew what any of it meant, only that from the moment of its outset, it filled us with fear and trembling. Only Jace's presence next to me kept me from bolting from the shore, although in which direction and for what purpose I could not have said. All I knew was that I wanted to run, run as fast and as far as I was able. But contrary to that desire, my feet were planted in the sand as the blood-sea rolled over them.

I turned and looked at Jace, the bravest person I'd ever known and what I saw on his face just then shocked me. His expression was a mask of fear, of confusion; his face showed him looking out at a world turned upside down on a moment's notice.

Fear was not an emotion or feeling that I had much familiarity with. We did not inhabit a world that evoked fear. Our world was safe, protected, controlled.

At least, it had been.

"What's happening, Jace?" I screamed again.

He was frozen, his face that horrible mask, his grip on my hand so tight that I nearly cried out in pain.

And then there was the heat. All around us, heat suddenly weighing on us like a heavy blanket.

"Jace! Jace!" I screamed, pulling on him, dragging him further onto the beach and away from the water. "We have to go home!" I shouted. I knew that my father would know what was happening.

But each step was a struggle. Moving Jace was like moving a stone statue.

"Jace, Jace!" I cried, hot tears burning my cheeks. "Please!"

What had happened to him? Why was he so frozen? Was it something within him, or was it some bitter magic in the air? And what was this crawling, unrelenting heat that seared our skin? This was not a familiar sensation at all. Climate was controlled in our world.

I worked to calm the panic rising within me. "Think, Ari! Think!" Although there was nothing in all the books and lessons, I'd ever learned that had prepared me to understand what was happening, at least one part of my training was helpful – all the exercises that helped me not to panic! But even with all the training, I could feel that I was fighting a losing battle, this was no normal circumstance though.

"Ari!" I shouted out loud to myself. "Focus!" I turned my attention away from the sky and the sea and looked directly at Jace. "Breathe!" I shouted at him. To my great relief, he seemed to respond. His chest rose and fell a bit more rhythmically. Somehow, I managed to pull my hand from his grip. I shook my hand a couple of times to try and get the circulation moving in it. When I could feel my fingers without pain, I pressed them against his wrist, trying to assess his pulse.

It was easily one hundred and fifty beats a minute.

"Jace! Jace! Relax!"

He did not seem to respond. Not knowing what else to do, I raised my hand and brought it across his face, slapping him. His cheek reddened slightly, but his expression remained unchanged.

"Jace!" I grabbed him by his cheeks and pulled him toward me. I kissed his right cheek and then his left cheek. "Jace, please," I begged. "Come back to me. Don't leave me alone like this!"

I couldn't believe that I hadn't got through to him. This was not the Jace that I had known all my life. "Jace, Jace," I cried, kissing him full on the lips. I could not think of anything else to do.

He still did not respond. Desperation was taking over my thoughts and my actions as I shouted his name as loud as I could while, at the same time, drawing back my fist and then bringing it crashing against his cheek. His head snapped back. His eyes widened as he repositioned his head. Instead of the frozen mask of terror on his face, his expression shifted to one of amazement.

"Ari," he said.

"Oh, Jace…" I stared at him. "Jace," I whispered, reaching out to grasp his arm, "what's happening?"

In all the years I'd known him, I'd never before known him to be as confused or worried as he seemed to be just then. "I don't know," he confessed, his eyes wide and his body tense.

We stopped, unsure of where to go next. Nothing seemed like it was only a few moments earlier. What had begun as a hint in the air, as gentle and soft as a summer breeze rustling through the smallest of leaves, had begun to whip those same leaves and branches now, causing them to dance madly above our heads. The air itself, only a short while ago so still, now seemed electric with uncertainty.

"What's that?" I asked, unable to keep the jittery tremble from my voice.

"What?" Jace asked, turning too late to see the brief slice of light that cut through the still darkened sky.

"I thought it was a firefly…"

"A Firefly? In the morning?"

Of course, he was right. But I couldn't imagine what else the small bursts of light could be.

"There!" I cried when another appeared. I poked my finger toward the burst of light and, although the light was gone as quickly as it appeared, I felt a curious buzz, like an electric jolt, on my finger.

"Oh!" I exclaimed, pulling my hand back.

Jace watched me but remained quiet and thoughtful.

"Did you see?"

Even though he did not answer, I knew he had. I could tell by the confused expression on his face. He was trying to understand what it could be. But, like me, it didn't make any sense to him. "It's as though infinitesimal pockets of gas are being ignited…" he said, almost to himself. I will say one thing, his tone was one of fascination, not alarm. But even his objective observation was unsettling. I could feel the small hairs on the back of my neck stand up. What could be causing these "pockets of gas"? Even as we considered this unusual phenomenon, it seemed to increase in frequency and severity. Soon, even as the breeze picked up, the air became more electric and constant microbursts of light and energy filled the air above and around us. We twirled around and around, trying to determine if there was a single source of energy.

"Finally," Jace stated with some fascination, "I remember reading about Ion storms in the library. Although I've never seen one, this comes pretty close to how I'd imagine it to be."

When I stopped, I shook my head. "I don't like this at all," I said, giving voice to the fear that was gathering in my thoughts. "Not one bit."

He drew a deep breath. I could tell that, although he was brave, much braver than I could ever be, he too was unnerved by everything that was happening. It was as if nature herself was trying to warn us about something. But what?

Just then, a distant rumble moved across the sky.

"Did you hear that?"

My question made him smile. "Of course, I heard it. Whatever else is happening, I have not gone deaf."

"Very funny," I said, sneering at him.

The noise faded, only to have another rumbling noise move across the sky. And then another. Soon, as it became louder, it also became more familiar. It was the rolling of distant thunder, growing louder and more ominous as it neared. Over and over, again and again, until the noise no longer came in rumbling waves but was a constant din. Crack! Crack! The next crack of thunder shook me so hard I almost lost my footing. That last crack of thunder was followed by a bolt of lightning that, despite the early dawn light, lit up the world around us, creating shadows in every tree and shrub.

Then another.

And another.

We found ourselves unconsciously ducking down as if to dodge any possibility of being struck by lightning. Hiding from the lightning and even from the anticipation of the lightning. The noise and the light were enough to make anyone cower. Only Jace's renewed courage and determination allowed him to continue to keep his eyes open and observe what was happening all around us.

"Fascinating," he managed to say, in between the crashes of thunder.

"What?" I cried out, barely able to make out his words over the thunder and crackle of lightning splitting the sky.

"I said, it is fascinating," he shouted raising his voice as loud as he could, leaving me still straining to hear.

"It's horrible," I shouted back, not at all fascinated by these strange events.

"But look," he said, pointing into the lightning shower. No longer just chromatic darkness and light, the lightning produced the colors of the rainbow.

I grasped his arm tighter. Perhaps under normal circumstances, I would find the color shower interesting, even beautiful, but the truth was that it had me completely unnerved. The hair on my arms was standing up. My flesh was goose-pimply. I was shivering. I felt cold and hot at the same time. I could not stop my heart from racing. It took all my concentration simply to keep my eyes open and to not collapse into a quivering ball. Which I probably would have done if not for Jace. I would be too ashamed for him to see me completely fall apart. After all, I was a strong woman and had spent many years ensuring that he knew that.

"It's because of the pollution," he shouted after a moment.

"What is?"

"The colors. The dust and pollution are acting like a prism and bending the lightning into all these colors."

"What pollution?" I quipped back at him… he knew the pollution levels of the earth were now nearly nonexistent.

"But what about the lightning itself?" I wanted to know. "This is like no storm I've ever experienced." I could feel hot tears rolling down my cheeks, and there was nothing I could do to stop them. "What is happening?"

He nodded his head. He combed his strong fingers through his thick hair. "Can't say I don't agree," he said.

"Oh, my!" I screamed out when the rumbling grew even louder, becoming so pronounced that it actually knocked me off my footing, causing me to let go of Jace's arm and to stumble. I barely managed to keep my balance and catch myself before I fell. The thunder – if indeed it was thunder – reverberated through the sky. The earth itself quaked in distress.

As Jace reached out to help me steady myself, a crackling sound like a whip being cracked filled the sky, only louder. It was as if the heavens were being torn apart. No, not the heavens, the earth.

"Oh no..."

The growing crackling sped faster and faster. Until it hit the curtain at the speed of sound only to rip through, causing a noise that was beyond deafening. I screamed, but I could not hear my own scream above the noise, a noise that came from no place and every place, from deep within the earth and from the reaches of the heavens above us, a noise that was so loud, so penetrating, and so massive that it had an indescribable physical character.

We looked to our left and then to our right. Before us and behind us. But there was no sanctuary and no escape. No place to hide. The noise was everywhere. On and on and on, ever louder, ever more frightening, as if it were proclaiming absolute dominion over the earth and the sky.

I felt lost in the noise. I could no longer stand. I was tumbling and rolling. I was descending into what seemed to be a pit filled with noise. Louder! Louder! Louder!

And then it was gone. Completely, utterly unavoidably gone.

Its absence was the more stunning and disturbing for how absolutely it had been there. If possible, I would have to say that the silence was even more frightening and overwhelming than the noise had been. The noise had pushed me out, but the silence drew me in, into an awareness that everything around me, everything that I had ever known and ever loved had been taken from me; drew me into an awareness of how everything I had once embraced had changed.

I was terrified. Lost. Even the things I could see and recognize seemed new, different. Alien and unfamiliar. A shiver went through me, one that seemed to come from someplace deep in my soul. I wanted to hide. To curl up in a ball and make whatever was happening simply go away. Nothing I had ever learned had prepared me for whatever was happening around me.

I wanted it to be a dream, even a very bad dream.

I longed for a time of better dreams when my dreams told of a world yet to be realized, not a world stolen away. I longed for the dreams I'd enjoyed when I was a small girl, when, each night my father would tuck my covers around me, and before he would kiss my forehead and wish me sweet dreams, he would tell me stories.

"The one about the forest?" I might ask. Or, maybe one of the great wars from long, long before. Or even some other event or great person, heroic or otherwise. But he never repeated a story, not once. Each night was a new story and a new lesson; a new story of how the world had been, before the change. Then my dreams that night would magically take me to that once existing world so that, as I grew to be a young woman, it seemed I had inhabited both the world that was and the world that once was long before, both at the same time.

But neither the world that was, or that once was resembled the world that presented itself to me now. No story my father had told me, nor lesson he had taught in any way prepared me. No place I had visited in my dreams, nor thought I'd ever had, nor wish I'd ever wished, prepared me for this horror before me.

No pearl of wisdom passed along from generation to generation over the course of time; passed along unchanged and unchanging, filled with wisdom and truth, visions and precepts, could give meaning to these events that were happening around me.

I was lost.

The memory of my father's voice and his image did not serve me at all. Did not comfort me. Did not guide me. The sound of his voice, once so real in my memory, trembled and vanished. The words of my teachers, so dear when I committed them to memory, could not help me. My studies mocked me.

All that I had striven to learn; all the hours I had devoted to the books of wisdom, the late nights, straining my eyes as I committed the words and lessons to memory; all that now proved futile.

Where once there had been pure white sand, crystal blue water, and exotic fish swimming amongst beautiful multi-colored corals, darting playfully through the strange shapes, now there was only a barren landscape on the ocean floor. Or what is left of it anyway?

There were no fish and no colorful corals. No crystalline blue water. Just rust-colored pools of water, grit black sand and ... and not much else. It was all gone. Everything.

Where had it all gone? What had happened? That I could not fathom; could not imagine...

The sky was leaden, dark grey. Heavy, it weighed on me and my thoughts. And still, there was silence, deep and unrelenting. Even my own heart, still pounding in my chest, was silent.

No bird chirped. No leaves sang in the breeze. No animal made its presence known. No cry, no moan, no breath.

The world that had witnessed my most innocent moments was gone.

I had the sense of familiarity if not familiarity. A vague déjà vu sense of having been in this place, but there was nothing about it that felt safe.

"Jace?"

I was surprised at the sound of my voice. It *was* my voice. It felt so odd, speaking. It sounded like something spoken in a vacuum, which is to say, it sounded as if it had no sound at all.

"Jace?"

He didn't answer. Didn't wait for me to say another word. He grabbed my hand and pulled me towards his transport. I don't know what his thinking was, but I was thinking only of leaving, getting back to the safety of my home and the care of my parents. Whatever excitement that had accompanied our journey that morning was long gone. Now all that remained was a hollowness I'd never known before.

Once we were safely strapped in, Jace started the engine. It too seemed to hesitate, as if the events occurring around us affected even its performance. But then it sprang to life, and we lifted off and sped away in the direction we once knew to be home.

CHAPTER TWO
THE ACADEMY

Never Bow Down

That was the Academy's motto and a lesson to us all; never bow down; not to anything or anyone. One was to always be the master of one's self.

As we flew home, I tried to focus on those words, whispering them to myself over and over again.

Every day at the Academy, regardless of core lessons, the same message was drilled into our minds and our hearts... *Never. Bow. Down.*

From the time I was a child, I had known that the Academy was one of the elite institutions of our society. However, it was only when I began to study there that I would come to learn just how elite. Our Academy, *Pandec,* was one of a handful of Military Academies that were strategically positioned across Pulchra.

The name *Pulchra* is derived from the ancient root meaning, "pristine" and in the case of our moderately-sized island-continent, it was an apt name. Located in the middle of the South Pacific Ocean with Australia, the USA, and Chile – or, at least, what was left of them – as our closest neighbors.

The formation of Pulchra was the result of the same seismic activity that resulted in those massive land formations being nearly decimated. As it was, by 2025, climate change had already driven the majority of humankind into habitable bunkers deep in the ground and safe from the unrelenting heat and solar rays that had turned the Earth's surface into a roiling desert of heat and dangerous gases.

The long process of creating and perfecting the bunkers began decades earlier, near the turn of the century. By then, human disregard for how their actions impacted global climate patterns reached a tipping point. The polar caps and other ice sheets melted in an ever more rapid process; sea levels rose significantly and, with no prospect of a refreezing of the ice caps, it never reduced.

Life on the surface became more challenging. Not only were vast population centers inundated with flooding seawater but more and more severe weather patterns lashed out against the interior plains of the continents. Tornadoes once thought unimaginable became the norm. Sleet the size of large stones damaged every structure. Violent thunderstorms brought about regular power outages. Crops were threatened as were supplies of potable water.

As was the way it had always been, the wealthy and elite managed to hang on longer than most. They were able to purchase or take land that remained relatively safe and to build homes that were protective against the ravaging changes. Meanwhile, the poor and the workers were moved to the crude spaces being carved out underground. Ultimately, as more and more activity was conducted from safe bunkers hundreds of feet below the surface, they took on the feel of true living spaces. The wealthy began to migrate from the surface to the bunkers as they continued to grow in complexity and luxury. Soon, the bunkers became vast networked communities and cities.

With ever-quickening certainty, reality made the decision for the final hold-outs above the surface. Life had become a subterranean reality as the majority of the Earth's elite inhabitants finally went underground.

Then, in 2080, seismic monitors within the bunkers picked up new, unusually violent activity. Seth Forester, a senior seismologist, working for the governing council, was one of the first to chart the activity.

As he moved through the rows of earnest young researchers, diligently studying their holographic monitors, several of the researchers hit their alarm buttons at once, calling attention to "something of note" appearing on their monitors.

Seth moved quickly toward the scientists.

He did not need their interpretations to understand that they had picked up something of concern. Still, he was too senior a researcher – and too experienced – to feel particular alarm.

"Let's monitor this closely," he said, looking over the shoulders of a number of associates who were watching their three-dimensional monitors. "Right now, it might simply speak to an anomaly. But if you note increased activity, please inform me immediately."

And so, those first researchers stayed glued to their monitors, reading and interpreting the data as it streamed in. Soon, other researchers began to pick up similar disruptions. In those first hours, the seismic activity seemed to dance around the globe, showing up in disparate places, making it difficult to discern a pattern to the activity. After all, living so deep in the ground, seismic activity was a way of life. No one in the bunkers was immune to the regular tremors that accompanied life below ground on the ever-more challenged planet.

"Dr. Forester!" one of the technocrats shouted out suddenly, real alarm in her voice.

He lifted his attention from another monitor and looked in the direction of the young technocrat. The urgency in her voice had him moving quickly toward her monitor. He was soon standing behind the slight girl with long, straight black hair. Her almond-shaped eyes were wide as she moved her hand toward the three-dimensional, holographic display. "Here, sir," she said, indicating a shelf deep under the sea. "The activity is following a pattern that is not dissimilar to what I'd seen when I studied the great earthquake."

He leaned forward, peering intently at the display. He could not help but feel pride in her ability to recognize a pattern in the disparate seismic activity. Even so, he shared her alarm. "Yes, you are right," he said after a moment. He drew a deep breath to make sure his voice was under control. Then he touched the communication device at his shoulder. "Please inform the President that there is significant – and dangerous – seismic activity." He waited a moment before continuing. "This is *not* a test. I repeat. This is *not* a test."

He had no sooner completed his message than an overhead alarm began to sound in the speakers that were placed throughout the bunkers.

"Code Alert Red. Code Alert Red. Please proceed according to instruction…"

As the alarm sounded and was repeated, the quiet bunkers quickly came alive with activity. People moved quickly, but calmly, as they found their way to the most secure areas of the bunkers. Regular training and alarms had prepared the population for events such as this. When the alarms sounded for an actual event, the time spent in the secure areas was almost always limited to a few short hours – hardly enough time to worry about the next meal.

This time, it would be different.

Above the bunkers, at the earth's surface, computers were adjusting the position and placement of the vast solar arrays which provided energy to the bunkers and oxygen.

While the increasing temperatures made habitation on the surface more difficult, the ability to efficiently harness solar energy had transformed subterranean life into something that more and more resembled what life had once been like on the surface albeit with significant differences. Comfort was never an issue. The bunkers were calibrated for temperature and humidity. Crops were planted in vast greenhouses. CO_2 was removed via huge exhaust operations while oxygen produced by the plants was concentrated and pumped through the bunkers.

Meanwhile, the people moved calmly and efficiently from their home and work pods toward the more secure areas.

'This is not a drill. Repeat, this is not a drill. Please move to your designated area with appropriate haste. This is not a drill'.

"Come along," mothers urged their toddlers as they pushed and prodded them along the tiled hallways. Even though they had done this any number of times, there was something about this alarm which unnerved them. As they moved their children on, they looked up nervously at the speakers embedded in the high ceilings.

Although no one said so out loud, they had reason to be nervous. Regular drills were part of life in the bunker. Occasionally, a tremor would necessitate a section of the bunker to spend time in the safe areas. However, this was the first time in anyone's memory that the message, *'This is not a drill'* had been broadcast with such urgency.

It was clear that something of note was happening.

But what exactly? No one knew.

For most of the people in the bunker, the earth's surface might just as well have been a distant planet. Most had never ventured above ground or even shown much interest in it. The bunker was a comfortable cocoon. Born after the great migration to the bunker, the vast majority of inhabitants never experienced the changing seasons or the way that day and night followed one another, making regular twenty-four hour periods, seven days a week. They did not know what it meant to see the leaves on a tree change color, or for the world to "come back to life" in the spring. They knew about life above ground only intellectually, through reading books or experiencing multi-media studies. They had never experienced "fresh air" to know what it smelled like.

They could, however, reasonably produce a chart of its chemical components.

Three-dimensional displays in school and holographic experiences were the closest they'd ever come to navigating a mountain pass or standing in the pounding surf as the waves broke against them.

The smell of flowers came from those raised in greenhouses. All flowers and plants, whether for consumption or research were genetically modified. The only samples of pure breeds of anything – plant or animal – were safely locked away in a number of redundant scientific labs where DNA structures and species' stem cells were stored in the very unlikely event that they were needed. And to ensure that our race, the human race would never be lost to history, a second lab called the Doomsday Seed Vault was hidden away in the Arctic and contained not only the seeds of every known plant but also the DNA of many Arc residents and animals. Everything had been thought of.

The bunker was, for most people, both a real and figurative cocoon. It was a climate-controlled space where all needs were quickly and effortlessly attended to. A ski vacation was "taken" in one's living room, before a huge screen. Experiential glasses and amusement park quality "skis" allowed each member to enjoy a very realistic experience of skiing – without traffic jams, lift lines, cold, cost, or the potential for broken bones. Indeed, the idea of a ski vacation requiring warm clothes was laughably retro! Some people were said to enjoy "nude" skiing vacations – without fear of the snow chilling their nether regions.

Indeed, for most of the inhabitants, the image of the bunker as a cocoon fell short. In truth, it was more analogous to a womb, safe and all providing. Only a few with youthful curiosity pushed through towards the surface and away from the restrictions of bunker life, away from the safety and the direction of the bunkers. For most of these, the strict educational and socialization program effectively rid them of their curiosity. For the small handful of those who the behavior modification did not prove successful, there were more dramatic methods. Ultimately, the extremely small number of people for whom such relentless curiosity could not be curbed became part of an exploratory elite.

As bunker scientists had come to acknowledge and appreciate, there were a very small number of traits and qualities that they simply could not control. Some were, of course, pathological. But there were others that had promise. Those that had the potential to benefit the community needed to be nurtured rather than blunted.

To acknowledge that there existed any variant that could not be fully manipulated and controlled was to acknowledge a reality rife with risk, but upon deep study and debate, it was determined that it was a risk that carried enough potential benefit to be considered worthwhile.

The vast majority of the students at the elite academies were individuals who were the progeny of the elite. However, there was a vital minority who had demonstrated such innate qualities. Only a very small percentage of the academies' students were both children of the elite *and* holders of such innate qualities. But these individuals were the ones who were ultimately recognized to be vital to the bunkers' survival.

Of course, none of this was on the minds of the people or the governing committees as the seismic monitors continued to show increased activity, and the population entered the safe areas of the bunker, a massive, global undersea earthquake rocked through the landmass on the ocean's floor. The land surrounding the Pacific Rim, already reeling under the pressure that global warming imposed on its ability to stand, began to erode and crumble into the sea. This collapse set off a complementary chain of events. The initial seismic events undermined the landmasses surrounding the rim and gave rise to a tsunami that threatened land one hundred miles inland from the coast. Also, the collapse of land further raised the sea levels, creating an additional storm surge that flooded the remaining land two, three, even four hundred miles from the shore.

The aftershocks, nearly as strong as the initial quake, continued to destroy large chunks of land, decimating much of what still remained of North and South America.

The bunkers, designed to withstand a force equal to multiple nuclear warheads, found themselves challenged to withstand the force the quakes unleashed.

The bunkers, stable entities deep in the bowels of the earth, suddenly became living, writhing things. Hallways that were level to the micron buckled and torqued. People moved on all fours to avoid being thrown to the floor. In the safe rooms, people were thrown up and down. It was worse in the control and science room, where the technocrats and researchers monitoring the events of the quake were thrown about like rag dolls. Few, if any of the researchers were without injury. Even those belted to their desks were bloodied from hitting their heads on monitors or from being hit by flying objects. Others suffered more serious injury, some of them mortal. Bodies were left inert in the hallway. The strangeness – and horror – of the situation was forgotten in the chaos and determination to monitor events and minimize the damage.

Forester had been tossed to the ceiling and then dropped back to the floor, sustaining a serious concussion.

"Dr. Forester are you all right?" Marybeth, a young intern asked, kneeling alongside him.

He held his head in his hands. "Yes, yes," he said. He tried to stand up, but he could not. He dropped back into a sitting position.

"Dr. Forester, you must rest," she insisted. She looked around for assistance, but she could see that there was no one able to help. She quickly assessed whether he had any other injury, broken bones or serious bleeding. Thankfully, he did not.

"I can't rest," Dr. Forester insisted, but his voice was foggy. He tried to get to his feet but could only remain unsteady on one knee. "There's no time. I must..." He pressed his hand against his head. The pain was blinding, but he had to work. His responsibilities were too important.

"Help me," he said to Marybeth, not noticing that her own hair was matted with blood from a similar injury. "Please."

She got him to his feet and to a desk with a functioning holographic display.

Everyone in the safe rooms felt the upheaval of being thrown about. Children cried for their mothers. Mothers clutched their children tightly, looking around anxiously for their husbands – all of whom were called up to their specific duties in the bunkers.

Ultimately, even though the arc was engineered to withstand such powerful forces, the bunker system was critically compromised. Above ground, solar panels were flung about like toys. Venting systems were crushed by shifting rock, and air vents were lost. Exhaust systems had been destroyed, and whole passageways had caved in.

The bunkers convulsed along with the earth. Ceilings could not be distinguished from floors as the bunkers twisted and turned with the seismic catastrophe. The numbers who perished were essentially uncountable. As with most "perfect" systems, when compromised they turned out to be worse than no system at all. The systems designed to sustain life transformed the bunkers into death chambers. Those who survived the initial quakes suffered horrifically in the days and weeks that followed, most perishing at the end of their suffering.

Only a small percentage managed to survive and, almost exclusively, their survival had more to do with luck than intelligence or design.

Meanwhile, the upheaval that caused so much damage to the bunkers also brought about fundamental change below the ocean. The seabed, roiled by the twisting and turning of the earth, pushed up from the bottom of the sea to the surface a new, large continental island mass.

And so it was, that Pulchra came into being; a new world had been born and was pure from any contaminants left behind by man. It would become a pristine and beautiful land, free of human habitation after the purge of 2025... but, I find I digress from the story I mean to tell...

On the first day of the Academy, Jace and I sat next to one another, anxious and nervous to begin, but just as anxious not to betray the jitters we felt. We were in a large auditorium in which every seat was filled with other sixteen-year-olds, each no doubt as anxious as we were. Of course, we did not know that then. As I glanced around, all I saw was resolute and determined faces on serious, prepared students.

"I don't belong here," I whispered to Jace.

"Shh. You most certainly do. You of all people are better prepared than all of us no doubt."

I shook my head. I was about to say something when the auditorium was plunged into darkness and before us on a large screen, the image of the Military Academy's Headmaster, Colonel Williams appeared before us.

"Youngsters," he began, using the term almost as a pejorative, "welcome." Never had a "welcome" sounded less welcoming! He cleared his throat as if that was the final comforting word we would hear from him. "You are here because you represent the best and the brightest of your cohort. While it is true that every one of your peers will attend an education program, few will be confronted and challenged, yes challenged, with the level of learning and training that you will have.

"We have learned over many generations that children, or 'young adults' as you no doubt preferred to be called, need support when it comes to disciplining their thoughts and actions.

"In short, children are reckless with their thinking and their actions. Anthropologists tell us that there was a time when such recklessness was permissible, even lauded." He made a face as if he had bitten into something very sour. "But we are long past such societal foolishness.

"You are here, in this Academy, because Military Academies are perfect environments to discipline thoughts and actions. Here, you will learn to be brave, to be smart, and to be ready…"

I glanced sidelong at Jace. Ready for *what*? I wondered.

"Idleness in thought or action only leads to trouble," Colonel Williams continued, his voice dry and harsh. "Here, you will be on a non-stop learning curve, morning and night, seven days a week, four seasons a year, keeping your minds focused and sharp. Otherwise," he went on, his voice taking on a cautionary tone, "it is very possible that you will fall by the wayside. And that is something none of us can abide."

He went on to present the psychological, developmental and societal statistics which demonstrated clearly that age sixteen was the exact time when the academy could be most successful; sixteen, the most important formative year before one became an adult.

"Lose the sixteenth year, and you lose the adult," he intoned.

Studies had shown definitively that between the ages of sixteen and twenty-one the final developmental aspects of learning and personality become set. To the extent that if society controls those years, society controls the adult. Perhaps more importantly, the studies made clear that if you teach a young adult to learn during those years, he or she will be able to continue to learn until they are eighty and beyond.

Lifelong learning is a direct function of the actions taken during those five formative years.

Initially, the research had been dismissed. For decades and decades, there had been the presumption that it was during the earliest years that such formative learning took place. Society had devoted incredible resources to early childhood education and training and only saw marginal positive results. Rather than question the assumption for too long, the response to these weak results was to throw more resources at early childhood concerns. Only when creative thinkers who were willing to quantify research results were able to be heard above the "common knowledge" was there a sea change.

As a result, the entire structure of education shifted.

Every significant aspect of personal and communal development come to focus during those years. Teamwork, a sense of community, responsibility… all took hold. Teach a young adult to care about others during those years, and the individual will have a sense of group responsibility and community for the rest of their lives.

For most of human history, lack of real appreciation of the vital importance of this period in a person's life allowed peer group pressure to exert the greatest control over the forming adult.

That was no longer acceptable.

As Headmaster, Colonel Williams continued, "Peer pressure weighs down on all of you at this time in your lives. Look around you. What these people think about you really matters to you. Unfortunately, they are no more capable of benefitting you than you are of benefitting yourself. So," he went on, his fingers forming a pyramid in front of his angular features and steel blue eyes, "we do not intend to allow your peers to determine your thoughts."

"And how do your peers exert their influence? Passively and actively. Through gestures, facial expression, advice and, of course, bullying. As our social scientists have taught us, peers tend to bully each other into some form of social order."

"It is only natural. However, we do not intend to allow the bullying that comes naturally to you at this age – a function of insecurity, you should know – to impact negatively on others. You are all born with incredible potential. Our goal is to make sure you realize that potential – whatever it may be."

"It is unacceptable to us, to you and to our society that you do or be anything less."

I sensed a number of students in the auditorium fidgeting in their seats. At sixteen, none of us wanted to be told that in essence, our freedom was not our own; that it belonged to an institution, even one as exalted as the Military Academy. So we heard the Headmaster's words about bullying with mixed feelings. No one liked bullying. We all had learned of the damage bullying did. But we also understood that it had been declared illegal years ago and few, if any of us, had ever felt the bite of its harshness. The penalty for bullying was harsh, and one feared not just by individuals but families as well. For it was incumbent upon families to teach their children not to be bullies.

Unlike the many years of human existence when young people were made to feel responsible for their actions, now, until the sixteenth year, it was the family that was responsible for nearly every aspect of a child's development and behavior. Parents, not school, served as the primary source of direction and education. Although many of us did attend instruction, education – of any kind – was not compulsory. Even though I did benefit from some formal lessons, my own early years were spent in the company of my mother, who guided me in my understanding of the world – a task and responsibility that she took great pleasure and seriousness in pursuing.

Once a woman had a child it was considered her responsibility to care for, raise and educate that child until their 16th year. She left all else behind until then. The father played an integral role in a child's life also, using his spare time to impart wisdom, historical events and the moral code to which the child would conform. These roles were considered the highest priority for any family, and it was gladly embraced by both parents.

My education did not begin with letters or books but with the world itself. From when I was still in the sling that my mother carried me in, she would take me out to explore the world. For it was the world itself that was the greatest classroom that could be imagined.

The fundamental lesson she taught from the beginning was survival.

"Do you see these?" she would say to me, lifting my hand to touch the edges of a brilliantly green leaf. "These are the Eidenhorn. They carry good medicine within them."

Aloe Vera. My first experience with the aloe vera plant was when I was three and fell, cutting my knee badly. Pressing a cloth on my leg, mother carried me to the woods where she came upon the aloe vera plant. She set me down and, as she broke open the plant and extracted its thick, milky sap, she reminded me of the lesson she'd taught me about the plant's healing powers. Then she gently dabbed the liquid on my knee, soothing it.

The marsh mallow plant was used to ease colds and respiratory ailments. Gotu kola. Chamomile to soothe my belly when brewed into a lovely tea. Peppermint.

So much of the natural world was beneficial. She wanted me to know, and to recognize the beauty and benefit of these plants. In particular, she loved to have me identify and take the bloom of the Echinacea, crushing it into a paste or using it as a leaf to steep in hot water.

"Echinacea is one of the most beneficial plants in nature," she taught me.

When I was older and able to walk, she made sure to point out not only the beneficial plants but also those that could be harmful if not used wisely. The more I came to understand the natural world, the more complex and fascinating it became. When I was a young child, I thought of plants as being good or bad, healthy or poisonous, beautiful or plain. But as I grew older, mother taught me that sometimes the danger with certain plants had less to do with their intrinsic qualities and more to do with other things.

"When you see these…" she told me, pointing out the sharp, orange-colored leaves sticking stiffly from low, bristled stems,

"… steer clear of the path." Then she looked forward and back carefully as if to make sure that the path was clear.

"Why, mother? Are they poisonous?"

She shook her head. "No, they are benign, neither good nor bad to humans. But they attract the low boar, and you do not want to be nearby when a low boar comes rooting for food."

The lesson taught me that plants were, of course, valuable not just for their medicinal uses but also as food for humans and all sorts of animals. And sometimes it was not a good idea to be close by when animals were feeding. To demonstrate the truth of her statement, she made sure that I was close enough – though far enough away to remain safe – to see two low boars approach along the dusty path in search of food. They were ugly, horrid creatures. Their fur was dung brown with dull, grey highlights. Their eyes were beady and black, moving back and forth constantly. They had long, pink snouts with two horns on either side, as well as a horn in the middle of their foreheads. And, true to their name, they stood on four very short legs, so short and low to the ground that their round bellies looked as if they grazed the path as they waddled along.

"Watch," mother whispered to me as we waited from our safe vantage point, upwind and behind a thatch of trees. "They have very poor eyesight and rely on their sense of smell, so they don't know the other is nearby... yet."

I shivered as I felt her arm instinctively tighten around me.

The two low boars approached along the path from opposite directions, both seeming focused on the plant and not on each other.

"The smell of the plant still overpowers their smell of each other," she whispered. "But that won't last much longer."

Their sense of smell seemed completely focused on the plant, but then, when they were no more than thirty feet on either side of the plant, they both stopped at once. They tensed and suddenly looked uncomfortable. They craned their heads, snorting softly. Then, they began to paw at the dirt path.

Mother gripped my shoulder, making it clear that something was about to happen. She brought her face close to mine.

Suddenly, the two low boars let out pained, screeching howls and began to charge toward one another. Faster and faster, they charged. It was remarkable that they moved so quickly and nimbly. Their low, squat bodies seemed like blurs of muscle. Faster and faster until it seemed to me they reached full speed just as they crashed together, head to head.

The concussion and thud of their collision with one another seemed to compress the air all around me. It wasn't until they bounced away from one another that I realized that I'd been holding my breath! I looked into mother's eyes and saw a reflection of my own feelings – although she had likely witnessed a scene like this many times.

The air was electric with their violent determination to attack one another. They butted each other. They gored one another with their horns, spilling blood on the path, staining it a dark, red color. Each time they fell away from one another, they pawed the soft path and readied themselves to attack again. Over and over, they continued to ram one another until they were so numbed and stunned and bloodied that they wandered off in opposite directions, tottering on their short legs.

My eyes were wide after witnessing that event. My mother's eyes were also filled with the fascination of the event. However, in addition to her feelings about the event, she was smiling knowingly. "Did you notice," she observed, "that neither of the two boars ever got to feast on the plant."

It was only when she pointed it out that I realized that she was right! In addition to being battered and bloodied, the two boars were still hungry!

"Cooperation, rather than conflict, would have seen them both satisfied," she noted with a knowing smile.

Point taken.

However, as important as that lesson was, it was not the essential one. Survival was, after all, always the foundational lesson my mother was teaching me. She emphasized that point the morning she held me as we watched the two boars. "What I want you to never, never forget, the most important thing about this morning is to be always vigilant. Remember, if instead of one of those boars you had been on the pathway, the boar would have rammed you as violently and determinedly. And," she went on, her voice dropping to a soft whisper, "I'm afraid, you would not have been able to batter back to a draw."

She gave me a gentle nudge. Although she made her point with some gentleness, I understood what she was saying, and I took it to heart. Whenever I saw that plant, I looked carefully around me, and I made sure to stay clear of the path.

In fact, no empty path saw me approaching without being very wary and cautious.

For mother, nature was a living, breathing lesson – not just information. She taught me to recognize the colors of different flowers and to understand *why* those colors were so important, whether to attract buzzing bees or to deceive possible predators. She taught me how different kinds of leaves are able to hold moisture differently and how certain plants turn themselves to face the sun throughout the day.

She taught me to respect the differences in clouds that some portended violent storms while others were as benign as the fun shapes I conjured up in them. She taught me to read the movement of the breeze and to weigh the moisture in the air. I came to know, along with the sailors on their sailing ships, that a red sky in the morning was a warning of rough weather to come whereas a red sky at night was a delight.

I remember laying on the cool grass with mother, as she pointed out the shapes and constellations in the sky, one of my favorite pastimes. I remember asking her one time if she believed that there may be life out there on any other planet. Mother simply responded, "I believe there is, but we have not yet proven ourselves worthy of a visit." And she let out a small laugh. To mother anything and everything was possible. "Although," she spoke gently and convincingly, "many years before the purge a spaceship was said to have crashed in a place called Roswell in New Mexico. For many years it was rumored that the government had found two aliens at the crash site, one deceased the other was detained in a bunker deep beneath an area kept for such paranormal oddities. It was never proven." And so just like that, we moved on to other things that mother had to show me.

"Do you see," she would ask me, "there, those three stars? That forms Orion's belt."

She pointed to other stars. "And there, Perseus, the Hero. And Ursa Major. Do you see there," she went on, pointing to the heavens, "Ursa Minor."

For a long time, I could not visualize the shapes and characters of the constellations, but over time I began to see what the ancients had seen in the night sky, a continuous play of characters and images. The stars seemed to come alive for me then. What's more, mother taught me that the stars were of practical use in addition to how they enlivened the imagination. She showed me how to use the stars to find my way in the pitch dark night.

"If you pay attention to nature, you'll never be lost," she advised me.

She showed me how, by staying as still as the night itself, I could hear the crickets to know which direction to go in.

The education I received from my parents was not limited to the natural world. It included visits to museums to observe artwork or the history of inventions. I was fascinated by the displays in the museums. To see how people thought about religion and god so long ago was an eye opener, later I would learn how many wars were waged over this diety. God is no longer a part of our society which is probably why we live so peacefully. I could not truly grasp the concept of who God was and why people had so many religions, so I cast any thought of it aside.

And how they lived! It was in the museum that I learned how people in primitive times, in the early 2000s and before, managed their lives. So primeval, so challenging, so wasteful, no wonder the world as they knew it collapsed on itself, imploded. To say that humankind as a whole was to blame for the problems that escalated them to the point of no return is an understatement. Each person had a role to play, each person had a responsibility, as they still do now, but most were willing to let, but a few carry the whole burden for them.

As you can imagine, even at my young age, my parents were dedicated to my education. Being so dedicated, they would not, nor could not, rely on my mother's insight alone. And while there were some formal tutoring sessions, so much of how I learned about the world was through play.

It surprised me to learn that the primitive understanding of play was that it was essentially frivolous activity, little more than a distraction during idle hours. We have come to understand that play is not only a very important way to learn but perhaps *the most* important way to learn. Remembering that survival – of both the individual and the community – is fundamental to everything I was taught, the lessons I gained during play took on exaggerated value.

By playing, I internalized lessons about teamwork and cooperation, lessons that were vital to how I grew up, as it was to all those I grew up with.

Play was relatively unstructured, which was, I supposed, the real definition of play. Whatever structure play took on was the structure those of us playing imposed upon our activity. We determined rules. We determined objectives. We determined the best or most successful way to achieve those objectives. We learned to win with grace and lose with dignity. We learned to communicate.

One thing we shared with primitives was a sense of longing for those long-ago days of play. When long days running about in the warmth of the sun, and days spent in what might have appeared to be activities without rhyme or reason was, in fact, providing the groundwork for all that we would become in the years to follow.

Sometimes play did benefit from some "facilitating" from an adult, someone to help articulate goals, rules, and successful teamwork. Play could also be an activity spent alone. Both outside and at night, when mother would let me spend time in the relaxation pod.

Primitives could only dream of something like the relaxation pod. Ah, even now the memory of the relaxation pod slows my heart rate and calms the racing of my thoughts. When I was young, it felt like it was the most natural thing in the world to settle myself into the cushions of the soft, reclining chair, place the cap brimming with electrodes on my head, slip on the bubble goggles and headphones and engage in a full, three-dimensional, multi-sensory experience.

Although it was called a "relaxation" pod, there were times that the experience I had while using it was anything but relaxing! One afternoon, I might experience the acceleration of gravity as I skydived from an airplane at twenty-five thousand feet.

Another time, I might find myself deep sea diving or swimming with great white sharks. And other times I might find myself floating on those big, fluffy white clouds across a clear blue sky.

Whether my experience was adrenaline producing or relaxing, every aspect of it was real, from the sensation of gravity to the smell of the sea's salt water. The Pod included both historical and modern activities, which was another way to open up my views on the world both as it had been, and as it was.

My parents were committed to my getting a complete education. In this regard, they stood out from some of their peers. Unlike many other parents, who chose to keep their children out of any formal educational environment until the compulsory age of sixteen, my parents had set very real goals for me, based on their own experience.

My father had become a successful professional, and he expected nothing less from me. "Not succeeding is not an option," my father declared simply. "You will do at least as well as I have done."

Even so, participating in a formal education like primitive Western society expected their four and five-year-olds to do, would have been barbaric! It wasn't until the tender age of twelve, just as I began to develop the physical and emotional signs of pubescence that I was sent to a study center to learn the fundamentals of mathematics, Pulchran society studies, history and the structure of scientific inquiry.

Some of my parents' friends could not understand my parents' determination to send me for formal education at such a tender age. Neither could many of my own peers.

"Ugh, how can you stand it?" Penina, the red-haired girl who lived close by, asked after I had been attending the center for several weeks.

More than her words, I knew by the tone of her voice and the expression on her face that she was expecting me to find the experience tortuous. Although I felt a pull to answer according to her expectations, the simple truth was that I enjoyed the studies.

"I like it," I said simply, shrugging as I skipped around her.

"You *do*?" she asked.

She made a face as if she'd bitten down on a sandwich with sand in it. "I cannot imagine…"

To me the rest periods in-between lessons when we got to play together were my favorite time, my skinny legs and arms had the lines of a child and no lean muscle. However, I ran and played with the boys as well as girls proving I was a genuine tomboy and quite the adversary.

"I would positively *die* if my parents forced me to do anything so horrible." Penina retorted.

"But it's not horrible," I told her. "It's really quite fun. And exciting, actually."

There was a part of me that wanted to point out that *of course*, she couldn't imagine… that was her weakness, a lack of imagination and curiosity. However, I already sensed that such a response was not only pointless but snarky and totally unacceptable.

For me, the studies were far from tedious. The truth was, I felt absolutely invigorated by my studies. Often, I wished I could go to *more* classes, not fewer. There were times when, even with the workload, I wished I was able to attend more than just the two days a week when classes were scheduled. The truth was, I *did* enjoy the material enormously. And it had nothing to do with the fact that these studies were designed to ready me for the selection test at the Military Academy. When it came to learning, I was fortunate to find the learning itself to be satisfying, absent any other goal.

The only way Penina and some of my other friends could even fathom my enjoyment of the classes was if they presumed me to be so slavishly goal-oriented as to want desperately to get into one of the premier academies – another goal they found hard to understand. Even so, however that factored into my parents' decision to send me to lessons, it had nothing to do with my own enjoyment. As much as I appreciated my parents' ultimate goal in sending me to these studies, that goal hardly colored my enjoyment of learning which, as it turned out, I loved doing for its own sake.

An added benefit to the classes was that a boy who had grown up in the neighborhood was also in the classes. That's right, Jace.

Living in the same neighborhood as Jace, we had crisscrossed paths many times during our hours of play and learning. As often as we were on the same side, we were on the opposite side in our games. Mostly, he was just another boy in the relatively large scrum of children who played together in our neighborhood. But as we got closer to going to classes, and I learned that he would be going as well, we spent more time talking, and I found him to be fun and funny, and totally interesting.

In class, we often studied together. It was then that we became good friends – although he said that he had always thought I was special. I was certain he was only saying that, though. It turned out that, in addition to enjoying our group playing, he and I both shared a love of learning – and sometimes the most esoteric things.

"Did you know," he asked me one day as we walked in the hallway between classes, "that when a butterfly flaps its wings at one corner of the world, it causes a hurricane on another."

I didn't know whether to take this literally or figuratively.

That it might demonstrate a physical reality struck me as being odd. What would happen if there were butterflies at various places on the globe all flapping their wings at once? So I asked him if he thought that the observation was a literal one. That gave him pause.

"Hmm, interesting question."

We went back and forth for a while, and it was the most remarkable give and take! I would say more than his intelligence in considering his positions and articulating them, it was his absolute pleasure at having the chance to challenge himself and me with the conversation. I actually think it was during this discussion that we formed our first, deepest bond. Jace was a remarkable person, extremely intelligent, focused and determined. As a child, he had enjoyed the way his mother and father introduced him to the world, just as mine did for me. But, like me, he sometimes felt lost and that no one else seemed to enjoy learning as much as he did. Like me, he depended on adults for his intellectual stimulation – or through his own devices. It wasn't until we were engaged in our discussion about butterfly wings and hurricanes that he felt he'd found an equal.

Curiously, it was during the conversation that I first thought of myself as intelligent. I mean, if I could parry with Jace, who was *obviously* intelligent, then maybe I was intelligent too. I mean, I guess I always knew I was smart but I didn't feel the edge of it the same way Jace did. I was able to get lost in my adventures with my mother, or in the museum pieces, I observed. I guess the best way to understand the difference between us was that I was usually focused on the "what" and the "how" and Jace was focused on the "why."

Together, we found comfort with one another, but there was also enough competition in us to challenge each other and make each other laugh. In short order, we discovered that we enjoyed being with one another more than with anyone else. We were best friends. It was natural that we often found ourselves reviewing material together. We studied together, not because it made the material easier to understand but because we found new ways to think about it. Quite often, when the assignment asked for one perspective, we provided three. If we were asked to come up with a method of teaching youngsters a task, we would come up with two, each more than satisfactory to accomplish the goal.

As you can imagine, more than once, the headmaster called us into his office, questioning the reason we worked so closely together. The first time, he was in no mood to be amused by us; not at all. His questions were colored by suspicion.

"Can you not find other students to study with?" he asked, leaning forward on his glass desk.

I looked at Jace and then back to the headmaster. "The other students are not intelligent enough, sir," I replied as though the answer should have been as self-evident to him as it was to me.

His eyes narrowed, and he straightened in his chair. He was clearly not amused by me or my tone. He looked at me with a withering, critical gaze. "We do not encourage that kind of perspective," he said. "Such judgments are frowned upon."

I had not been raised by my parents to be a smart, thinking girl only to be cowed by the first authority figure who felt it was his place to intimidate me! He might have been in charge, but I knew I was right. I drew a quick breath, and then I matched him, straightening my thin, young girl's body as much as I could. "It is not a judgment," I said, doing my best to match the steel in his voice and doing a pretty good job, despite the fact that my knees felt a bit weak. "It is a statement of fact."

It was impossible to discern at first just how this assertion was going to play. His sharp eyes held mine for another moment before the smallest flicker of a smile twitched across his leathery skin. "I see," he observed softly, relaxing his ramrod straight posture and easing himself back in his chair. "And you?" he asked, turning his undivided attention to Jace. "Do you agree with this so-called 'statement of fact'?"

I glanced quickly at Jace. Up until that moment, it did not even occur to me that he did not see things the same as I did. But in that millisecond, I felt fear course through my soul. Not because I feared the headmaster if Jace disagreed with me, but because my world would have collapsed upon itself if my assumptions about Jace and me were not perfectly matched by his own!

And even if he did agree, he might have taken a position that was less confrontational. After all, Jace was not the one who had been referred to as "impetuous" through most of his life! Perhaps Jace felt no need to prove his mettle like I did. Certainly, he did not straighten up any straighter before the headmaster than he was already standing, which was expected of any of us in the presence of our teachers and superiors; here, showing respect to the headmaster. His reply bore none of my determination or verve.

I held my breath, waiting.

I felt relief wash over me when, rather than replying, he simply laughed with delight.

"You're amused?" the headmaster asked, not as harshly as I would have thought he would have asked.

"Sir," he said, both respect and familiarity in his voice, "I might not have said it quite so boldly as she did, but I know, and I'm fairly sure that you know only too well that what Ari says is absolutely true."

There was a moment of uncertain silence after Jace spoke, a moment when it seemed the headmaster himself wasn't sure how he would react to these two students standing before him. He was a man who carried himself with absolute authority. Even if he had not been the headmaster, and in possession of an office that would have commanded respect, he would have received it. And yet, here we were, two youngsters, essentially challenging the way he preferred to have students behave and speak.

Although I kept my eyes down, as did Jace when we glanced up we could see the headmaster still considering exactly how he was going to respond to our impertinence. And even I could see that it was an impertinence. I felt the weight of the possible consequences of my words. He could, of course, choose to punish us. And the punishments he could choose from could be from reprimand to expulsion. Or, equally possible, he could commend us. He could praise us for our intelligence and self-confidence.

One or the other. Black or white.

Surprising me, he chose neither. Rather than render judgment, good or bad, he instead decided to query us about our position. "You say your superior intelligence is absolutely true. Is this truth tautological? An empirical fact?" he asked, trying to inject doubt into our observation by his tone.

I nearly cheered out loud when Jace spoke, not even hesitating as he qualified his statement. "Insofar as it is a provable one, yes sir, it is indeed."

The headmaster leaned forward and rested his pointed chin on the pyramid he'd formed with his fingertips. "So, it is provable, is it? You have no qualms about putting Ari's assertion to the test? No doubts that her ... ahem, boldness... will prove to be ill-founded?"

Jace glanced at me. Our eyes locked. Looking into his eyes, it was as if I was looking into my own soul. He turned to the headmaster. "As you wish, sir."

Whether my statement was empirically true or not, I knew, and Jace knew that the Academy did not like to consider any of the students better or different than the others. Indeed, our entire culture didn't. That was at the heart of the "no bullying" laws. Communal efforts required equality in thought and status. Which was not to say that people were blind to differences amongst members of our culture. Just that identifying those differences had more often led to negative outcomes than to positive ones.

Colonel Williams had emphasized as much during that first day address, "Those in charge, 'the Ministry', want alert, responsible, thinking individuals who are sensitive to the needs of others and our planet, and who want to share the responsibility of caring for our earth and living in peace together as one race, one Government.

"You will learn a great deal here, but information is not enough to help you develop into the people we need. For the Ministry's vision is not of a society of humans with fixed habits of response to authority. Although," he continued ominously, his piercing eyes seeming to focus on each of us, "every now and again some fall through the cracks." He straightened up. "Those are dealt with swiftly."

The Academy had a very clear philosophy about fostering community while at the same time finding the balance to encourage and support individualism. Jace and I were quite clear that claiming to be more intelligent than other students was, at best, occupying a grey area.

Still, it *was* the truth.

It would be a mistake to think that either Jace or I felt "special" because of our intelligence or dedication to learning. Both of us were absolutely committed to the same goals and aims as our society, the Ministry, and the Academy. We'd even talked about it on occasion. We didn't feel special, and we didn't *want* to feel special. However, even with that understanding, I could not see why that should run counter to *facts*.

From the day I began prep courses, I felt fully alive. I was like a finely tuned athlete finally allowed to run without hesitation. The only one who I had discovered capable of keeping up with me when I chose to run – was Jace. Even my instructors, on occasion, found it impossible to keep up with me.

In the headmaster's office that first day, I felt myself beginning to twitch with impatience – not my most endearing trait – as the headmaster continued to eye us, wondering if we were prepared to defend the audacity of my claim, I couldn't remain silent any longer, I began to speak.

"Sir, I certainly did not mean to be disrespectful. And the last thing I want to do is to suggest that being smarter than our peers makes us *better*. Both of us are quite clear that that is not the case. But the simple fact is, our peers find studies to be work. For Jace and I, it is joy.

"I don't know how best to assess that joy quantitatively. I am sure we would have trouble measuring that to your satisfaction, but it is true nonetheless." I quieted down for a moment and looked down. "I know it to be so."

He considered me closely. Then he looked over at Jace. It was clear that he had a preference for how he wanted to deal with us, but he was either interested, amused or troubled by our assertiveness. "You two present a very unique case," he conceded. "I will consult with your instructors," he went on, speaking simply. "You will return to my office tomorrow at 1400 hours."

"But... warfare exercises..." I started to protest, knowing that the scheduling of such a meeting would mean missing the beginning of the warfare exercises, one of my favorite activities.

Jace, however, was more focused and disciplined and quick to speak over me. "Yes, sir. We will be here. Promptly at 1400 hours."

The headmaster's eyes went back and forth between us. "See that you are." Then, with the wave of his hand, he added, "dismissed."

The reality of how close I'd probably gotten us to expulsion hit me when we were out in the hallway. Suddenly, I broke out in a cold sweat and had to lean against the wall. "Oh my God, what did I do?"

Jace laughed.

I breathed a sigh of relief, realizing that somehow, in spite of my audacity, we had survived the meeting with the headmaster to face another day. "I can't believe I was ready to protest returning!"

Jace chuckled. "You're crazy, you know that, don't you?"

I made a face. "And why would you say that?"

"Really? I need to explain? You are called to the headmaster's office, and you practically tell him he doesn't know what he's talking about!" He shook his head and then swept his hair from his twinkling eyes.

"Well, I'm not the one who laughed in his face," I pointed out, making it clear that I was certain that if there was any trespass made, it was by him and not by me.

"I couldn't help myself," Jace said with a shrug.

"Nor could I."

With that, we laughed at once and then walked out of the building and did what we always did – we started working on our assignments together as though nothing had changed. In fact, nothing *had* changed. Nor would it before 1400 hours the next day.

I slept only fitfully during the night. There was no outcome of the next day's meeting that was not inconceivable to me. Certainly, I could not imagine that we would actually be expelled or even punished for our behavior, or our attitude. That seemed to be an outcome that was contrary to reality. But *not* being punished seemed equally inconceivable. We had been called to the headmaster's office because our behavior fell outside the approved boundaries.

There *had* to be consequences.

I could tell from Jace's rumpled hair the following morning that his night had been no more restful than mine. Our glances to one another made it clear that though we attended our morning classes, our thoughts were elsewhere.

We walked silently to the headmaster's office, arriving exactly forty-five seconds before 1400 hours. His secretary nodded to the door when we arrived.

"Go in. He's waiting."

We entered and stood at attention in front of his desk as the headmaster reviewed some papers on his desk. It was all I could do not to have my knees buckle from beneath me. I felt as if my future, my life, pivoted on this moment.

And, in some sense, it certainly did.

What could he be reading that was more important than our meeting? I wondered, willing him to look at us and speak. Yet, when he did look up, I couldn't help but look away, if only for a moment. When I did find the strength to look directly at him, I saw the same steely grey as I had the day before, but also a hint of amusement in his eyes.

"Well," he began, taking an exaggerated breath, "I have spoken with your instructors and queried them on the 'absolute truth' of your assertion." He paused. "Do you have anything to say before I share with you what *they* had to say?"

I glanced at Jace. Was this the time for a defensive maneuver? We had studied such strategies in our classes. Should I suggest that maybe I had been hasty in my assessment, if only to deflect the criticism we were sure to face? Before I could decide, the headmaster cleared his throat.

"I'll take that as a 'no'," he said. Then he sighed. "Well, it seems as though your instructors agree with both of you," he said, a quick smile flaring across his stern features. "Which," he added quickly, "is very fortunate for you." He returned his attention to the papers on his desk. "So, you are free to continue your collaboration…"

Jace and I looked at each other, our eyes wide with astonishment and relief. "Thank you, sir," Jace said quickly.

The headmaster glanced up and raised an eyebrow. "…so long as there is never, and I mean *never*, any suggestion that such collaboration compromises the integrity of either of your work and studies." He paused for several seconds, allowing his words to sink in. "Do I make myself absolutely clear?"

Was he warning us against cheating? I did not understand at first because the notion of any kind of cheating was completely foreign to my nature. "Sir, are you suggesting that we would ever….?"

"Make sure you do your own work," he said sternly, not answering my question directly. "I have given you permission to collaborate, but collaboration should never mean compromise. Understood?"

I stared at the top of the headmaster's head as he studied the papers on his desk, my mouth open but no words coming out. How could anyone ever suggest that Jace or I would *cheat*? I felt anger rising in my chest. I gripped my hands in tight fists.

Jace no doubt felt the same as me but, as was his nature, he was better able to control his emotions. "Yes, sir," Jace said to the headmaster. As he did, he quickly put his hand on my elbow and led me from the office. There were some social cues that I did not pick up on so easily. Clearly, I did not understand that the headmaster was dismissing us. Jace knew, and he was only too glad to be out of the office.

"Whew," he sighed when we were in the hallway. "We were lucky that time," he said.

"What do you mean?" I snapped angrily. "Don't you realize what he was suggesting…?"

He nodded. "Of course I do," he said. "But you really don't understand how close a call that was, do you?"

Now I was confused. I was angry, but Jace seemed more relieved and grateful. I shook my head.

"We could have so easily been expelled."

My breath left me. I knew that punishment was a possibility and I'd even feared expulsion, but somehow expulsion never seemed like a real possibility to me. What had we done that could have resulted in expulsion. I was so certain of what I'd said and done… But, as I said, in so many ways I did not understand the ways of the world. In this context, Jace was more of a guide than a collaborator.

Whatever else Jace accomplished by telling me about how close we'd come to disaster he certainly did a good job of getting rid of whatever anger I was feeling!

So, it was clear that our academia supported and encouraged individuality but only within a context defined by the greater good. We were like fish swimming in a river. We were free to explore how we wanted to swim and how deep we wanted to dive, but the river was controlled by the Ministry.

Later that evening, when I thought about everything that had transpired, I realized that there was something strange about the way the situation was handled. The headmaster had taught us a lesson, but I wasn't sure exactly what that lesson was. Not yet. I would have to discuss the situation with Jace. After all, by the time we had arrived at the Academy, the Ministry knew us very well. Each one of us had a defined path to follow; each student moved along a tailored educational plan designed to take advantage of his or her strengths and minimize his or her weaknesses. When we arrived at the Academy, the Ministry knew where it wanted us placed and articulated our requirements with that in mind.

I did not know at the time that there were only two students who, in the history of the Academy, did not have such a strictly defined path – me and Jace. Whatever the Ministry had in mind for us was different than for the other students.

We had followed the same testing and evaluation as all the others, but we had scored qualitatively differently. Although ultimate occupations were not necessarily determined by the Ministry, the simple truth is that while individuals had some limited input in their destiny, the comprehensive exams we all took upon entrance to the Academy were remarkably predictive.

Mine took place in an airy office that was not much larger than my own room at home. The difference was that there was absolutely nothing on the walls of the office. Likewise, other than the computer tablet that my proctor brought in with her, there was nothing in the room other than the large, transparent, video glass-topped table, a chair for her and a chair for me.

My proctor was a slender woman of indeterminate age. She could have been twenty-three or forty-six. Advances in medicine made it hard to tell. Her face was pretty and friendly, and her dark black hair was cut in what was called a "pixie cut". I would have thought she was in her twenties but for the stray gray hairs that highlighted her dark hair. Her eyes were deep brown, and she wore eyeliner. When she smiled, which she did often, the lines at the corners of her mouth and her eyes betrayed more years than I would have guessed.

I was waiting at the door when she arrived, promptly at 0900 hours, the time of our session together.

"Well then, you must be Arianna," she said, extending her hand to me.

I took her hand and shook it. "Yes, ma'am."

"I am Annette Polin," she said with a smile as she continued to grip my hand. I had the feeling that she was not so much greeting me as assessing something about me. Holding me with her eyes, she added, "You may call me 'Ann'."

I smiled and nodded. "Very nice to ... um, Ann." I felt awkward speaking to an adult in such an informal manner. We were all taught respect as children, and that extended to our interactions with adults.

She smiled and released my hand. "Nice to meet you too, Ari," she said, immediately taking my more familiar name. "Let's go in, shall we?"

She opened the door and led me toward the desk. She indicated which chair I was to sit in and then took the opposite chair. As she did, she rested a small valise on the floor and took from it her tablet computer. She set that on the desk, turned it on and then looked up at me.

"All right then, shall we begin?"

I nodded.

"Let's take care of the basics first, shall we?"

I nodded again, but I really wished she'd stop asking, 'shall we?' when she knew that we were going to do whatever it was she wanted. But maybe she was doing little things to annoy me; maybe this was all part of the assessment as well. My parents coached me before the session, telling me that the most important thing I could do was to just stay relaxed.

"There will be a lot of formal testing, of course. But a great deal of what you will be doing will be informal. Everything and I mean everything that happens in that room is relevant so just stay aware. You'll be fine."

I could tell that she was trying to keep me relaxed, but my father's efforts were actually putting me on edge. My mother, however, did manage to relax me.

"It's the easiest test you'll ever take," she counseled. "After all, you are only being tested on being yourself."

That made me laugh. "And I can hardly fail that, can I?"

She laughed too. "It is impossible to fail at that."

But then I stopped laughing. "Still, a lot is riding on this assessment." I looked at my father, whose expression clearly showed that he agreed with me. My mother, however, continued to smile.

"Nothing is riding on this test," she said simply. "What will be, will be." She came close and kissed my forehead. "Worry about only those things you can control." She glanced over at my father who, seeing the look in her eye, finally relaxed as well.

"Mother is, of course, completely correct," he said, smiling warmly. "You are a remarkable creature..."

"I'm a girl, father!"

"...my apologies," he chuckled. "You are a remarkable girl, and your exam cannot help but demonstrate that. Sleep well, my child. Get up refreshed and ready."

I did sleep well. So well, in fact, I almost didn't remember what it was that I was to do that morning. When mother came in to wake me, I was startled when she reminded me of the day.

"Today?"

She smiled. "Yes, today."

I jumped out of bed, ate a good breakfast and got dressed.

"Would you like me to accompany you?" mother asked.

I shook my head. "No, I am fine," I said. And even though I had flutterings in my stomach, I knew that I spoke the truth. I was fine. And ready.

Ann asked me to say my name and address, which she checked against the record that was in her file.

"How tall are you?"

"I was just over 175 centimeters at my last exam," I said. "But I am quite certain that I have grown since then."

Ann smiled and made a notation in the tablet. "And how much do you weigh ... or did you weigh at your last exam?"

I returned her easy smile. "Almost 63 kilos," I said.

"Perfect. Okay, your home address?"

I gave her my address as well as the information about my parents and other family members. I told her about my family history which, I was certain that she already knew. But I could not help but swell with joy and pride as I shared with her the many walks my mother took me on when I was a small girl.

"How old were you on the earliest walk you remember?" she asked.

I described a walk when I was still carried in my mother's snuggly carrier. As I spoke, she looked at me suspiciously.

"Are you certain that you remember this walk? Might you not be remembering being told about it?"

I shook my head. "No, I have a very specific sensory memory of that walk. The feel of the carrier's material against my skin. I remember the color of the fern when she lifted me up to it."

Ann simply logged into the tablet that she carried with her and accessed my chip. Ann could watch the recall of my memories on her screen, as could I on the table in front of me.

She listened closely with a twinkle in her eyes. "Okay, I think you're right." There was a moment of silence as Ann prepared my examination. I looked down to the table in front of me and saw packets unopened on the screen. "Before we begin, do you have any questions for me?"

I shook my head.

"All right, let's get started then, shall we?"

I stiffened at her words, but then simply nodded. Each packet on the screen in front of me had its own label. One said: NUMERICAL. Another said: VERBAL. Another said: NON-VERBAL. I couldn't see the others, but I would come to know that they included, Shapes, Mechanical, Cognitive, and Memory.

CHAPTER THREE
THE ACADEMY/
APTITUDE

You will have twenty-five minutes for each section on the aptitude test," Ann explained. "There will be an optional five minute rest period in between the tests." She looked at me. "Are you ready?"

I nodded.

"Okay. I will need you to lean forward scan your iris." She reached across the screen and slid the first envelope toward me. "You may begin."

The first envelope was titled SHAPES. As soon as I opened it, she said simply, "Time has begun."

The first session had a series of shapes in a row followed by a question, "What must the next shape be?" Of the four choices,

I chose one. On and on it went through twenty-five questions. Inverted stars. Octagons with corners bent. Mirror images to be matched. Odd shapes. Missing shapes. Ovals in concentric rings. The time passed so fast, as I gestured to complete the group of questions that had been put before me.

One after the other, I went through the questions. When I had finished the last question, I sat back in my chair and looked over at Ann.

She was watching me with curious eyes. "Do you want to double check your answers?"

I shook my head.

"Are you sure? You have time."

I shook my head again.

"Okay." She signed the packet off on her tablet, and we proceeded to the next packet.

Three minutes of the twenty-five allotted minutes had elapsed.

The next packet was NUMBER GAMES. This exam measured my quantitative abilities. I was confronted with numerical sequences, odd word problems in which there were eight siblings of varying relationships and I was to determine which was the youngest. One question I thought was so amusing that I couldn't help but laugh out loud, had to do with pay amounts – a basic RTD type problem – but this one presented such ridiculously low pay that it had to have been taken from a century or two earlier.

Again I sat back in my chair to let Ann know that I was finished. Once again, Ann asked if I wanted to double check my answers. I shook my head. She noted that I had ample time to do so if I wanted. I shook my head.

Three minutes of my allotted twenty-five minutes elapsed.

So it went, through the word games, the VERBAL and NON-VERBAL assessments. I found the SPATIAL assessment to be a lot of fun. Hands turned this way and that, shapes in varying degrees of size representing distance and depth. Forms that could be constructed from presented bits and pieces.

The last assessment, the SPATIAL assessment, required the least amount of time of all. Two and a half minutes.

And then I was finished.

"Do you have any questions for me?"

"No," I said, shaking my head.

She allowed herself a smile. "You know, you are the only one who did not ask me one very specific question," she observed.

"Really?" I asked, finding that observation interesting. Not, mind you, that I had not asked something but that everyone else *had*.

She nodded.

"And what was it that they wanted to know?"

She cocked her head to the side. "They wanted to know when they would be getting their results."

I sat back in my chair. That seemed a very uninteresting question. "That's it?"

"Yes," Ann said. "Why do you think you don't find that a very compelling question?" she asked me.

I shrugged and responded, "Because I am already fairly certain what my result is," I said this without any particular emotion. I was neither bragging nor being humble. It was a simple statement that I made.

Her eyebrows arched and her eyes widened. "You *know* what your result is?" she asked, her voice tinged with a chiding quality as if she found my statement to be amusing, like a statement that a small child would make after giving a star a name or something.

"I didn't say I knew what my result is. I pointed out that I was fairly certain what my result would be," I chided back at her.

"And what would that result be?" she asked.

"I am fairly certain that I answered each question correctly," I said.

She leaned forward. "Ari, you are just sixteen years old, how can you be so 'fairly' certain?"

I shrugged. "I don't see why I would have answered any one of them incorrectly," I answered with an answer which seemed to infuriate her in a way I could not understand.

"That's ridiculous," she said. "The way you've rushed through the exams... there is no way..." She shook her head. "I've never had a student move through these assessments as quickly as you have done. It was almost reckless..." Then she checked herself. "In any case, we have more assessments to complete."

She pushed another packet towards me on the screen. This packet contained photographs that I had to provide narratives for. Inkblots that I had to describe. Odd sorts of tests it seemed to me. After all, what had any of this to do with what I was or was not qualified to do?

Rather than think about how tedious the process of testing was, I started thinking to myself that Jace must have found this whole process to be mind-numbing indeed.

Which was funny because, when we saw each other afterwards we'd both been through the process, so we "compared notes". Both of us had the exact same thought – that the other would find the whole process tedious.

"And could you believe how they doubted us about being correct in our answers?" Jace asked me incredulously. "And why? Because we finished in less than the allotted time?"

As it turned out, our exams showed nothing so much as the two of us were perfectly paired in our exceptionalism. Not only had we both scored one hundred percent – unheard of in its own right – but we had both done so in times that were equally unheard of. Mind you, we did not move through the exams at exactly the same pace. Jace showed exceptional speed in a different exam than me. He was incredible in the non-verbal assessment. Even so, every other exam took each of us exactly three minutes.

"Basically," the headmaster said in presenting our cases to the Ministry, "their times were a function of the mechanical need to actually *type* the answer down or for their proctors to do the same. They processed the information and came to the correct answer significantly faster than that."

When it turned out that Ann was my instructor in an ancient literature class, she took the opportunity to hold me after class to apologize for having doubted my confidence that I'd gotten all the questions correct.

"It was really quite a remarkable experience, proctoring your exam," she said, smiling at me. "You are a special young lady."

"Thank you, ma'am," I replied, never presuming to call her 'Ann' while we were at the Academy, no matter the circumstances.

"All of your instructors share my pride and admiration," she added. "Keep up the good work."

"Thank you, ma'am," I said again.

"I was wondering…" she began, somewhat hesitantly.

I straightened up. "Yes, ma'am?"

"Well, as you know, generally speaking, each student is assigned a senior advisor to help you progress through your course of study. As I say, generally the advisor is assigned. However, this year two students have demonstrated such exceptional potential that they will be given a say in who their advisors will be…"

"Jace?" I cried out excitedly.

She sighed and smiled. "Yes, your friend Jace is one of the two. And, of course, you are the other. So, I was wondering, well I'd like you to consider me as a candidate for your senior advisor," she said.

I smiled. "I'd love that, ma'am."

She returned my smile. "That's wonderful. Really wonderful."

CHAPTER FOUR
THE ACADEMY/
APTITUDE

And how is it going for you both?"

Jace and I sat across from Ann Polin, in the same office where I'd taken my aptitude exams a week earlier. Right after I took the aptitude test, I met with Jace in the gardens by the administration building. We had agreed before the test that we would meet after. It was a coincidence that we happened to finish and come out of the building at exactly the same time.

"Well, what did you think?" he asked as we turned toward the quiet spot we had discovered on a small lawn behind the building.

"I liked the shapes," I told him as we sat down.

He shrugged. "I liked the mathematical questions."

"Yes, those were all right. Wasn't the one with the hands turned all different ways curious?"

He smiled. "I know it wasn't supposed to be, but I thought it was fun. I kept imagining arms and people attached to those hands. In my mind, I made up little stories about the people I imagined attached to those strange limbs."

"Me too!"

"And those bloody ink blots! They were the most ridiculous things!"

"Did your proctor become impatient with you for answering so quickly?" I asked.

He laughed. "Yes, absolutely infuriated I would say!"

We were both laughing about the exams, comparing notes as it were. We knew that we were not to discuss the test with anyone who had not yet taken them, but we did not think there was any restriction on our talking about them with each other.

Jace looked at his watch. Technically, we were both still scheduled to be taking the exam for another two hours. Both of us had finished that quickly! So, we reasoned that the time we had right then was our own.

We talked for about an hour about the test, certain that even if we had not done as well as we presumed, we had done exactly the same as one another. Still, neither of us could think of a single question or challenge we'd had trouble with or which posed any sort of a real challenge.

Of course, that's exactly what we learned from Ann several days later when she called us both to her office.

Although she had not proctored Jace's exam, she had introduced herself to him in the days immediately after the test, asking if he would consider her for his advisor as well as mine. He said he would certainly think about it.

"I am Ari's counselor," she then added with a smile.

His face brightened. "Well then," he said. "You should be mine as well!"

So it didn't particularly surprise us to be called into the little office and have her greet us. Still, I was a little concerned by the serious expression on her face.

"Please have a seat," she said to the two of us when we came into the office.

We looked at one another and then sat down. We didn't say a word as we waited to find out what was going on.

Ann was quiet for several moments. Then she cleared her throat.

"Is there anything you'd like to tell me?"

Jace and I looked at one another, our eyes widening in surprise. Her voice seemed to suggest that we had done something wrong but neither one of us could figure out what she might have been referring to.

It was not often that either Jace or I was dumbfounded and almost never that we were *both* dumbfounded, but this was one of the occasions. "I don't understand," I said. "What do you mean?"

Her eyes registered a curious recognition. "You really don't know, do you?" she asked.

We shook our heads.

She laughed, which surprised us both more than anything else she could have done.

"I'm sorry," she apologized. "It's just that you have really astonished me now. I have finally come up with a question that you don't know the answer to!" She continued to chuckle. "Come with me," she said firmly. It was impossible to tell from her tone if she was angry or amused.

She stood up from behind the desk's screen and went to the door. Jace and I looked at each other. She paused at the door, her hand pressed against the scanner that allowed for entrance and exit.

"Well? Are you coming?"

We clamored to our feet and hurried after her. She walked quickly through the tiled hallway, her face was focused straight ahead. Her eyes looking neither here nor there. She did not pause as she exited the building and walked down the steps and onto the flat stones of the pathway.

Jace and I looked at one another, our eyes showing our growing confusion. Where was she leading us? What had we done?

She continued past the administration building and across the athletic fields. Upon the lush, nearly endless expanses of lawn where many of our classmates were engaged in sporting events and mock battle engagement. Although the focus of our education was on our intellectual development, social research had determined that in order to maximize intellectual potential, it was necessary to fully engage the body as well.

Although there had long before been some differing perspectives on the mind-body relationship and connection, by this time, there was no dispute. Mind and body were inexorably linked. Absent a disability, it was nearly impossible to develop one without the other.

Just watching the other students running along the fields made me long to be out there with them. In perhaps one of the few other differences between Jace and me, I was significantly more physical and athletic. I could run and run for hours, enjoying the sensation of my muscles being engaged. I could push myself to run faster, jump higher, swim harder and revel in the challenge.

Jace thought such activity to be more of a nuisance than enjoyment.

Of course, his attitude seemed to have no bearing on his physical skills or ability. He was the only one of our cohorts capable of out-dueling me, out-running me, or climbing higher and faster.

"How can you do that?" I asked him one time after we had concluded a match with the long lances, a match that he had won by points.

"Do what?" he asked, nonchalantly removing the padding we wore for the games.

"Beat me?"

He shrugged. "I don't know. I don't think about it," he added.

That, as you can imagine, infuriated me. "That's what I'm talking about! I never see you engaged in any physical activity other than what is required. You don't practice. You don't work out. You don't even *enjoy* it, and yet you're the best out here! Even better than me!"

He nodded. "Ah, so *that's* what's gotten you upset," he observed with an objective coolness that had me ready to jump on him and pummel him! "You're upset that you lost the match."

"Of course I'm upset that I lost the match," I snapped at him. "Isn't the entire point of a match to win?"

He laughed. "And you're not even just a little bit happy for me, having won?" he asked.

"Not at all," I growled. "In fact, I'm quite certain that I'm even angrier *because* it is you who has beaten me."

"That's wonderful!" he said, clapping his hands.

"Wonderful? What's wonderful?" I demanded, wrapping my arms around myself if only to keep them from throttling him.

"You're angry that I beat you and angrier still because I make it look effortless, right?"

I scowled at him. "I suppose."

"Let me ask you a question. When one of our classmates feels upset because we score so high on our tests – without studying – are they justified?"

"Hey, we study! At least I do."

He smiled. "Our classmate doesn't know that."

I looked at him suspiciously. "Are you saying you practice and that I just don't know it?"

He shrugged. "I'm saying that it may be good for us once in a while to realize we might not always be the best – for whatever reason."

I could feel a frown tugging at my lips. "Well, if I'm not the best then you are. I can live with that."

He laughed. "And when I'm not, you are," he noted. "But there may be a time when neither of us is, and we have to be able to deal with that too," he said.

I shook my head. "Not going to happen," I said casually.

"Maybe not. But the whole purpose of our training is to be able to deal with the very thing we never expect. Any computer can amass data and spit it back – even in creative ways. But it takes an interesting mind to be able to prepare for something that's never been."

I stamped my foot. Just when he was being infuriating, Jace always managed to prove himself to be more thoughtful and insightful than anyone I'd ever known. I couldn't stay mad at him. I was just grateful that he was my friend.

I sighed.

Jace nudged me. He knew what I was thinking as we walked along the fields but he wanted to keep me focused. We had fallen a bit behind Ann and her quick pace. Well, *I* had fallen behind. Jace slowed down to make sure I caught up.

We hurried to catch up as Ann walked past the Science building and then toward the Information Complex.

I looked at Jace as if to ask, "What are we doing here?"

Ann stopped in front of the Information Complex. She studied our expressions. "Still no idea?"

I looked at Jace and then back to Ann.

"Jace?"

He looked at the building then at Ann. She nodded with an expression that seemed to suggest satisfaction.

"Come on," he said, heading into the building.

We didn't take the elevator. As soon as she headed to the staircase, I felt my breath draw in.

"Ah, figured it out, have we?" She turned and smiled at me and then at Jace.

Two weeks earlier, I had been reading in my room when Jace knocked on the door. "It's open," I called out, recognizing his knock.

He came into my room.

"What's up?" I asked him.

"What are you up to?"

I nodded at the computing pad in my hand. "Differentials," I said.

He looked around the room. It seemed like he didn't know exactly what to say next, which was highly unusual for Jace. If there were anything I would say about Jace, it would be that he always knew what to say.

"What's going on?" I asked him. "You're acting funny."

He opened the door and looked in the hallway. Then he came back in. "Come with me," he said.

I shrugged. "Sure." It didn't take much to convince me to tag along with Jace. Besides, I was way ahead with the differential material. I shut off the computing pad and put it on my bed. Then I slid to the floor and followed after Jace as he went out the door.

We followed the path from the dorms for a little while but then, when we came to the playing fields, rather than walk around, we cut across the lawn.

"Where are we going?" I asked him. He remained silent and thoughtful.

Having spent a number of years trusting Jace in his adventures, I didn't really expect him to answer, but I always asked. I just followed along, past the Science Building and toward the Information Complex.

He pushed open the door, and we stepped inside. The air was cool and dry. It felt unlike any other building I'd been in at the

Academy. And why would I have been here? We had no classes here, no instruction. It was one of the handful of places at the Academy that didn't capture my attention at all. But clearly, it had captured Jace's.

"Shhh," he hissed, putting his finger to his lips as the sound of footsteps approached us. "Come here," he whispered, pulling me into a doorway.

The footsteps came closer and then passed, receding away along the wide, tile floor.

"What's the matter?" I asked him. "Aren't we supposed to be here?" Even though I hadn't been in the Information Complex, it was my understanding that every place on the Academy's campus was available to us unless it was locked or specifically noted to be off-limits. I had seen no such sign suggesting that we were not to be in the building.

And yet Jace was behaving as if we were doing something wrong. "Jace?"

"Everything's fine," he said. "Come on," he added, stepping out from the doorway.

We followed what seemed to me to be a maze of hallways. Left. Right. Right. Left. Until we came to a staircase. Jace started to go downstairs. He looked back once to make sure I was following him.

Staircases at the Academy were strange, wondrous things. For the most part, we went in elevators or escalators if we had to move from elevation to elevation. There were also times when we moved along lateral walkways. We almost never took stairs. When we did, the stairwells were well-lit.

After the first flight down – which was lit like every other staircase I'd encountered at the Academy – we entered another staircase. This one was not as well-lit, or as wide as any of the others. The railing was wood, polished it seemed from many hands running along it.

One flight down. Another and then another.

"Jace?"

He didn't answer until we'd gone down four flights. At the landing, he pushed open a door.

"Oh my…"

He stepped aside as I entered a place I had never experienced before. Even so, being there took my breath away – just like Jace knew that it would. We had entered what had been called a "library."

Of course Jace and I were familiar with books. It was just that in our experience, books were old and inefficient. We viewed everything on computer tablets. Pages were turned virtually. And what did it matter? The words were the same.

Well, it did matter. I liked the physical sensation of turning pages. What was lost in the inability to immediately cross-reference every possible text from the tablet was more than made up for with the simple, physical pleasure of holding a book, touching its pages and taking delight in the exquisite scent that a book often gives off.

I loved it, and I knew that Jace did as well.

Now, here in this place, there was floor to ceiling books. Shelf after shelf, after shelf of them.

"My God, Jace! How did you find this place?"

He shrugged in that mysterious way of his. "I just happened upon it," he said.

I looked at him then, and I narrowed my eyes. "Just happened upon it? Seriously?"

Jace looked just the slightest bit sheepish. "Okay. I came into the Information Complex just to explore. I'd never come in before and I was curious what was in here.

"I wandered for a while, just looking around. No one seemed to particularly mind that I was here. For the most part, it seemed to me that there were just offices here, cubicles and workstations.

"Nothing particularly interesting." He sighed. "I was getting ready to leave when I heard a door open. I took note of it because the door *creaked* like we'd been taught doors had done long ago."

It was true that doors opened and closed nearly silently now. Just a soft *whoosh* of air. So to have a physical sound. A creak. That was fascinating. It gave me a shiver and made me imagine what life must have been like when *all* doors opened and closed like that. Just the thought of it fascinated me so I could imagine what actually hearing it did for Jace.

Jace and I shared a love of the "old world" and how things were. There were times when Jace wished he could have lived then. Not me. I liked learning about the past, but I was pretty happy with the world I inhabited.

"Just imagine what it would be like," he once said, "actually working on a farm. Growing *fresh* food." He closed his eyes and let his imaginings become real for him.

I shrugged. "It would be all right I guess," I said acknowledging him, but I wasn't enthusiastic about it. Even if I didn't share his enthusiasm about *experiencing* the past, I really liked his nostalgia for it. Not only did I find it fascinating, but I also took to heart the old adage that one not able to learn from the past was destined to relive it.

And based on what I knew about the past, I did not want to relive it!

"Are you sure we're supposed to be down here?" I asked Jace.

He just kept walking. I stayed just inside the doorway for a moment but then when he'd disappeared around one of the stacks I felt very vulnerable, so I hurried to catch up with him. I found him kneeling down on the floor with an oversized book in front of him.

"Look at this," he said, staring down at the pages opened before us.

He had taken an atlas out from the stacks, and it showed land masses that did not correspond with current land masses.

"This is what the world looked like," he said, half to himself.

I was drawn to the pages and could not help but kneel down so I could look closer. I drew my finger along the coastline of various continents.

Jace jumped up and, leaving the atlas on the floor, motioned for me to follow him to another place in the stacks. He stopped and pulled a volume from the shelves.

"Look at this," he said, handing me the small book.

I studied the cover. There was a picture of a girl, not much older than Jace and I. She had dark hair and dark, haunting eyes. I read the title. "Anne Frank: The Diary of a Young Girl." I turned it over in my hands and then looked at Jace.

"What's this about?"

"I am not one hundred percent sure," he admitted. "I've only read a small bit of it. But from what I've read – and from what I've managed to learn *about* it, there was a terrible period during the twentieth century..." He went on to briefly talk about a cataclysm known as the Second World War.

"Barbarism," I shuddered when he was finished. However, even as I rendered my judgment, I knew that such qualities still existed in people. Society could work very hard to teach and breed such aspects of human nature out of us, but ultimately we are still what we are. Even the tamest dog retains the ability – and nature – to bite.

In all that I had read and learned, I knew that people had a marvelous ability to engage in a broad spectrum of ways, from love to hate, charity to cruelty.

Jace and I had even spoken about it over the years.

"Do you really think people are capable of terrible cruelty?" he asked me one time.

I thought for a moment, not about my answer but about how I wanted to best communicate it. Neither of us was the kind to simply make assertions or to mimic the lessons we were taught. We were both too relentless in our curiosities and our intelligence even at the young age when we had the conversation.

The question itself had grown out of a scene he and I had not long before witnessed. We had been walking through the woods and had come upon some foliage that I had learned about long before with my mother.

"When you see these..." she told me, pointing out the sharp, orange-colored leaves sticking stiffly from low, bristled stems, "...steer clear of the path." Then she looked forward and back carefully as if to make sure that the path was clear.

"Why, mother? Are they poisonous?"

I related the lesson I had learned that day. As if to make the lesson that much more powerful, two short-legged boars approached from different directions.

I saw them before Jace. "Come!" I whispered hurriedly, dragging him behind some bushes where we could see without being seen. Then, just as had happened that long-ago day with my mother, the two boars fought themselves to a benumbed draw and staggered off, neither of them enjoying any of the meal they had both come looking for.

That day, my mother had witnessed the scene and taught me a lesson about cooperation. Jace and I, seeing a similar scene, spoke about a different lesson.

"Such violence," he sighed.

"They are hungry," I noted.

"Do you think it was hunger alone that caused them to behave in such a way or do you think it is in their nature to be violent?"

I thought it was a smart and compelling question. After all, if it were the *nature* of the boars to be cooperative, they would have cooperated as a *default* response. Instead, their immediate response was to violence.

We talked about it for a while and then Jace asked what I thought our natures were. "Are we violent or are we cooperative?" he wondered aloud. He looked me directly in the eye. "What do you think, Ari? Are we peaceful creatures who cooperate or are we violent and dangerous?"

I gave it some thought. "I would have to say we are both," I decided finally. "Certainly we are capable of violence." I nodded toward the small volume in my hand. "This episode in history demonstrates it. And we are, after all, still human beings at the base level," I noted.

"But…"

"Yes, but," I said, cutting him off. "But we are also capable of recognizing that aspect of our nature and of trying to blunt it. We can create music and art. We can cooperate – indeed, we have learned that our survival is dependent on cooperation.

"Still," I continued, thinking out loud. "If we were not so prone to violence and selfish behavior, the Ministry would not devote so much energy to teaching us *not* to behave in such negative ways. Clearly, if we have a gift greater than the short-legged boar…"

Jace laughed at the comparison. "Ari, don't be ridiculous!"

I raised my hand in protest. "I'm not being ridiculous. I am speaking about essential natures. Some of these we share with the beasts of the fields. There can be no doubt about it. However, where we rise above the boar is that we, *recognizing* the limitations of our natures, can seek ways to minimize those weaknesses and maximize our strengths.

"The boar has the capability to butt itself silly while fighting over some food. It cannot elevate itself above such non-productive behavior. But we, I think, while possessing plenty of barbarism in our natures also have the ability to recognize that barbarism cannot move the human enterprise forward."

As we removed ourselves from behind the bush, both deeming it safe to return to the path, Jace softly applauded. "That was a brilliant exposition, Ari," he said, genuinely pleased by what I'd said. "I fear though that it is not the entire explanation."

"What do you mean?" I asked as we continued on our way.

"Well, while I think it is certainly wise to teach and train us to work cooperatively and to the larger benefit, there may indeed be downsides to how effectively we remove or hide essential aspects of our natures."

I looked at him curiously. At the time, I could not grasp what he was suggesting. In fact, I don't think he fully appreciated what he was trying to sort out. But over a great deal of time and thought, the importance of his insight would become more apparent.

Meanwhile, I weighed the small volume that I held in my hands. "What do you think it was like for her?"

"You mean, hiding in the attic?"

I shook my head. "No, not just during the fighting. I mean before. Living in the 20th Century. Do you think she was happy before all these terrible things happened? Did she go to school? Did she have brothers and sisters? What were her parents like?"

He shrugged. "I don't know how much we can tell by one book. But there is so much here about how different people lived..."

He walked down the aisle and took another volume from the shelf. This one had many more pages than the first. It was by a writer named Charles Dickens. "David Copperfield."

"It's heavy," I noted.

He nodded in agreement. "It was written many years before the Anne Frank diary," he said. Then he told me a bit about the world inhabited by David Copperfield, at least as portrayed in the book.

"That's horrible!" I cried out, thinking about the conditions that so many young people experienced. "Not having enough to eat? Living in such squalor? It's horrific. I can't imagine…"

"I know. But that was just how people lived. That wasn't even a time of war. It was just the way society was structured."

"People were so greedy," I said.

"People *are* greedy," he pointed out. "At least, if we are considering essential natures," he added.

I tried to impose the world of David Copperfield on our own and I couldn't. The way all people were treated and cared for in our society just did not compare. The idea of allowing anyone to flounder and to squander their potential seemed so… so… barbaric. Almost crueler than the war in its way.

"And this," he said, hurrying down and around the stack, coming back with another book.

I tried to pronounce the name of the writer. "Doy… doy… Dostoevsky?"

He smiled. "Dostoyevsky," he said, pronouncing the name fluidly.

"How did you do that?" I asked him with wonderment.

He crooked his finger and bade me to follow him. We entered another room, this one with workstation after workstation equipped with primitive recording equipment. "This is how people once learned to speak foreign languages," he said. "It allowed me to not only pronounce this Russian writer's name but to read the book in its original language."

He smiled, very proud of his accomplishment. Clearly, Jace had been putting his spare time to very practical use!

"I still don't feel right about being in here," I noted. I looked around. In the ancient, fluorescent light Jace's face had an unnatural appearance, almost like a mask.

"I'm sure it's all right," Jace said confidently. "After all, there are no notices restricting access."

He was right about that. But by the same token, nothing was suggesting that we *belonged* in the room. And it wasn't as if it was easy to find, after all.

"Who do you think uses this room?" I asked him, looking beyond the recording devices and into the larger, book-filled room.

"Researchers, I would think. Although in all the time I've come here, I've never seen anyone else."

"I think we should put everything back where we found it and leave," I said.

He nodded. "You're probably right. But it's cool, isn't it? I mean, look at all these books," he said as he closed the door to the recording room.

I had to agree that it was pretty amazing. Still, I was ready to leave. When exiting the library area, I noticed on the wall near the door a notation made by an author – Angela Clarke who simply said, "A library is not just a reference service: it is a place for the vulnerable. From the elderly gentleman whose only remaining human interaction is with library staff, to the isolated young mother who relishes the support and friendship that grows from a baby rhyme time session, to a slow-moving thirty-something woman collecting her CD's. Libraries are a haven in a world where community services are being ground down to nothing. Libraries are vital, their worth cannot be measured in books alone." This small passage moved me more than anything else that I had seen that night with Jace. What a lonely world it must have been, and yet somehow I felt that I fitted comfortably right into it. It all made sense to me. Our libraries were very different to the one that I found myself in and taught many cultural and societal antidotes, but none shared such desire and pain as this one.

Still, I was ready to leave, and I was very happy when we were back by the playing fields again.

I did go back with Jace several times after that. I ended up reading a great many books that I would never have read, and learned about a great many things I never learned in my lessons with mother or in my formal lessons at the Academy. Even so, each time I went to the library with Jace, I was relieved to leave again. I always carried a feeling that we were doing something we should not do.

That feeling was at the heart of my reaction to Ann bringing us to the door of the library that day, when she asked, "Still no idea?"

I swallowed hard. Unlike our interaction with the headmaster, when I had been perfectly certain of what I was saying and of being right, I felt very unsure about whether we had been doing something appropriate.

"It was my idea," Jace volunteered, his voice never wavering. "I discovered this place and then when I saw how wonderful it was, I just couldn't imagine not sharing it with Ari." He then looked Ann directly in the eye. "Do you know how wonderful this place is?" he asked her.

There was a twinkle in her eye as she started to answer. "Yes, Jace," she said. "I do know how wonderful a place this is. I should. I am responsible for it."

Well, you can imagine how stunned we both were. It must have shown on our faces because Ann, whose expression had remained quite serious, suddenly laughed. "Close your mouths, both of you." She tsk'ed and shook her head. "You look ridiculous like that."

We dutifully closed our mouths, but that did not end our surprise at what she'd said.

"Ann?" I began.

She raised her hand to quiet me. "I suspected one or both of you would discover my little project sooner or later. I should not have been surprised that it was much sooner. You two are the most inquisitive and intelligent students the Academy has seen in its history..." She said this with no particular emotion but as a statement of fact. As a result, neither Jace nor I really reacted to the statement.

"In any case, I am pleased that you've discovered my project. I had discussed with the headmaster whether or not to simply bring you here myself but felt that it would be wiser to wait until you had discovered the library on your own."

"The headmaster knows we've been here?" I asked, surprised again.

"Of course," she said easily. "There is not much that the headmaster does not know. He is responsible for this Academy and everything and everyone in it. It is in his – and our – best interest that he is aware of everything." She brought her hands together. "In any case, let's go inside and see what we can learn."

Jace and I followed Ann along a path that was very familiar to us. She led us first to the stacks that held the atlases. While Jace had found a number of atlases that showed maps of the world as it used to be, she took out other volumes, volumes that helped to understand not just the land masses and the changes that they experienced but also many of the factors that contributed to the changes over the years.

"Looking back," she said with a steely distaste in her tone, "it is astonishing to think of how foolish the people and their leaders had been. Even as an environmental disaster unfolded right beneath their noses, they did not act to stop it. Even worse, their actions and behavior was so short-sighted as to actually *accelerate* the destruction." She closed her eyes and shook her head.

"Our social scientists have spent years and years trying to discern the how and why of such self-destructive behavior so that we can better remove it from our own practices."

I glanced at Jace. This was exactly the conversation that we'd had many times before, never with a clear resolution. But something in his expression made me certain that this was not the time to note that.

"You read about some events and social conditions that plagued mankind for hundreds and thousands of years. Poverty. Cruelty. The unequal distribution of resources." Ann continued.

"Greed had been endemic to the human condition for so long," Ann sighed and shook her head. "We have striven to remove it from our own condition. Our social scientists and political leaders have been single minded in their determination to create a world in which everyone is treated fairly." It was decided before our ancestors exited the Arc that a universal basic income would be introduced to ensure that no person or persons were left behind, or wanting for basic needs. Even though the income is scaled depending on your standing in society, not one person is left without food, shelter or their daily needs. What could be fairer?

I felt something deep within myself bristle. Fair? Was fairness all that we aspired to? I knew that I did not want to be treated – and forced to be – like everyone else. I was certain that Jace did not.

"Have you found these volumes interesting?" Ann asked Jace and me.

Jace did not hesitate. "I have," he said honestly.

"And you?" Ann asked, turning to face me directly.

I thought for a moment. "I don't know that I have felt as strongly about them as Jace has. They have confused me at times, which I don't really enjoy."

Ann laughed. "No, I don't suppose that being confused would be a sensation you would enjoy. Certainly, it can't be something you're used to experiencing."

She was, of course, right. While there were many things that I confronted for the very first time in my life, few of them actually confused me. Between my prior experience and my logical thought process, I could easily accommodate new and even strange things into my worldview without being confused or troubled by them.

But the things I was seeing in the books that Jace had found left me feeling a bit lost. The cruelty of primitive people disarmed me and, their seeming pigheadedness in the face of an environmental disaster. Their short-sightedness in dealing with global hunger. Their seeming insatiable desire to fight in wars – the results of which almost never accomplished any significant betterment to people or the world.

"I just do not understand the motivation," I said, still searching for an adequate way to explain what I was feeling. "I mean, they were people. We are people. And yet, our society is so different. Our people act so differently." In quiet reflection though I knew it was because we were socially conditioned to behave in a certain way. I would never dare voice that opinion though.

Ann nodded sagely. "Well, we have had the benefit of learning from their disastrous experiences," she noted. "And after they had caused so much harm, we really had no choice but to change the way we behaved. Over time, with a determined change in behavior, there came about a change in being."

"So the psychological follows the physical?" Jace asked, listening intently to Ann's explanation. "The body has the advantage in the mind-body equation?"

Ann was quiet for a moment. I don't think that even knowing how special Jace was, she expected the question from someone as young as he was. I would hazard that she would have not expected the question from *anyone* regardless of age. In our society, some things were simply taken for granted. That the authority of the person speaking was never questioned, neither tacitly or overtly. Neither Jace nor I were very good at showing that kind of deference.

"Not exactly. And not always," she said after a moment of consideration. "However, I think it is accurate to say that when the individual has been trained to react a certain way, then his or her mind ceases to seek the old way of thinking."

Jace nodded. "But we have seen instances when, for example, even the most tamed of animals react in fierce ways when presented with the right stimuli. Why would we suspect that humans, much more complex, would lose their ability to react in a manner that is essential to their nature?"

Ann smiled. "Perhaps I did not explain myself quite as clearly as I wanted to," she conceded. "I do not mean to suggest that anyone completely *loses* aspects of their essential natures. Rather, their tendencies are blunted. It is less and less likely that they will resort to more primitive manners of behavior.

"For example, the many generations that our system has been in place has seen the spirit of cooperation overtake a natural tendency to think selfishly. That is not to say that we do not sometimes have to contend with instances of selfish behavior. But our cultural imperative is to blunt such behavior while," she paused and turned to the books on the shelves nearby, "we know from these works of fiction and nonfiction that the cultural imperative not only allowed such greed and selfishness but actually promoted it. As a result, instances of greed, selfishness and violent acts were not only common but essentially excused."

The answer seemed to satisfy Jace. At least for the time being.

I appreciated what she had to say, but there was still the niggling concern of *what was lost* with the cultural blunting of this aspect of people's nature. Even without the benefit of Jace's discovery of the library, I had learned about the greedy behavior of primitive people of centuries past. What hadn't been as clearly answered though was, what became of the positive aspects of those individualized motivations?

After all, there had to be those as well.

Little did I know that the next few moments would begin to help me understand my question more fully and, in the process – and in ways that I doubt that Ann intended – make me question the work of the Academy and our society.

CHAPTER FIVE
A "VISIT" TO THE PAST

I n any case," Ann went on, "I did not bring you here just to show you that I was aware that you'd visited the library. As I said, we knew that you would discover it soon enough. The question was, what to do about it when you did?" The works contained within this knowledge base are limited to a very few people.

Jace and I looked at her with a shared look of astonishment. I could not have been sure at that moment, but later, when we spoke about what happened, we both discovered that we'd shared the same reaction, that we were trapped in some disturbing dynamic. We had spent our lives wanting to excel in all our studies. The Academy was our singular goal. We had achieved all that we'd hoped to achieve up to that point in our lives. We were somewhat celebrated for our gifts. And yet, in this instance, it became apparent that even our "missteps" were anticipated and planned.

I had read in one of the books that Jace had shown me, the feelings of someone who longed only to be *'free'*. I felt exhilarated by that passage and the emotion that the character captured. I felt such a life and experience was available to me. But, as soon as Ann uttered those words, I felt as though that exhilaration extinguished.

Jace felt the same.

Perhaps more importantly, we both knew as one that our disappointment was one thing that had to be held close to ourselves and not shared with Ann, or any other authority figure.

It seemed either that our reaction was very successfully hidden or that Ann had not even been looking to see how we might react to her statement. I personally thought that it was the second of the two possibilities. Although I had only begun to get to know Ann, there was something about her that I related to very well. There was no question that she was a perfect authority within the Academy, attending to her duties with precision and certainty. She not only taught with great determination but her counseling of some students was exemplary.

In particular, her counseling of Jace and me.

The question was, did she *know* just how fundamentally different Jace and I were? And if she did, was she surreptitiously encouraging a kind of rebellion within us that was unheard of at the Academy and our society or was she trying to hem us in?

She had the confidence of the Headmaster, and that was something that she needed to keep. Perhaps even *he* understood that it was in the exception that the rule was proven and that Jace and I were truly "exceptions".

I was only beginning to have a sense of these questions and many others. For a long time, I would not bother to fully articulate them. Sometimes they would feel as a sensation brushing through my thoughts. It would only be later, after the Event and all that followed that these questions and thoughts would come to dominate my imagination.

"The Headmaster was not as certain as I about what to do after you'd had a chance to discover and explore the library. He felt that anything less than censure would just 'encourage' you in what he called deviant ways. But I impressed upon him that your ways were hardly deviant and that you were simply exercising the gifts that you'd been given, gifts that our own tests had demonstrated to be real.

"You will have to be aware," she added, her voice dropping just a bit, "that the Headmaster is concerned with how far and how fast to let you explore." Her expression impressed upon us that even though we were respected and recognized for our intelligence at the Academy, there was a limit to how far we could go. It brought to mind something my mother had long ago taught me when we were in the fields, exploring.

We had come upon a family of wild beasts. One of the calves seemed to have taken it upon itself to be nurturing to a smaller, weaker sibling.

I watched in fascination and delight to see such generosity in nature. But then, even as the calf brought food to its weaker sibling, the sire attacked, killing both the calves, the generous one and its weak sibling.

"Mother!" I cried out in astonishment.

She hugged me and hushed me, telling me to dry my tears. "You see, my child," she said softly, "in nature and the world, what is different can only be tolerated within reason. Then it becomes freakish and finally dangerous." She held my face and looked deeply into my eyes. "Remember that, my dear daughter. Always."

I had not thought of that moment since. Until now. It occurred to me that Jace and I were in danger of becoming the "other". Different, bordering on freaks. How far could we go before we were considered dangerous?

Jace and I spoke about my concern later that day. We agreed that there was a real danger. That afternoon we made a pact. We would carry on as much as we could *just like everyone else.* Normative behavior would be our cloak. Our protection. Only with one another and, perhaps with Ann, would our full sense of who we were find full expression.

Ann watched us both, measuring our reaction to her words. Satisfied that we had heard her message clearly, she gestured for us to follow her.

"I am quite certain that you have not discovered my other collections," she said as she led the way deeper into the bowels of the library until we came to a series of doors, each protected by a graduated security system.

Finally, with a particularly meaningful smile, she paused before a final set of doors. "Are you ready?"

Jace and I looked at one another and nodded.

"Good." She stood before the iris-identification pad and then pushed open the door.

I felt the breath taken from me as the door opened on to a huge, warehouse-sized room. The first thing I saw was what looked like a stampede of wooly mammals. But then, on closer examination, I saw that they were elephants.

Elephants!

These magnificent creatures had been extinct for hundreds of years. I only knew them from images in books and on electronic displays. Noble creatures standing fifteen feet high with their mighty ears and massive trunks.

"Would you look at them," I said, my eyes wide with wonder as I circled around the display of life-sized, real, but stuffed elephants. Ann allowed us to freely interact with these beautiful creatures, life sized, but taxidermied animals. She explained to us that the DNA of most creatures including these was carefully stored in the ARC and when the earth was repaired enough, scientists would start to repopulate the world with them. As yet the earth was not considered healed.

"Back when people hunted these magnificent creatures for sport," Ann said, "a man who would become an American president went to Africa and killed this whole family." Her voice was filled with a sadness and longing I had not heard before.

I looked at her and then I looked at the elephants. A large bull elephant led the herd, his huge tusks reaching fifteen feet in front of him. Behind him followed a couple of females and younger elephants. In their midst was a small baby, small enough to have as a pet! At least that is what I thought.

"Why would he do such a thing?" I asked.

"For the same reason that people did most of what they did at the time – selfishness, greed, thinking that all existence existed for his personal enjoyment and pleasure. It was an extension of the individual. *I* am most important therefore *my* family and tribe is most important therefore *my* beliefs are correct and my comfort is more important than anyone else's and everything that exists, exists for me and mine." She sighed. "Frighteningly, we still have those same emotions and feelings. It is part of our genetic make-up as human beings. No amount of engineering seems to be able to fully erase it from our being.

"However," she went on, "we have come a long way toward blunting that fierce individualism."

It would be later, when only Jace and I were there, that Jace looked at me with his most earnest expression and asked me what I thought about what Ann had said.

"What do you mean?" I asked, trying to think of the particular thing he was asking about.

"The bit about getting rid of individualism," he said, his tone off-hand but his expression deep and thoughtful.

"What about it?" I asked, trying to anticipate what his train of thought might have been. That was often the way it was for the two of us. Jace would raise a topic, and I would try and figure out where he was going with it. Most of the time I could figure it out. Sometimes, I caught on quickly. Once in a while, I was completely lost until he told me. I think I liked those times most of all. Of everyone in the world, even my teachers and parents, only Jace could genuinely delight me with the excitement of discovery.

Until the moment he asked, I hadn't given her comment much thought. I had just been caught up in the moment, trying to take everything in. After all, it was not every day that students were given a private tour of an unknown museum! But, now that he had asked, I realized that her comment had struck me as very odd, and somewhat troubling too. But I wasn't exactly sure why.

After all, she'd made perfect sense when she cataloged the negatives of human greed and materialism – both fully the consequence of the heightened sense of individuality. We had been taught how man's behavior had brought about the degradation of the natural habitat, forcing the population into the bunkers.

And yet, I could not help but consider that along with those profound negatives, it is our sense of self, our individuality that contributes to everything wonderful about being human – our ability to create art, to make music, to fall in love.

Certainly to "erase" the sense of self and individuality, to erase human greed and avarice is a positive aim, perhaps even a noble one. But if that effort also removes every vestige of our human ability to create art and music, or to fall in love... perhaps it is not such an appropriate goal.

But then, even with Jace's incisive questions, my faith in the Academy was absolute. If the Headmaster determined that ego was the source of the avarice and greed that had done such damage to the world, then I did not doubt him. And to have Ann in agreement... well, that seemed to settle the matter for me.

I looked Jace in the eye. "But do you really think that is the true goal? To get rid of individualism?"

The truth was, I knew that our academy supported and encouraged a degree of individuality by allowing each one of us to move through a tailored education plan that had been individually-designed, specifically with each child's requirements in mind. I felt quite certain that it was not individualism or ego itself that was the object of the Academy's focus but rather the unhealthy expression of it. After all, I did not think it was possible, let alone desirable, that the things that made us unique were erased.

We all had tasks that we would be trained to do. Our futures, occupations and role in the larger enterprise were not left to the whims of emotion and random events as had been the case in the past. While we each had some input into the direction our futures might take, the truth was that the options available to us were determined by the series of very comprehensive tests that we'd each completed upon entrance to the Academy.

As Jace and I had learned from our own experiences, these tests take into account objective knowledge and learning, our interests, personality, creative expression, skills, mental aptitude and unique abilities. The tests are followed up with a number of well-structured counseling sessions with a senior advisor who is assigned to the student based on personality matches. However, the student still may reject the advisor and request another.

Of the thousands upon thousands of students who had passed through the Academy over the generations, only Jace and I had presented ourselves as the kind of enigma that called the process into question. That said, in some way, the Academy took solace in the old adage, "The exception proves the rule" in assessing our aptitudes and capabilities.

The simple truth was that the process had served our community well. The match between individuals and their career had proven to work in the best interest of the person and the community.

The community moves forward; the individual feels rewarded by satisfaction in the task.

No longer did people feel the need to search for a career based on potential income. Because the system of matching had been so well-perfected, and professions so expertly allocated, earnings – and indeed, money itself – was no longer a viable system of assessing worth. It had, after all, been an imperfect system throughout history, creating class tensions, philosophical debates, wars and the unequal distribution of resources.

In our community and society, satisfaction resulted from the ability to contribute to society as a whole. A responsible bartering system functioned to fill in the small, everyday gaps that inevitably resulted in human interaction.

Lest anyone believe that this system was foisted upon the people, imposed upon us in some dark conspiracy, the teaching of the Academy was clear and verifiable. The allocation and education system came about over the course of many hundreds of years during which our civilization spent time in the underground bunkers during the purge.

Survival first. Then philosophy.

Underground, conflict was a luxury that we simply did not have. Each had to do his and her part. Disagreement could result in disaster – real disaster, not some vague sense of unhappiness. The disagreements and arguments that preceded the purge had to be surrendered; otherwise, the doom of all was guaranteed.

It was logical that this period would see an explosion of regulations. We were teaching ourselves and learning how to live together. Some decisions had to be made about how best to negotiate the transition.

The transition was not easy, but it was necessary. Humankind learned a great deal during those years; and has benefitted mightily from the process. It was not a certain outcome, but with hard, hard work and great expense, we moved forward rather than backward.

At the Academy, our raw scores were combined with input by proctors, and all the scores were entered into vast and complex computer algorithms designed to place everyone on the correct career path. The algorithms had been designed to account for thousands of variables, from age, union of parents, genetics and effort; physical capability is assessed along with mental acuity. Proctors are trained to observe every aspect of the test taking, from a subtle eye movement to the more obvious, such as signs of frustration or impatience.

Once the data has been entered into the programs, it cannot easily be manipulated by human intervention. Only in the event of a gross error, the kind that had not occurred for many, many years, is a candidate ever retested. Certainly, such retests are not entertained based on any of the "non-merit based" criteria so often used in the past.

In formulating the future, the program does not care about the "influence" or "importance" of a family member. Everyone in the society is important. No one's influence weighs more than anyone else's.

Once set upon a course of study, the curriculum – which has been developed using the same complex algorithms – is followed exactly. In this way, learning plans are both "individualized" and communal.

We are all taught according to need and talent. No two children are taught the same. Yet, when all is said and done, we are all trained according to the same standards and creed. This training is deemed necessary and is compulsory for everyone.

There are no exceptions.

"It was not always like this," Ann explained to Jace and me during one of our regular visits to the museums. "Many centuries ago children went to schools and were taught to think and act the same as each other." She smiled as she studied our expressions. "It's ironic, is it not? Jace and I had ascertained from the many books we had read that back then, the idea of 'individuality' was practically a form of idol worship, there really was no individuality at all. In the history of mass education, a child was simply taught to be a non-thinking and compliant unit, the fear of our forefathers was that having too many free thinkers would not be good for the world. Not in curriculum or in teaching method anyway.

"People then were raised to become compliant workers and, more detrimental to all involved, compliant consumers." Ann shook her head in mild approbation. I was certain that I heard a slight "tsk" in her not-so-subtle judgment of how "primitive" people had been in the past. "And what consumers they were! They wanted *everything*, even when there was nothing left to be had!"

She described the weaknesses of an educational system where there were universal lesson plans based on government requirements with each and every child moving through the system as one. Some excelled. Some coped. And some, who could not keep up, were left behind, often turning to crime and theft as a means of survival. There were entire social castes doomed to lives of crime and substance abuse for no other reason than the "system" sought to force them to learn and be just like everyone else.

An obvious impossibility.

Meanwhile, there were others who were truly gifted children. These children rose to the top like cream no matter what their circumstances. Invariably, they were placed in situations and schools that valued their individuality and the possibilities that they brought to society. It was often hard for many of them because the process of finally finding a learning environment that matched their gifts often resulted in too many negative experiences that scarred them in one way or another.

And then there were those who, because of societies inequalities and the fact that they happened to be born into households that possessed great wealth, also benefitted by being placed in learning environments which treated them as individuals, although in many instances they were still pushed to be what they were not.

In short, it was an inefficient system which caused more harm than good; it was patterned after assembly lines that had been devised to efficiently produce widgets, cars and shaving cream. In addition to being wholly inadequate to educating students, they spoke to the underlying philosophy that held young students to be little more than the products manufactured by these assembly lines.

"It is a wonder," Anne added with a sigh, "that any of them could so much as stand upright in such a system." She gave an involuntary shudder.

However, even with our own highly touted individualized system of education, much of our early education shared the "group mentality" of previous methods of educating. While the process by which some of us learned was different than others, there was still a common body of knowledge that the community felt it vital that we shared.

"Shared information is shared destiny," the Headmaster made clear.

So, during our first year at the Academy, we were directed to move from one area to another as a group. Other than the guiding hand of our advisors, there was a scarceness of individuality about what we learned. Nor should there have been, as best I could tell. Our world demanded that we learn about war, warfare, defense, advanced armed combat and survival techniques.

No matter our final task in society, we were all, first and foremost, required to be soldiers even though we live in a peaceful, friendly world. So it was that by the end of our first year studies any one of us was capable of killing another person with a single blow. So was the *cookie cutter* model of the past.

Of course, the ability to kill another is never the same as having permission to do so. We were taught that we must always be prepared to act, but acting was a matter of profound discretion. The ability to kill another was a skill we were required to have. We were also taught that actually killing another, except in warfare, was absolutely unacceptable.

Our first year lessons were so that we all embraced our shared history and destiny, and that we had the tools to ensure our own personal safety. Underground survival was the first lesson we had to become expert at so that we could respond appropriately to any of the possibilities that could arise.

Even as Ann showed Jace and me the many horrors that befell the generations before our own, she took pains to make plain that even though these things happened in the past, there was always the danger in the world that it could happen again. Indeed, because the danger is always present, the Academy was sure to expose us to the numerous atrocities that the Ministry does not want to see repeated.

When Ann took us through the museum exhibits, there was a cool, safe fascination. The displays, even those that had been created to depict real life situations, were remarkably sterile. They allowed for cool detachment and study – which both Jace and I enjoyed. However, the atrocities that Academy exposed all students to that first year of study were immediate, visceral and gut-wrenching.

None of us who experienced the lessons were quite the same afterwards.

While the content and process was the same for each student, the experience itself was individualized. My teacher, Norman Sitzman, was responsible for my introduction.

"Ari."

I turned to face him. His voice had an atonal, flat quality. Which made his ability to command my attention all the more remarkable. Perhaps it was his physical presence. He towered over most of the students and, indeed, the faculty as well. His skin had a sandpaper quality, rough and reddened. His dark hair was cut close to his scalp, forming a flat top. His eyes, generally hooded and making it difficult to read his emotions or thoughts, were deep and dark.

"Yes, sir," I replied, standing at attention.

"Follow me."

"Yes, sir."

Although each of us knew that we were to be introduced to the atrocities of past times, none of us knew exactly when our individual experience would be. Part of the goal was to surprise each student, making him even more vulnerable to the power of the presentation.

I hurried along after Mr. Sitzman, struggling to keep up without falling into a loping runner's stride. His legs were so long that his normal, efficient strides made it extremely difficult for me to maintain his pace.

But I did. I had no choice.

When we arrived at the student's lab facility, he led me into a small room. Inside the room, there was a chair with a total immersion helmet and a small tray alongside it.

"Sit."

I sat.

"Put the helmet on."

I put the helmet on. As soon as I brought it over my head, I was immersed in total darkness.

"You can hear me now," he intoned. "Soon, you will not be able to hear me. Instead, you will be completely immersed in a sensory experience. Are you ready to proceed?"

I felt a shiver pass through me. Then I nodded slightly. "Yes, sir," I said, trying to firm up my voice so that I sounded absolutely certain. In truth, I was feeling very uncertain. Jace had gone through the experience only a few days earlier. It had shaken him. When I asked him about it, he just shook his head sadly.

That unnerved me.

"I am placing a device in your hand," he said as he pressed a small object into my right palm. "If at any time, the experience becomes too disturbing, you are to press the device. Do you understand?"

I nodded again. "Yes."

"Yes, what? You have to say exactly what you understand."

I knew that he was following a script, but the preciseness of the script was unnerving as well. I swallowed hard. "I understand that if at any time the experience becomes too disturbing to me, I am to press the device," I said. I also knew that I had to pass this session so that it was not presented to me again. From Jace's reaction, it was something that I knew I would only want to experience once.

"Good. I will not be far away." His voice trailed off.

With that, the pitch darkness gave way to a gray fog. My body was immersed in a chill as I found myself outside a primitive hut, looking in through a window. Without knowing how I knew, I knew that I was in Russia at the time of the tsar, but which tsar, I could not say. What I did know was, that before me in the primitive hut, were three soldiers dressed in heavy coats, their horses champing outside, sending fierce clouds of vapor from their nostrils. In front of these soldiers, a woman of undetermined age crouched in a posture of supplication and fear.

She held two children, one an infant, close to her. Behind her, with looks of terror on their faces, were two other children, wearing little more than rags; they looked to be six or seven years old.

"I don't know, I swear," the woman cried to the soldiers. "If I knew, I would tell you."

"I don't believe you," snarled one of the soldiers. "You know where he is and we want to know... *now*!" He took a menacing step toward the woman, causing her to shriek and pull back.

"I don't, I don't!"

"I can make her talk," one of the other soldiers said.

The taller one, the one who had been addressing the woman, turned and looked at the younger soldier. In truth, the younger soldier looked little more than a boy, perhaps even younger than Jace or I. The older soldier's lips turned up in a cruel smile. "You can?"

The younger soldier nodded, his pale blue eyes showing a cold cruelty I cannot adequately describe.

"How?"

"May I show you, sir?"

The older, taller soldier stepped back as if to give the younger soldier free range. There was a curious, artificial quiet in the small hut. The young soldier stepped forward. He smiled at the woman clutching to the baby and the young child. The other two children cowered deeper into a shadowy corner.

"We don't want to hurt you," the young man said, the strange smile animating his features in a cold, harsh manner.

A slight whimper escaped the woman's lips.

"We just need to know where your husband is. We don't mean him any harm. We have to ask him a few questions is all."

The woman clutched her children tighter to her breast. Just then, the infant began to whimper and cry. Perhaps he was hungry, and the closeness to his mother's breast made him aware of his hunger. Perhaps she simply squeezed him too tight. Who knows? Who can ever know such things?

The young soldier frowned at the baby's cries. "Shhh, shhh," he intoned. Although the sound was a comforting sound, nothing was comforting about his posture. He smiled. He went to great lengths to present himself as a "friend" who wanted to do no harm and yet his entire presence spoke of such terrible menace that I couldn't help but shiver as I observed these things.

The soldier extended his hand. "Let me comfort the baby and stop him from crying," he said.

The woman visibly trembled and pulled back.

"Don't be like that," he said, his voice cold as ice. "I only want to help. The child is unhappy." He leaned forward and grabbed the baby's arm and, after a struggle, wrenched him from the woman.

In the struggle, the baby began to cry louder.

"There, there," he said, his eyes focused on the baby. "Stop your crying."

The baby, of course, did not stop crying. He actually began to screech louder.

"Shut that creature up," the older soldier snapped, clearly tired of this little scene.

But the younger soldier seemed not to listen. He was following a plan that only he fully understood. He shook his head at the older soldier. "She will tell us what we want to know," he said, his voice certain.

He turned to the woman. "Where is he?"

The woman's eyes widened in terror. "I don't know. I told you I don't know. Why won't you believe me?"

"Because you are lying," he said in a calm voice.

"Quiet that baby!" the other soldier shouted.

Holding the baby in one arm, the young soldier stepped back and pulled out his sword, the cold metal substance glittered in the firelight. Holding the child in one arm and his sword in the other, he began to bounce the baby. "There, there," he cooed. "Mama won't tell me what I want to know."

"Please…" implored the woman, sensing that something terrible was about to happen. "Please."

The young soldier stared at her. "You want something from me, but you won't give me what I want?" he snapped. "One last time. Where is he?"

The woman sobbed. "I told you, I don't know."

The soldier shrugged. Then, with no more emotion than if he was tossing a soccer ball in the air, he tossed the baby up and caught him. "Tell me!"

The woman sobbed.

He tossed the baby in the air again, this time higher. But rather than reach out to catch the baby with his arm, he repositioned his sword under the baby so that when the baby came down, the blade pierced cleanly through the child.

The woman shrieked a shriek that was animalistic in its agony. The soldier shook the baby free of the bayonet, letting it's small frail body fall to the floor of the hut with a thud.

I felt a sickness in my stomach. I squeezed the device in my hand. The helmet was pulled from my head and I gasped for air.

"Are you all right?"

I felt as if I might pass out but after a couple of breaths, I was able to nod and then look up. "Yes, sir."

"Good."

"How could he be so cruel?" I asked, half to myself.

I had seen just one example of the horrific cruelty that people had visited upon one another. Others saw other examples. These horrors were gut-wrenching, they far surpassed the worst nightmares I'd ever experienced. I know that I woke up for several nights running, my heart pounding and my skin drenched in a cold sweat, an image of that young soldier's cruel smile slowly fading from my mind.

I knew that every other student was experiencing what I was. For weeks after we were exposed to this violence, students were distracted and came to class with dark circles under their eyes. None of us could erase these images from our memories; some things cannot be unseen.

There was nothing in our histories or our upbringing that could have prepared us for such ugliness. Not even the long talks that we had with our parents before we left home. No, nothing came close. But those first immersion exposures were only the first step. The purpose of our exposure was not only to disturb us, of course. It was to prepare us for our exposure to the realities of warfare. For, without the ability to exact profound cruelty upon one another, how could there ever have been wars?

The lesson sunk in.

The first class lesson I attended on the history of warfare demonstrated what happened when wars took place centuries ago, before our current millennium. I was not sure why we were shown the wars. I suppose we needed to garner our knowledge from some point of view and, when it came to the barbarism and cruelty of war any point of reference was as good as another – all that changed was the technology of cruelty. But why that time, and those weapons? I would later learn that the reason we live the way that we do was a direct historical consequence of these wars.

As soon as we were instructed to don our immersion helmets in class and we were cast into that deep darkness, we all re-experienced the barbarism we had been individually exposed to. Our heart rates increased, and I for one could feel a prickly heat make the skin on my arms and back pucker. I would later learn that every student reacted to the sensation in a very visceral way. Some got dizzy. Some became short of breath. One student vomited. Another nearly collapsed and had to remain on the floor with his legs propped up until he had regained his inner balance.

The instructors, understanding what our reaction would be, waited several moments before our inside screens came to life and we were shown footage of foot soldiers entering cities. They fired their weapons indiscriminately – into small gatherings of people, huddled together for safety or at individual citizens fleeing the scene. They seemed not to care a whit if their "targets" were civilians or soldiers. In their practice of warfare, everyone was a legitimate target. So it was that these soldiers, cloaked head to toe in thick body armor, shot at people for no discernable reason at all. Their weapons glittered in the harsh sun, metal guns that demonstrated clearly over and over again that they were capable of cutting a person in half. When these weapons weren't being fired, they were carried at the ready, draped onto the backs of the soldiers roaming the streets like packs of vicious predators. In jackboots and heavy gloves, they roughed up citizens they did not simply shoot down.

A recurrent behavior was for a soldier to arbitrarily grab a citizen and shove him or her to the hard ground. The soldier would then place his heavy boot against his victim's back. Then with calm cruelty, he would bring the barrel of his weapon forward, pressing it finally against his victim's head.

Sometimes the soldiers spoke. Sometimes they demanded something from their victims, usually an admission of guilt in something or for something. Other times, they were silent. But however they approached the situation, the ending was always the same. The head of the victim would be prodded with the barrel of the gun. The camera would show us a close-up of the victim's eyes, wide with terror. And then the soldier would pull the trigger. Bone, blood, flesh and brain would splatter. The soldier would laugh and kick the lifeless body aside before moving on to his next victim.

There was an almost numbing monotonous rhythm to these killings, but every once in a while, something would be different. A child would be shot. And grandfather would have his beard torn from his chin. A young woman, clearly in the bloom of her femininity would be pushed down and, sometimes before and sometimes after the trigger was pulled, would be wantonly displayed and her body toyed with in the most immoral and disturbing ways.

I felt sickened by the display.

And the laughter of the soldiers! Were there no morals then? No decency? Did these people place no value on their fellows?

If this "hand on hand" nature of cruelty was bad, the scale of the cruelty was even more astonishing when the other tools of warfare and destruction were demonstrated. We saw gargantuan machines that drove men into combat situations that could easily roll across or over everything in their paths. They were surmounted by huge guns capable of blowing out the sides of houses or buildings. From my view, it didn't seem to make one bit of difference if there were people inside those buildings or not. "Collateral damage" we learned to call it in subsequent classes.

"You mean," I asked, "that it was simply *acceptable* for non-combatants to be slaughtered?"

"Yes."

I was stunned, not just by the answer but also by the absoluteness of it. No additional information. No explanation. Just, "yes."

It seemed to say it all.

But of course, when it came to the destruction and cruelty, there was *always* something more to say. As we continued to learn, at the time such murders and deaths were dismissed with the antiseptic label, "collateral damage". Which, from what I could understand, meant that these poor people just happened to be in the wrong place at the wrong time through no fault of their own. People who, only weeks, days or hours earlier had had every reason to go about their daily lives, eating, sleeping, dreaming, loving, hoping, and then suddenly had it all wrenched away from them. And for what? What had their deaths and misery done to add to the perpetrator's strategic aims? Not a thing.

It was beyond horrific. I could not help but feel disgust when I considered how our forebears behaved, how, despite their literature and art, their high moral prognostications, their surety about "right and wrong" sunk to such despicable immorality and degradation. That such a label as "collateral damage" was not only allowed to exist but seemed to have been embraced as an excuse or even a reason for militaristic brutality nauseated all of us.

Of course, there was more – as we were coming to learn. There was something known as MOAB, "affectionately" called the "Mother of All Bombs" but which really was an acronym for Massive Ordinance Air Blast. The MOAB was a large-yield conventional bomb – that is to say 'non-nuclear' – that was developed for the United States military.

This explosive device could be dropped on hills and mountains and penetrate deep underground, blowing the mountainside out similar to the eruption of a volcano. Because it was not a "nuclear" weapon, it was somehow considered "allowable" during the warfare of the period.

Of course, it would be easy to point to the United States in its determination to exact the greatest destruction on its foes, the fact was that each country was as bad as the other, all stockpiled weapons that could kill and maim a whole generation of humans in another country.

"And for what purpose?"

Our instructors asked the same question that had been forming in our own minds. For what purpose and to what end? What was accomplished by the use of these terrible weapons? What had been gained? Financial wealth for a few? Momentary advantage for one country over another?

Sometimes, the instructors asked the question and waited, waited long minutes as we stammered some inane excuse, trying desperately to fathom some explanation for the use of such violence and weaponry.

Ultimately, none of us were able to come up with anything near to an adequate answer.

"Do you know why you cannot answer the question?" our teachers asked.

We waited. Perhaps a deficiency in our learning or prior education, we thought.

"Because," they said, "there *is no adequate answer!*"

And that was, of course, the point of the study. As we were presented with the awful and barbaric behavior, all we could do was sit and stare in shock at the barbaric nature of these weapons and the aftermath of their use. Gasps were heard around the auditorium, an occasional shriek. At different times, students ran from the room to the corridor outside. Some felt faint. Others, sickened. It made no sense to any of us.

I felt so nauseated thinking of the devastation and loss of life, I was thankful that we possessed no such arsenal of weapons now. I could not help but feel grateful when I reflected on the fact that we lived the way we do, protected from such senseless violence. I took pride in our being a peace loving people, that our neighbors were our friends who in times of need – and there have been such times – have pitched in to help us as we have pitched in to help them. I was thankful to live at a time when there were no longer many races, just one. The '*Human Race*'.

Nobody was left behind. Not a person, nor country, nor living being – human or animal. I shuddered at the conclusion of the presentation, unable to imagine ever treating another living being in the manner that I saw humans treat one another in the presentation.

Having been confronted by the reality of war's brutality and cruelty, we were then taught that, despite the violence and the destruction, wars never solved anything. In fact, as history made only too clear, they only ever made things worse.

Many generations ago, wars were waged against innocent countries by governments controlled by greedy corporates wanting to control resources, food supplies and much more. The corporates were controlled by the banks, and in the end, they were all controlled by the persons with the most wealth, who could not buy anything more with their money, so they wanted power at all costs.

Those in charge went to great lengths to disguise the true reasons for these wars, claiming that they were religious in nature or that one person was a Dictator and should be removed for his crimes against humanity. Or simple greed and perceived opportunity triggered them. Uneven resource distribution was a common trigger. One country may not have had enough food so they would attack another.

Many wars were fought for control of fossil fuels – the very things that would wreak such havoc on the environment. To our minds, we could not understand such brutality for fuels like oil and coal. Surely they had the means to develop technologies that allowed them to do without it.

Perhaps the most disturbing cry for war was when leaders employed what came to be known as "false flag" events – events when they committed crimes against their own populations and blamed another country or group. This allowed the leaders to rally their populations around their leadership, convincing them that they were actually solving problems when it had been them that started it all. The leaders ended up with a "mandate" to start another war.

This technique was perfected until leaders were so good at barraging people with all types of conflicting media that they managed not only to brainwash their citizens into believing in their cause but convinced the population to go and kill each other for the love of their country!

When we questioned how people could be so gullible as to accept this brainwashing, our teachers explained that the residents of earth had been made amenable to this type of brainwashing. Most had been programmed from birth to sit in front of media boxes that entertained their minds, or to escape from their realities into electronic devices that took away their interest in what was happening in the outside world around them.

"Some sat in front of these devices, all day!" our teachers explained, their voices betraying their own astonishment that people could live in such a manner. Such a waste of precious time, such a waste of life.

As a result of this onslaught of media, they became violent and hostile, often desensitized to the pain they could inflict on another human being. Not only with their fists or weapons, but their words also.

"People of all ages simply lashed out at others, hardly conscious of the harm they were doing. As a culture, they hurt other people for fun. Yes, that's right, for fun. As you might imagine, with this cruel desensitizing, crime rates soared, mostly murders, rapes and other assaults." Nobody could escape, nobody was spared, every person was affected in one way or another.

The Governments of the day had developed a plan, and that plan played out far better than they had ever expected. The manipulation of media and cultural cues had given them a result they could only have dreamed of. They had a pliable, desensitized generation of foot soldiers more than willing to do their bidding.

"Is it any wonder they ended up destroying themselves?"

We sat dumbfounded, considering the question. Perhaps it was only rhetorical, but each of us, certainly Jace and I, struggled to conjure up a response. *Was* it any wonder? Could things have been different? Why hadn't people rebelled? Was the brainwashing so effective?

I could not imagine how our ancestors lived and survived in such dark, primitive times. Of course, my astonishment was just a function of the same arrogance they felt then, thinking that they too lived in the most enlightened of times. Sitting in my classes, listening to my teachers, striving to be the best I could be, it never occurred to me that we were on a collision course with the past and that my knowledge and training would be the only thing to keep me alive.

CHAPTER SIX
THE PURGE

There is much that I value far above the way our forebears lived. Certainly, I have no respect for them when I see how they fought or became passive. But there are other aspects of their experience and lives that I think would be wonderful to experience. There have been times when I have secretly desired to hold a domestic cat and feel the small creature's warm body and soft fur beneath my fingers or hear its soft purr in my ear.

Years before, when I was little more than a small girl, my mother and I traveled to a museum where they had footage of this small domesticated animal. They showed the cat in the arms of a human, the cat purred so loudly it could be heard on the screen. Even when my mother took my hand and tried to pull me away, I resisted. I could not take my eyes off what I was seeing. It seemed almost magical. Not only did the cat seem very relaxed in the human's arms, but the human seemed very relaxed holding the furry creature also. Looking at the film, I felt I understood for the first time what a symbiotic relationship really was.

My chest was filled with such a sense of longing as I watched that film that I didn't know what to do. I could almost *feel* the relaxation that the cat and the human felt. It was such a delightful sensation.

After that day, one of the most selected scenarios chosen in my relaxation pod was of a small kitten purring.

To my understanding, cats seemed to be the epitome of all that was good in the natural world, particularly as it intersected with human experience. They were so loving and so precious, something that should have been protected at all costs. But they too were wiped from the face of the earth by the arrogance and foolishness of human behavior.

Which seemed to be a repetitive theme in human history. Arrogance and foolishness. Sadly, it seemed our forefathers did not truly care much about anything – (unless they were able to get something from them), not their neighbors, not the animals that roamed the earth and, ultimately, not the earth itself.

They loved themselves in the individual but not the communal. They treated each other abysmally but, as we had come to understand, that lack of compassion or care could not help but reflect upon how they treated themselves. Unable to truly care about another, it was impossible for them to truly care about themselves.

Whatever ability they had to bond with others extended only slightly. They loved themselves and, perhaps their family and kin. Beyond that, they held everyone in suspicion and as potential objects for conquest. For too many, the same feeling defined their relationships with family and kin.

As a race of people, they were petty, clannish, and ultimately self-destructive. They wanted the one thing they could not hold, the one thing that would prove to be their undoing the more they approached claiming it – they wanted power.

Such a being capable of much cruelty to his fellows certainly cared even less about the other creatures with which he shared the earth. However, for some, the cruelty toward other people did not extend to animals. Our teachers taught us about small pockets of animal protection activists, people who put their own lives in danger in order to save individual animals, as well as animal species. Extinction was their greatest fear – for every species that inhabited the earth. But in the end, they could not stop the relentless consequence of man's foolishness and pride. When push came to shove, they lost. As a consequence, the animals lost. Ultimately, humanity lost.

For many creatures, extinction was barely noted. For others, the ending came with a grudging acknowledgment. The final indignity for cats came when the species was charged with a decline in smaller wildlife and so were found guilty and sought out for destruction. It wasn't that they were particularly worried about the wildlife but more the food source that the cats were destroying. The irony was completely lost on those making the determination, that the greatest agent of extinction was condemning another species for doing nothing more than trying to survive. Those cats that were not out and out destroyed were eaten when food supplies ran out.

As a result of all these actions, there were very few small creatures who survived. Of those that did, the few that were saved exist now in the ARC.

The natural world essentially vanished. So too the artificial world that humans created for control, for commerce and for distraction. The devices known as personal computers filled landfills to brimming. Televisions, which they watched to distraction in their determination to lose touch with reality are long since gone.

We have no such personal devices. They had been banished for many years while society re-ordered itself within the ARCS. We do of course have computers, but they are solely used for appropriate occupational needs and as a study-based device. The closest technology we have to any device that assists us with our lives is a PAD – a Personal Assistance Device.

PADs are useful aides. Each of us has one, and it links to the implant that each of us is given at birth. It wakes us up, turns our lights on and off, and gives us weather reports and suggestions of dress for the day based on what is in our wardrobe that is matched to the weather. It alerts us to incoming chats and calls and plays music to us based on our individual preferences. It measures health parameters and can direct us to seek medical treatment when required. It can also provide information to us that we might not have for the lack of our PAD, we only need to ask. It is individually programmed to be responsive to each of our needs alone. It is comprehensively responsive, or as much as an inanimate object can possibly be.

It records all of our personal details and, most importantly, keeps track of the population.

PADs are vital to our individual functioning but also to our larger, communal needs. As such, it is illegal to not have a chip or to remove one. Not that any of us would ever knowingly compromise our PADs. To do so would go against everything that we have been taught.

Despite knowing Jace for as long as I had, I remember having the distinct sense that I truly *met* him not long after we began at the Academy. Perhaps it was that during those first few days something *within* me changed. I was no longer a child and so I no longer reacted to him solely as a friend. From not long after we had first gone to the museums with Ann, I began to view him differently and, I believe, his feelings about me grew more complicated as well. There was a new tension in our relationship, one that was not entirely unpleasurable.

I remember timidly looking over at him during our very first lesson on the history of warfare. His soft curled brown hair fell messily around the strong outline of his face. His large almond shaped, chocolate eyes were animated with excitement and shared an easy smile with his lips that turned up at the corners to greet me, as he turned toward me and mouthed, "This is remarkable!"

Oddly, my stomach did backflips. Never had that happened before. I could feel my face grow warm.

So much of our time at the Academy seemed destined not only to continue our friendship but to see it blossom and grow into something more. We both wanted – and were assigned – Environmental Geology as our occupations. Our unique talents and intelligence levels were so singular that our teachers had never seen *one* student at our level let alone two at once. As a consequence of all this, we were almost always joined together in our learning and study.

I don't think either of us ever minded. I certainly did not!

During the warfare lecture that day, Jace sent me a small note. It simply said, "Call me later." He had drawn a cute little flower in the corner. Passing notes and even communicating with eye contact and facial expressions was nothing new for us. But the flower? That was something new.

I tried very hard not to engage him or look at him for the rest of the lesson, but it was very difficult. When I did manage to avoid looking over at him, I kept glancing at the note and the small drawing. Every now and again I felt compelled to shift in my seat to glance at him and, each time he would catch me looking his way, and give me one of those cheeky, flashy smiles of his.

I made a face each time, but the truth was that I felt shy each time. I slunk down in my seat and stared back at the instructor standing at the podium. Each time I could feel the heat rushing across my face. I could not understand what was happening to me. "What a stupid display you are making of yourself," I snapped at myself.

I tried to calm myself down. "It's just Jace," I told myself. But somehow it was the fact that it *was* Jace that was the crux of my new feelings, which were both disconcerting and extremely pleasant.

As we knew from the very moment we met, Jace and I were a perfect match. We enjoyed the same things, and both of us had a passion for environmental studies. My passion had come to me from the many hours I had spent with my mother, exploring the world and having her as my first teacher, teaching me about the plants and the way the world once existed. My father was another incredible influence, although his influence was often less direct. My father is an Atmospheric Scientist. His dedication to science and to the study of our atmosphere and our environment made my career choice an easy one.

I had been raised for such a path, and for success upon it. Many times, my father took me to the lab and introduced me to the equipment he used in his occupation and his study. Telescopes and electron microscopes – instruments and tools that allowed him to measure the heavens and the atom, the vast and the molecular. I found his enterprises to be both amazing and interesting. While it is possible that I would have simply possessed my nearly insatiable curiosity, there is no question that my upbringing honed my curiosity and molded it, along with the importance of a clear line of inquiry.

The truth was, I wanted badly to follow in my father's footsteps. I wanted to share his passion or, at the least, study something that I felt passionate about. It was a delightful and wonderful happenstance that I got my wish.

Not that being the only child of Noel and Zara Vayne was one joyful experience after the next. Despite the intellectual and emotional gifts bestowed upon me, I was more than a little bit aware of the expectations placed upon me and the vision that my parents had for my future. There was no question that I felt the weight of that pressure riding on me.

The expectations and pressure did not come solely from my parents either. The truth is that the community has a great deal of interest in marriage, partnerships and children. These things cannot be left to the whims or coincidences of individual caprice. When a partnership is formed as one was with Noel and Zara, my mother and father, and wedlock is entered into, the Ministry will allocate by requirement how many children that you can have as a family.

In the case of my family, it was one.

Me.

Not only do these decisions manage the need of keeping our overall population in check, but it also serves the purpose of guaranteeing that the union will produce children or, in our case, a child, for whom particular resources, gifts and the energies of the family can be focused.

Of course, with the population capacity so limited and the need to rationalize the number of children born each year, every effort is made to guarantee that there are no "illicit" children. As a result, sexual relations before marriage are absolutely forbidden. No child can be born outside of wedlock. To do so would be to limit the child's opportunities and limit its ability to contribute to the culture and society. In other words, the child would be shunned, as would the parents. Indeed, no child was to be conceived or born without permission.

There was minimal, if any, resistance to these policies. Everyone understands and accepts the limits of the world we inhabit. As a result, we are all committed to existing in the earth-wide community and to maximize the potential for success in that community. As such, we both explicitly and implicitly agree to live by established regulations that maintain the eco-system and the environment of the earth for ourselves and for future generations.

Undoing the damage earlier generations had done to the earth and its environment, left us with a long way to go before we could achieve the early pre-purge environment. There was still a great deal of work to be done. However we have made great progress. We were all aware of this. We knew that we, as a human community, all had to make the necessary sacrifices to undo the sins of the past.

Our commitment to success was not begrudging, it simply *was*. Like breathing, eating and sleeping, it was part and parcel of who we are. We had learned a long time before that the population needed to be carefully managed if we were not to outpace the limited resources available to us. In short, the lesson was clear: overpopulation is not a sustainable model. It was simple maths. How earlier generations managed to miss that simple fact was astonishing to us.

However, there were many, many things that made prior generations confusing to us. We simply knew that the population had to be monitored very closely.

Historically, the warning signs were in place. But, as I've noted, they were ignored. Whether due to ignorance, which is hard to fathom or arrogance, which at least is consistent with so much else about human behavior then. Whatever the reason, by the year 2014 the world had grown to seven billion people! Seven billion, on this glorious small rock called Earth! Those seven billion represented at least three billion more than the earth could safely and adequately sustain.

Estimates at the time placed the earth's population at ten billion by 2050. Of course, this estimate was so far off as to be farcical. In fact, our researchers are convinced that the number was deliberately wrong in order to lull the population into believing that the governments of the day could manage the ever-growing famines.

It had become painfully obvious to our researchers that the governments at the time had absolutely no faith in their populations. And why should they? They had spent generations consciously and quite successfully transforming them into numbed and ignorant masses, moved by trivial entertainments and oblivious to the havoc they were wreaking upon their environment.

So it was that by 2025 the population had reached an astounding 14.6 billion people! The number was astounding. How could anyone believe that such a number was sustainable? Even if each and every person was reduced to the minimal amount of calories and fluid intake, there were simply not enough resources. And, of course, the limited resources were not distributed fairly or intelligently. The very people most complicit in destroying the resources of the earth, most culpable in stripping it of its riches and its flora and fauna, were the very ones who continued to claim ever greater percentages of the resources for themselves.

Even as resources dried up. Food supplies vanished. Even as governments faced growing anarchy in their streets, with mobs roaming the cities, scrounging for food and water, with lawlessness becoming the law of every land, even then there was almost no effort to address the problems.

Not that such a reckoning would have accomplished much. The earth had long passed its breaking point.

There was no longer any need for housing as the growing population simply roamed the streets in small packs, like feral animals, sleeping on the streets, defecating in alleys or in collapsing buildings. There was no running water, no sanitation. The medical system was completely broken. Medicine delivery was non-existent in the cities. Only in the fortress-like, gated communities of the very, very rich and powerful was there anything approaching "normalcy", and even that was diminishing rapidly.

And still, the governments acted as if the day of reckoning was far off.

Powerful corporations and interests believed that they could still make money from fossil fuels. Climate change was no longer an arguable notion. It was real. It was present, and it affected every aspect of life.

By 2025, governments had long been using dramatic means to try to control the weather, which still continued to become ever more extreme. They had sent drones and probes high up into the atmosphere, spraying and seeding clouds, both trying to bring rain and, when the rains were too intense, they tried to stop it. They became quite good at turning the water supply "on and off", turning off rain in one country while flooding another.

The technology was actually quite effective, and for a while, allowed for greater food production. However, as with all things human, greed and arrogance took over. Eventually, the seeding got out of hand. Flooding in some countries was devastating while drought plagued others. Soon, the technology itself no longer proved effective. They could no longer effectively control the weather. Hurricanes of ever greater force pummeled the coastlines while tornadoes battered the inland areas. Snows twelve feet deep were common and stretches of drought lasting a decade or more was not unheard of. Cold summers, warm winters. The climate was turned upside down.

Nothing seemed to work. The fundamentals of nature were out of balance. The constant manipulation and interference had taken its toll. Spraying crops. Antibiotics in livestock. Genetic manipulation of seeds. For a short time, the correctives brought results – and great wealth and power. But their successes diminished.

Pollution. Overcrowding. Climate change. It was only a matter of time before the breaking point was reached and a terrible implosion occurred.

There was only one hope – to purge the population.

The elite and the powerful had created the problem, and now they would have to address it. And, as always, if their "solution" were effective, they would have to shoulder the least consequence.

There was, by this time, no choice. The apocalypse was on their doorstep. They *had* to act, and it was only because the necessity could no longer be ignored, that action was finally taken.

The world governments met and, after a period of emotional hand-wringing and finger pointing, the ominous reality set it. They were well past the point of blame. They had to act if they were to salvage any shred of humanity.

With this certainty weighing on them, they began to plan. The strategy they hatched was beyond radical, but there could be no more self-delusion, only radical action had any hope of success. In collaboration with one another, the governments agreed to sterilize certain groups of men and women by administering powerful chemicals directly to the water system.

That decision was the difficult one. The easier decision was *who* would be sterilized. This decision did not require debate or vote. The elite and powerful in government and world economies knew who would carry the heavy weight of their centuries and centuries of arrogance – the same people who had always borne the weight of their crass desires. It was understood that the sterilization campaign would be directed at the middle and lower classes of each country and society.

Children were dosed with powerful chemicals designed to cause them to succumb to a "sleeping sickness" that brought about a relatively painless death in a short period of time. The governments prided themselves on this benign and considerate path. They even went so far as to make sure the medicines were delivered in a liquid dose that had a very attractive "cherry flavor".

The strategy was to make these medicines available to every parent and to market it for low-grade fevers and any kind of cold symptom. Seeing as colds and other viruses were rampant at the time, parents readily dosed their children with the delightful new medicine. By the time the general population made the connection between the medicine and the deaths of children, it was too late.

Of course, the powerful and elite knew that they could not kill off *all* the middle and lower classes. Who would serve in their bureaucracies? Who would take care of their children? So, while it was clear to the governments who would be purged, there was a great deal of intercession for *some* people to be spared. Selected families who were able to support the government's plan – based on their purchase of health insurance on the open market – were often allowed to pay their way and be spared. These people were put on notice not to drink or cook with untreated water supplies.

The world governments worked hard and fast to build sustainable environments underground where the elite and Government officials could remain safe, along with workers to ensure secrecy, until the earth could purge the population and right itself. They called these underground bunkers ARCs, Autonomous Rescue Caverns. Scientists and medical researchers were each given a device to carry, which effectively put them on 24 hours' notice of the ARC's closure.

Of course, the elite and powerful had no intention of taking in the workers, only those soldiers they could trust to guard them. They simply were operating with all practical contingencies. They knew that even though they were in lock down, they would still need to seek answers as to how to clean up the world when the locks opened allowing them access to the outside world.

They built bunkers, many stories deep. Each country was responsible for their own bunkers, their design and capacity. The only commonality was with technology that allowed them to communicate and, in the event of a global catastrophe, to conjoin. Not that any of the people involved in the design of the bunkers had any illusion about taking anyone else in. Even in these circumstances, even with the apocalypse upon them, they were plotting and strategizing for their "best interests" never understanding or appreciating still that the "best interest" of each was the best interest of all.

Even at the end of history as they knew it, they were still bowing at the altar of power and money.

In order to guarantee a pliant workforce, from the middle of 2020, the government and elite began to kidnap young children. After careful screening, they determined who would become part of the servitude caste in the bunkers. Although they anticipated this aspect of the plan to face the greatest resistance, it was actually one of the easiest to implement.

Their plan was ingenious in its simplicity and cruelty. Under the guise of an outbreak of a perilous worldwide pandemic, normal blood tests were conducted, and children with specific markers showing that they had a resistance to the vaccinated termination serum were kidnapped. But not "really" kidnapped. The governments drafted a contract and, by telling parents that their children were being taken to designated "sanitariums" to keep them safe from the pandemic, parents gladly "signed over" their children, convinced that the "good" government was acting in their and their children's best interests.

In the ARCs, the children were educated in the tasks that would occupy their lives while they lived in the bunkers far below the surface of the world they had once known. They were taught to care for and nurture hydroponic plants and vegetables, essentially creating a new food source. They were taught to monitor and manage the engineering tasks associated with the complex nature of underground life, from the vast air devices and exhaust ductwork. They were taught how to maintain the underground water supply perfectly. Water was sterile so that it was safe for the elite to drink, cook with and bathe in.

Sanitation was an underappreciated but essential part of life under the ground. These children were responsible for the various tasks involved in keeping the bunkers safe and sanitary, safer and more sanitary than the gated communities that the elite had lived in above ground and certainly more safe and sanitary than anyplace they or their families had ever lived.

In addition to these essential tasks, the children were bred and trained for the more mundane tasks of life under the ground. Such as, cleaning the living spaces of the elite, caring for the children, cooking their meals and making their beds. Some of the brighter children were turned into a teaching force for the children of the elite.

In addition to the children, the ARCs were veritable arks for life as it once existed on the surface of the earth. The remaining species of animals, primarily those bred for food and work, were taken into the ARC. These continued to be bred as a necessary food source for the elite underground, providing protein and variation in their meals. Others were kept on specialized farms where they were allowed to reproduce to sustainable levels to ensure the continuation of the breed after the purge.

Those animals that either had been extinct on the surface or that took up too much space in the ARC "unnecessarily" were preserved in other ways. DNA samples of less valued animals and species were also stored for likely future use.

From my own perspective, it was sad that the domestic cat was not included in any of these salvation plans, but the common house dog was.

Plant species were preserved, and major hydroponic systems were operated by large solar farms on the surface which the government had built as a renewable energy source and a promise to the people that they would do their best to reverse the warming of the planet.

Of course, that "promise" like all the others made by the governments to the people was nothing more than a carefully crafted lie.

The truth was that the "promise" they made was really an excuse to create an underground food supply for themselves when they went underground. Even though their scientists – who still believed that they would be part of the underground society – did not think it was the most efficient or effective plan but they had to come up with some way to ensure a continuing food source in the bunker. It was the only idea that they could implement with the short notice they had.

Until underground cisterns could be created and safely fed, water was delivered to the ARC via underground reservoirs where the water was fresh and free from contamination. These water supplies were filtered naturally by nature. However, no chance was taken, so the ARC was fitted with massive reverse osmosis machinery to ensure that even the naturally filtered water was further filtered and safe.

They tried to think of everything, every possibility, every contingency, every threat and every benefit. When the call finally went out in 2025, only the chosen – the elite, the powerful, the connected and the necessary – knew to respond and arrived in time to be underground for the ARC's lockdown. All superfluous workers were sent to the surface on errands that would see them return too late for inclusion in the project.

Each 25-tonne blast door was secured by twelve, eight-foot titanium metal rods which embedded themselves into the blast walls at least a foot on either side; each was secured on a timer for 500 years.

Once the timer had been set, it could not be stopped or reversed.

* * *

We are now generations removed from those who survived and thrived in these underground bunkers. While we are anything but proud of the behavior of our forebears, both in causing the damage to the earth and environment and in the way that they allowed millions upon millions of people to die so that they could carry on, we also understand that when the apocalypse arrived there really was no other choice.

Many generations of people had a hand in the destruction of the surface. Only a few would have a hand in the continuation of humanity. For that, we are all eternally grateful. Of the billions of human population, less than one billion humans were saved in the ARCs worldwide.

When the generations finally left the ARCs five hundred years later, five hundred years after their ancestors saved themselves from destruction, the world they encountered was far different from the one that their ancestors left.

When they walked out from the bunkers in 2525, much had changed but, miraculously, much was restored. The advances made in the sciences while they were in lockdown helped rectify and reverse a great deal of the pre-purge damage, certainly much more quickly and effectively than anyone would have ever dreamed possible when they entered the bunkers in 2025.

And here I am, in the year 3014. There is still a very long way to go to fully restore everything that was lost. In many ways, we have evolved as a race, but we still have work to do. While we are much more committed to the success of our communal well-being, the same DNA that dictated the greed and arrogance lies deep within our beings.

We are a very complicated and fragile race. We are capable of so many good things, but we must also remain fully aware that we are capable of destroying ourselves again if we ever stop working together.

Sometimes to build a better world, you have to tear the old one down.

CHAPTER SEVEN
ADVANCED COMBAT; OCCUPATIONAL TEST

In the relatively rigid castes and strata of our larger community, it was rare – no, nearly unheard of – for people to cross over from one area to another. Once a career and life path had been set, the roadmap of one's life was certain. What was true for the individual was true of the entire family line. As the parents went, so too the children. People wed others in the same caste, raising their children with the same opportunities and expectations.

As much as what our aptitude tests showed, our histories defined how we would move forward toward the future.

Jace was one of the "one in a million" who crossed over. His future in science was a profound shift from his parents' background and history. There is not, nor was not, a particular judgment placed on our castes. Every person had a role to play in the sustainability and betterment of our community. Every person knew that and embraced their role and contribution.

Jace's parents were not scientists, as would be expected of a young man being trained and groomed for a future in science. They were firmly established in the manufacturing sector of our community. The skill set that had been honed and bred into his family over several generations was particular to manufacturing. Few of those skills were transferable. Little of the lore and knowledge was either. For Jace to become a scientist was tantamount to becoming a "blank slate" and rewriting not only his history but that of any children he may have in the future.

No, it was more elemental than becoming a blank slate. It was as if Jace recreated in the course of his few years the genetic and training profile that his family had passed along for generations. It was when I paused to give the accomplishment thought, I found it beyond astounding. I, of course, took who Jace was for granted. Why wouldn't I? What was singular about him was singular about me as well. As a result, he was "normal". But, of course, he was no more normal than I was.

Even so, my accomplishments did not call into question the fundamental, existential assumptions of our community. Jace, in effect, became a new person.

Despite the inherent pressure resulting from what he'd done, Jace was customarily nonplussed by what he did, what he was. After all, he reasoned, what else *could* he be? What else *could* he do?

"Things are what they need to be," he sighed with a shrug the only time we touched on the subject. Then he looked me straight in the eye. "It's not as if I made a decision to be who I am. I am, who I am. Just as you are, who you are.

"The only thing that gives me pause; the only thing for which I am consciously grateful for is that you and I are both on this adventure together. Everything else is... well, what it is."

Again, even though there were clearly "elites" in our community, there was no value judgment placed on the various sectors of the community. Like a body, our community depended on every facet to function well. Each facet of the community displayed real genius and leadership. In this regard, manufacturing was not in any way "inferior" to science. In fact, many important discoveries were originated in the manufacturing sector. Many "theoretical" insights would have been meaningless if not for the manufacturing sector discovering how to turn the theoretical into the practical.

So, while it has always been possible to cross sectors – if one's tests were compelling and the senior advisors felt strongly about it – it was exceedingly rare. No one was aware of anyone else doing so for two or three generations before Jace.

Possible. Not probable.

Of course, I grew up in the science sector. My genetic background and history was a powerful determinant as to the direction I'd follow. The greatest uncertainty had to do with *where* in the science sector? Wherever I was to end up, my parents had started early to maximize my gifts, placing me in a study center long before my peers engaged in formal study.

I was enrolled at the tender age of twelve. I was a gangling tomboy of a creature. Built like a boy and as fast and strong as any, I more than held my own during our first full year of "study".

Despite the many things we were learning with Ann, that first year was dedicated less to study than it was to preparing us physically for a world none of us wanted, but all of us had to be prepared to confront – a world at war. If at any point that should happen.

"I would emphasize," Mr. Frist, our instructor said, addressing us as we sat in a large amphitheater, awaiting the beginning of the next phase of our lives. Before the small, wiry man had taken his place before us, we were a curious gathering of nerves in our matching gym shorts and tee shirts. We glanced sidelong at one another. Some of us, of course, knew one another from our neighborhoods but most of us were strangers.

Who was that one over there? Was she stronger than I? Smarter? And him, he looks so intense and determined!

There were many moments that I wanted nothing more than to be back at home, under my mother's gentle tutelage. I tapped my foot nervously, awaiting the "beginning."

"Don't be nervous," came a voice.

"I'm not nervous," I whispered defensively, turning around to look directly at Jace's smiling face. "I'm not," I insisted. And I wasn't. At least, not anymore. Seeing his smiling face calmed me quite a lot.

And then Mr. Frist took his place before us.

"Ladies and gentlemen," he greeted us in a strong but not unkind voice, "we will be spending a great deal of time together."

There was a nervous buzz that seemed to go through all of us like an electric current. Mr. Frist allowed it to run its course. Unlike the military posture of the Headmaster, he was comfortable allowing young people to be young people… within reason.

"Okay… now our task is to prepare for the very unlikely and unthinkable," he went on. "We are going to prepare ourselves physically for the possibility of war."

Whatever electricity remained coursing through us died with those words.

"You two," he said, pointing to two boys. "Come here."

Nervously, two boys I didn't know cautiously approached Mr. Frist. He handed each a firm, padded object.

"Now, I am going to step back, and you are going to defend yourselves against one another with these," he said. Then he faced everyone else. "The object is to be the last one standing." He turned back to the boys. "Ready? Okay, go!"

We each sat up straighter as the dull thud of each strike echoed through the amphitheater. We winced with each contact. One boy then the other staggered but neither fell to the mat.

"That's right!" Mr. Frist shouted in encouragement, clapping his hands. "Give it to him! Good one!"

Soon, we were all caught up in the combat, cheering for one or the other of the boys. We took sides for reasons that we could not say. Unfathomable. Perhaps one of the boys reminded us of someone else. Or we'd cast our support during a moment when one seemed to hold an advantage, or, conversely, when one seemed at a terrible disadvantage. Soon, we were standing and cheering. With Mr. Frist, we cheered on each solid blow.

And then, one of the boys, the one with the darker hair – for that was the only way I could truly distinguish one from the other – dropped to one knee.

"Come on, don't give up!" Mr. Frist cried out.

With surprising enthusiasm, even those who were supporting the other boy took up the chant. "Don't give up! Don't give up!"

But the lighter haired boy pressed his sudden advantage. He swung his padded wand and connected with the side of the other's head. The boy tottered and then, unable to balance any longer, fell to the mat.

There was, among us, a sudden silence. Then a cheer went up. But the cheer faded on its own accord as Mr. Frist gazed at us with an expression we could not decipher. He gazed at us for a moment, and then he crouched near the fallen boy. He whispered something in his ear. Then he approached the victor and whispered something in his ear.

The victor went over to the vanquished and helped him up. They shook hands and then returned, somewhat winded, to their previous places.

Mr. Frist crossed his arms and considered us. "Well, that was interesting," he said, allowing his gaze to take us all in. "How long do you think it took you to become a bloodthirsty mob? A minute? Five minutes?" He chuckled, but his chuckle carried no amusement. "Fifteen seconds," he said evenly. "Fifteen seconds and you began to cheer for the defeat of one of your own." He waited. The large room was completely silent.

"That is the first lesson you need to learn about war and warfare. You take sides. Even after generations of training, we respond instinctively."

We were astonished and disturbed by our obviously flawed response.

"Don't feel bad," he told us. "It is understandable. But now you know. Never, never concede your reason and intelligence to your base instincts. For it is *that* which makes warfare so terribly cruel."

With that lesson learned, Mr. Frist went on to demonstrate techniques that we would use whenever we were in combat. Throughout, he emphasized that even in the very heat of battle we must not give in to base emotions.

"I am not speaking about morality," he said. "I counsel you to remain logical because that is the best way to gain and maintain an advantage over your adversary. Become embroiled in emotion, and you are lost."

So began our instruction in hand-to-hand combat. As we fought, we were continually assessed and taught. Stances. Approaches. Keeping an eye always to strategic retreat.

"Better to live and fight another day!" Mr. Frist taught us. "Never allow yourself to be trapped. Always have an exit strategy."

Mr. Frist tried to teach us that, in addition to the physical dimensions, war was a moral and psychological battle and that often if one can hold the moral and the psychological high ground, he or she can succeed even with inferior physical capabilities.

That said, we worked hard to maximize our physical capabilities. We worked with weights. We ran to improve our stamina. We went through obstacle courses designed to frustrate us. We battled in the cold and wet as well as on the cushioned mats of the amphitheater. We built not only muscle but flexibility.

More than once, in our exercises, I found myself opposing Jace. In fighting, as in almost everything else, we were extremely well-matched. However, I did have one advantage that I quickly learned how to press. He liked me and responded to me in ways I was only just beginning to feel toward him. I used his budding interest in me and my being a girl to my advantage and to put him off guard. This allowed me to put him on the floor quickly and easily.

"Really, Jace?" I would say after pinning him yet again. "You haven't learned to guard against your weakness?"

He would smile and shrug. "I guess there are some weaknesses better not strengthened," he said in an observation I did not yet fully understand but which sounded to me to be much wiser than our years.

Of course, Mr. Frist and our other instructors did not find his comfort with his weakness endearing. They counseled him on correcting for it.

"And you'd better," they made clear in no uncertain terms.

Jace, being Jace, took his lessons well. When we next opposed one another, I found myself on my bum before I knew what had happened.

"What was *that*?" I asked, gazing up at him.

Same smile. Same shrug. "I guess there are some weaknesses better off strengthened," he said.

He was like a Zen koan! It was a challenge and a delight to keep up with him!

Most of the time, we were not pitted against one another. Our advanced combat training saw us paired off against just about everyone else in our group, male or female, with no consideration toward size or weight differentials.

"Do you think your mortal enemies will ever show you the kindness of only fighting you if you are equally paired?" Mr. Frist chided us whenever anyone balked about going up against a larger student. "I don't. The task is to quickly figure out how to neutralize your opponent's strength relative to your weakness – and then make your move!"

Although we were all somewhat tentative during our first exchanges, we quickly lost any reluctance to fight and to fight hard. Our instructors urged us toward victory, real victory, not simply "feeling good" about our efforts.

"Remember, when it comes to war there is not a satisfactory second place. There is victory, and then there is death."

As a result, it was not long before we were all covered in various manner of bruises and cuts and scrapes. We were often hobbled by sore muscles and twisted limbs.

No matter how much pain we were in, none of us was willing to concede a point. Blood, sweat, tears. It did not matter. Our goal was victory which, in this context, amounted to impressing our instructors with our determination and skill.

We knew that there were no "practice runs" in the Academy. Everything we did was being viewed, assessed and analyzed. Every move we made, every success and failure was being weighed in the determination of our future occupations. I cared for no one in the group any more than I cared for Jace, but when it came to our one-on-one combat, I felt no more mercy toward him than he did toward me.

One day, I was paired with Ronan, a boy who had grown to nearly man-size at a very early age. He even bore the slightest trace of facial hair! He no doubt outweighed me – and just about everyone else – by thirty pounds.

For some reason, our pairing happened when every other pairing seemed to have been resolved, so all the instructors and students had gathered around our mat. As we warily circled one another, I could feel my heart beating in my chest and into my ears. The shouts of encouragement – to both of us – sounded muffled. My concentration was complete. I could smell the anticipation on his body as he moved closer.

"Come on, little one," he sneered. "What do you say? Let's get this over with quickly." He laughed.

It was an ugly laugh. I knew Ronan to be a considerate boy outside of our war games. But I also knew him to be ruthless during the games. He had yet to lose a single contest, and he meant to keep it that way when he faced off against me, a skinny girl.

"What do you say? I'll make this easy for you? Concede now and no pain."

I continued to circle him, keeping myself just beyond his potential reach. Just then, he pounced, and I danced back. I could feel the air move past me as his mighty paw of a hand came within millimeters of my face.

"You're quick, little one, but not quick enough."

He had no sooner ended his observation than I ducked low and scooted between his legs arriving behind him. I took my foot and kicked it hard against his back, sending him staggering forward. If I thought my maneuver would intimidate him I was in for a rude awakening. It seemed my action only served to amuse him – and to increase his bloodlust even more.

Even as the crowd around us cheered my audacity, he pivoted and stared at me with a gleam in his eye that I had never seen before. "Little one, you do yourself harm to prolong this."

"So says you," I said, sneering at him. I do not know where I found it, but I found my voice, and I was glad for it.

His face turned red and then purple. I sensed I was in grave danger now– but I also remembered Mr. Frist telling us that emotion in battle is our greatest enemy. In other words, I knew I had finally gained a small and only potential advantage.

He swatted at me again, this time catching me in the face with his powerful fist. In an instant, I felt a sharp pain and then a cold numbness. I could feel blood running down my face, and it was only later when I was in the infirmary that I learned that he'd broken my nose!

I staggered back from the force of the blow. I did not raise my hand to my face though. I knew I had no time for that for I was absolutely sure that Ronan would presume that, having connected such a strong blow, he could press his advantage.

I could not allow him that.

As he stepped forward, prepared to deliver another fierce blow, I leapt up and brought my foot across his head. The blow stunned him. I skidded across the mat on my belly, using his own size to give myself cover. In an instant, I was back on my feet. I delivered two quick jabs to the back of his head, and then, before he had the time to turn around to face me, I was on the mat and ducking under him. I became like a mosquito that he was unable to swat. Meanwhile, I delivered jabs and blows, weakening him not with an overwhelming strike but with a constant, unrelenting rain of blows.

"I will destroy you!" he roared.

But I no longer feared his roars or his size. I had only to keep moving, to dance beyond his fists and his feet, and to deliver quick hits. I brought my feet across the back of his knees, causing him to fall to the mat. I jumped on him and began to pummel him with my fists. Over and over. He rose up with me on his back, trying to ride him as I would a wild beast.

Unable to shake me loose, he fell back. The wind flew from my lungs as he landed on me. His head struck my still sensitive nose. I felt I was suffocating as I pushed up against him. I rolled left and right, trying to find an angle. I reached out and brought my arms around his neck and squeezed. Like a snake, I squeezed. He began to gasp.

Whatever else, his amusement in fighting me was now gone. We both knew that we were fighting for keeps! I didn't hear anything else, not the shouting of our fellow students and not the voices of our instructors.

It wasn't until we were pulled apart by Mr. Frist, with him calling a "draw!" that I once again became aware of my surroundings.

"You were fantastic!" Jace cried out, rushing up to me. He took a cloth and wiped at the blood on my face.

"Ari?"

I turned to see Ronan facing me. Only now he was the sweet, but very big boy who entered the Academy at the same time I did. "Ronan," I said, wrapping my arms around him in a hug.

He smiled. "I'm sorry about your nose. Do you think you need to go to the infirmary?"

I released him from my hug and gingerly touched my nose. "Ummm, maybe," I conceded.

"Mr. Frist," Jace called out. "May I accompany Ari to the infirmary? It seems her nose will need to be looked at."

Mr. Frist nodded and sent us on our way, but not before I gave Ronan another hug. Then, as we walked to the infirmary, I said to Jace, "I'm glad we don't have hands on every day!"

Jace laughed.

I knew I was lucky to have Jace with me, both going to the infirmary and every day we had combat – he helped clean my wounds and ease my sore muscles.

When our training wasn't focused on hand combat, we experienced the atrocities of war in our pods, or we gathered to watch film after film about wars and battles from a previous era. While it was possible for us to become numb to the horrors of war, our instructors were clear that we had to remain conscious of how horrible war was.

"It is so horrible it is worth our greatest efforts to avoid. However, when it is unavoidable, we must engage in it to win. There is no other option."

We learned to aim and fire disruptor energy weapons. Barreled guns such as those shown in the films were outlawed, we were never shown how to fire one and only learned about them in films.

"Never set to kill," we were taught. "*Unless* you intend to kill."

The disruptors were interesting weapons, small cylindrical-shaped and easily carried in a pocket. Its design was efficient. Lighter than a kitchen knife, a small slide button near the open end could be shifted left to right. On one side, it read simply "Stun". On the other, "Kill".

Slide the button to the left, and you could deliver a shock to your target. To the right...

We practiced long and hard with the disruptors until it felt as if they were extensions of our flesh. We "battled" target dummies with them, honing in on the upper torso for maximum effectiveness.

Using the disruptor seemed easy. And it was… in theory. In practice, it was more challenging. Jace and I practiced hour after hour, trying to model the instructors correctly.

Our time in Advanced Combat Training was quickly drawing to a close. Although there were times when it seemed to last forever. Now that it was coming to an end, it was astonishing how quickly the time had flown. We had covered so much material and gained so many skills, skills that we hoped we would never have to use.

"I am proud of you all," Mr. Frist told us. "You have learned well." He laughed. "And I hardly recognize you anymore!"

He was not kidding. The intensive practice had caused all of our bodies to become stronger, leaner… more warrior-like. The next time I saw my parents, they gazed at me as if seeing me for the first time, or as if I was a stranger who looked similar to their daughter!

With the conclusion of Advanced Combat training, we entered into re-evaluatory testing, this geared directly to assessing and reassessing our future occupation in light of what we'd already encountered at the Academy.

For this testing, Ann would no longer be an advisor for me.

The process was familiar in some ways, new in others. Rather than being administered, this test was done in the solitude of a small room with a chair, desk, and multiple choice screen display.

Question. Answer. Question. Answer. One after another. Despite being alone in the small room, there was no question that we were being watched. We were always being watched. "Evaluated." One of the great joys of the Academy was the discovery of small spaces where eyes could not see you.

The libraries and museums where Ann took Jace and I were such places – but, of course, when we were there, she was observing us! Still, that was at least *personal*. The cameras added a completely different feel to it.

As I read the questions, I came to understand that many of them were tailored to me and for my experience. I had no doubt that every other student was making the exact same discovery.

What distinguished this exam from the others we had taken in our lives was that there was no preparation that we could engage in to maximize success. No study. No practice questions. We were being assessed and evaluated on who we *were* and not solely what we knew or were capable of knowing.

We were, very plainly, being profiled based on genetics, history, experience and only a very small bit on performance. This was unnerving for all of us. After all, we had all been high achieving, focused and successful students and people.

That night, we all felt drained by the experience of testing but that sense of exhaustion was matched by relief, and a desire for celebration – the worst the Academy could throw at us had been thrown! The most difficult and unsettling of our lessons had been taught and learned.

In a very real sense, war was over for us. There would be no more hand to hand combat sessions. No more being struck by batons or electric charges. No more scenes of primitive times and their brutal practices.

We stood at a calm, at the moment between past and future. And we wanted to "let our hair down" and celebrate. So we did! With dance music blaring and sweet concoctions in our glasses, we laughed and sang. We talked about the future none of us could yet see.

In the next day or two, we would know the direction our lives would take. But for this moment, all was potential. All was promise. All was good.

"You'll get a good spot," Oliver said to Jace. "You're bloody remarkable. You too," he said, nodding over at me.

I didn't know what to say. I felt awkward and uncomfortable with being identified as "special" by someone in our group, even if I knew it to be true, even if I was pleased that the assessment was bestowed on both Jace and me together.

"We'll all get a good spot," Jace said, ever the diplomat, ever the one able to find the words. "Because whatever spot we get is the spot meant for us." He shrugged. "And there's no spot better than that, right?"

Oliver eyed him for a moment. "Maybe so. Maybe so."

"It is so!" Ronan bellowed, standing tall and raising his glass above all of us. "All is good! And right now, we are together. Bloody good!"

In the morning, we would all head our separate ways, back to our families to enjoy a four week seasonal break during which we would celebrate Nouvelle Terre, the day of the new earth. That day will see extended families and friends gather together to celebrate the opening of the time lock on the ARC.

So, when we finally grew weary of our laughter, our dancing and our singing, we began our farewells to our friends and fellow students, getting set to head home.

Although I was sad to say farewell to my friends, I was happy to be returning to my family. My greatest fear leaving for the Academy was worrying about how I might manage for such a long stretch without being with my mother and father.

As I was returning home, I felt a growing longing not only for them but for the familiarity of my home and personal belongings. While the Academy was comfortable in a spartan way, it was very clinical in its appearance.

At least it was thus far.

My mother assured me that it would get much better. With each passing session, we would be given more freedom. Rather than dormitories, we would be housed in individual rooms and allowed to have our own belongings around us.

A strange thing happened when I was home though. As much as I'd looked forward to coming home, when I was home, I felt "homesick" for the Academy. Well, at least *part* of my experience at the Academy. I waited each day for Jace's call. It was, no matter what else was happening, the highlight of my day.

As soon as I knew he was calling, my heart would begin to race, and I would hurry to my room where I would talk with him for ages!

"Well," Dad remarked with a smirk after I'd been home for several days, "I'm certainly looking forward to meeting the young man who is managing to steal my little girl out from under me!"

I could feel my face blush. "Dad, no one is stealing me…"

He cleared his throat and gave me a look as if to say, "I know more about this than you do."

I lowered my eyes. "I'm sure you'll meet him very soon," I said.

The days and weeks of break were lovely and over much too quickly. Even so, I would be lying to say that I wasn't looking forward to getting back to the Academy.

And to Jace.

* * *

We'd all changed in so many ways during our first year at the Academy, but it seemed to me that Jace had changed most – at least in my eyes. He was becoming a man. In another few months, he would turn eighteen. Long gone was his young boy's body, scarecrow thin and filled with restless energy. Now, in its place was the body of a man. Muscles replaced thin arms and legs. Power was conveyed in his every movement.

He was, in a word, striking.

My own body had, of course, changed as well. But there was more changing in me than what was most apparent, and those changes made it nearly impossible for me to keep my eyes off of Jace. For the first time in my life, I needed to *consciously* focus on the task at hand, lest I find myself distracted by him. Our constant banter and teasing had taken on a new quality, one that I could not yet articulate. All I knew was that it was compelling, powerful and welcome.

Upon returning that year to the Academy, we were once again ushered into the amphitheater where Headmaster, Colonel Williams stood before us. As we sat silently, he gazed across the seats, seeming to hold each one of us in his eyes and thoughts.

"Well," he intoned finally. "I see you have returned."

There was soft, nervous laughter that rolled through the hall.

The Headmaster allowed just the shadow of a smile. "I wasn't sure you would. I'm never sure." Then he straightened up and faced us in a way that seemed to convey a begrudging respect. "But you have. And that is worthy of comment. You were children when you first arrived here. Through our efforts – and yours – you are now on the cusp of adulthood. You are men and women in whom we will all place our faith.

"Do not let us down." There was a long moment of silence before he continued. "Now, we have a great deal to accomplish, and we've less and less time. Today will be devoted to a number of tests. Some of them will feel and seem similar to those you have already taken. They are not. How can they be? You are not who you were when you took the first series. You are new people, people reborn to the tasks ahead of you.

"With these tests, we will finalize our assessment as to how you will best serve the Community. There will be psychological tests, aptitude tests, special interest tests. There will be physical ability tests and mental stamina tests. When you have concluded your tests, you will speak with a senior advisor who will review your results along with a counselor. At that time, a decision will be made as to your future."

At this point, it was so quiet it would have been possible to hear a pin drop. Only the echo of the Headmaster's strong voice continued to carry into the far cracks and crevices of the amphitheater.

"One final note," he added. "The senior advisor and counselor will be new to you."

I felt my heart sink. I had been looking forward to seeing Ann again. There was much I wanted to tell her about my thoughts and experiences at home. Perhaps more, I had come to trust her. Now new people will decide my future.

"Now, just wait in your seat until your name is called."

I felt butterflies in my stomach as I waited. But fortunately – or unfortunately – I did not have long to wait before my name was called and I was led to a designated testing area.

"Relax, Ari, relax," I told myself, shaking my arms to release the nervous energy that was bursting from me. I was worried. Really worried. There was so much riding on these tests. For me, the worries centered not just on where I would end up, but where Jace would end up as well. If he didn't get into the Sciences, then he would be moved to another part of the Academy. The chances of our seeing one another would drop down to almost nil. That thought filled me with dread. I couldn't imagine the Academy or, if I was completely honest, my future, without Jace. I just couldn't.

He had taken a seat alongside mine as we waited for our names to be called.

"Don't worry," he whispered.

"I can't help it," I whispered back.

Through the corner of my eye, I could see him smile.

"Arianna Vay."

I sat up straight, hearing my name. A quick glance at Jace. He reached out and grabbed my hand. "Don't worry," he said. I didn't answer. I tried to smile. And then I was on my way.

My examiner led me to a small, soundproof room.

"Have a seat," he said simply, nodding in the direction of the small chair in front of the desk. "Just relax." He closed the door. For a brief moment, there was complete darkness. Then a small light positioned in the corner came on. A moment later, an illuminated screen came to life in front of me.

"Ari, relax."

I looked at the speakers, the source of the gentle voice.

"Breathe slowly. Place yourself in a state of relaxation."

The hammering of my heart was giving away my nervousness. Whatever was to happen, would happen. I had to relax. Taking the voice's advice, I concentrated on breathing slowly and deeply. I closed my eyes and tried to visualize my breath going in and out of my lungs. Slowly, slowly.

As I felt my heart rate slowed down, I knew that my monitors as well as – the embedded chip that tracked all aspects of my physical response saw to that.

As soon as my heart rate had slowed to an acceptable rate, the voice said, "We can begin."

I opened my eyes and looked at the questions as they appeared on the screen. I did not understand why I was being asked the questions I was being asked. "What colors did I favor? What kind of weather suited me best? What smells did I find offensive?

The answers to these questions were, of course, simple and straightforward. But *why* was I being asked such questions? That troubled me. But I had to push my discomfort to the background and simply concentrate on answering.

Honesty was always the route to go. One question after another. It became reflexive until the following questions appeared on my screen: Have you engaged in sexual activity? I paused. Not because I *had* engaged in sexual activity. I hadn't.

But I knew something was different about how I felt inside when I was with Jace. I knew my body was changing and sending me new, unsettling messages.

Were those messages *sexual?*

I was both frightened and excited about what the answer might be.

So, although I answered "no" to the question, my heart was racing, and I felt a heat in my cheeks. Had I been honest? If my feelings were sexual then wasn't much of my action with Jace somehow sexual? It was all so confusing!

"Breathe," I told myself, knowing that even if my actual thoughts weren't being monitored, my physical reactions were, and those were telling enough! I breathed slowly, and the next question appeared on the screen. And then the next.

If my most private thoughts were to be known, yes, I had thought about Jace *that way,* but I would never break regulations; I would never consider *acting* on my feelings. Such actions required marriage.

I sighed. Yes, my answer had been honest and correct.

During a short break after the test, I sat outside the test area. My examiner stayed close to me but did not engage in any conversation. Although there were a handful of other students in the area, none of us communicated with one another in any way. Such communication was forbidden during testing. Examiners kept a close eye on us, but to my knowledge, no one ever tried to communicate with another student.

And what would we have communicated anyway? What would I have communicated? It is not as if the questions I had been given had correct answers. They were questions about me. In truth, I had no idea what they had to do with my aptitude for any future position or career. This seemed to be about my personal life.

I gave up trying to sort it out. After all, these tests have been used for a very long time and seem to have accomplished what they were set up to establish. There was obviously more wisdom in the questions than I could understand.

Coincidentally or not, just as my "faith" in the tests was reestablished in my own mind was the exact moment that my examiner came over and tapped my shoulder, indicating that it was time for the next session.

Following the now-familiar procedure, I found myself back in the testing room before the monitor.

This set of questions centered around my character. Who was I? How might I respond to certain situations? For example, if there were a fire and I could only save my mother or my father, who would I save?

After this test, another and then another. Finally, when I was finished, I was brought to a dining room. Until I sat down, I hadn't realized how famished I was! While my tests were collated and analyzed, I ate a huge amount of food. I was so focused on eating that I almost didn't realize that the tables around me were filling up with other students, all as famished as I was. Soon, there was the collective noise of our eating and, after we finally began to feel sated, our conversation and laughter.

It was good to be with my friends and fellow students again! The testing had been so isolating. Somehow we knew that we could now talk about the tests and testing freely.

"Did you get a question about a red fox or a grey one?"

"Were you asked about the measure of a crate?"

Strange questions. Seemingly arbitrary questions. Although, from the talk around me, it seemed that at some point each of us was asked about sexual activity. No one came out and said it, but a number of people alluded to it.

"Did you get a question about…?"

Always a pause, awkward and unending. Always answered by, "You did too?"

I was finishing my third – or maybe it was my fourth – dessert, when I heard a chair sliding alongside me. I glanced up.

"Jace!"

He smiled. "How'd the test go?"

I felt myself blush. For some reason, even though there were hundreds of questions on the exam, the only one that came to mind had to do with sexual activity. Not trusting myself to answer, I just shrugged.

His smile never wavered. It was as if he knew something that I didn't. Of course, that was a quality of his that both endeared him to me, and infuriated me.

"I hear that there is only a little more to go," he said.

I nodded. "I'll be glad when it's over."

He glanced at me like he was trying to read what I meant by my comment. There was a moment of concern like he was worried but then that passed. He knew I would be all right.

Just when I felt most comfortably sated by my meal, my examiner appeared at my shoulder. "One last test," she said.

I nodded and got up. She led me to a small, comfortable room. The walls were adorned with beautiful, hand-painted pictures. Once again, there was a glass screen on the table. I would later learn that each of the rooms had different pictures painted on the walls. It was as if the rooms were hand-painted with each of us in mind.

In my room, the paintings seemed to be populated with small, furry animals. They were playful as they romped across the painted landscape. So friendly. So cute. I felt my body relax and a smile broaden across my face.

I found myself becoming completely engrossed by the painting. It was as if I was walking through the landscape, rather than simply looking at it. I was completely taken up by it. I could feel the warmth of the sun on my skin. I could smell the fecund smell of the plants. The flowers. I could hear the way the breeze danced through the brush and trees. I could hear the footsteps of the animals along the paths.

Then I felt my breath catch in my throat. Oh my! I approached slowly. There, before me, was a domestic cat! A cat! How did they know? How did they know what this creature meant to me? How it had danced through my thoughts and imagination for as long as I could remember? Even more than when I was posed the question about my sexuality, I felt suddenly naked and exposed.

Perhaps for the same reason!

My inner thoughts and dreams, my hopes and fears all felt as if they were being broadcast and bared to the world.

I had never told anyone about my love for domestic cats and certainly not the specific one that was here before me, painted on the wall! This cat, this very cat, was the same one from my leisure pod! What other information from my pod had they gathered, and why?

I reached out to pet the cat… and I felt my hand press against the cool wall of the room. The three-dimensional quality of my experience ended. The door opened, and Ann Polin stepped in.

"Hello, Ari," she said.

"Ann," I said, feeling a bit flustered.

She stepped aside, and two others came into the room, a counselor and another advisor. I quickly stood to attention.

"Hello, Ari," they said in unison. Then they stepped over to two chairs on the opposite side of the desk and sat down.

I looked at Ann who indicated that I could sit down as well. She, however, remained standing. "Ari, this is Arna and Joyla. They will be reviewing your results and discussing them with you. I will be available, but primarily to consult." She smiled. "It has been a pleasure working with you, Ari." With that, she slipped out the door and disappeared.

I looked at the two women in front of me. They were attentively studying the results of my testing.

A moment later, the two women glanced up at me.

"Good work, Ari," Joyla said. "Our understanding is that you wish to continue in the Sciences, like your parents. Is this correct?"

I nodded. "Yes."

"Because of your parents?" she asked, her tone more pointed.

"Yes and no," I answered. "Of course, my earliest exposure and understanding of science came from my parents, so in that regard, yes. However, I have come to love learning about science and have always found that the more I've learned, the more I had to learn. It has always been close to my heart."

"And if you were unable to continue in Science?" Arna asked.

The question dumbfounded me. For, in truth, though I knew I was being tested to assess my aptitude for a Science career, it never really occurred to me that I would not have such a career path. "I... I cannot imagine not pursuing a career in Science," I said finally. Then I looked at them closely. Leaning in, I asked, "Have you found anything that might compromise my going forward with Science?"

"We are not at liberty to say," Arna said. Even so, they seemed satisfied with my response.

Joyla asked the next question and then, one after the other, they seemed to alternate questioning me. The questions went on for another hour or so until, finally, they looked at one another in a silent agreement and then turned back to me. "Could you please wait in the corridor outside?"

Although framed as a question, I knew that it was anything but. I slid my chair back and, without a word, went into the corridor where I sat on the bench and reviewed the session, considering and reconsidering each of my answers and responses.

As I thought of each one, I could not think of a single word I would have changed. Having quickly reviewed and been satisfied with my communication, I found my thoughts returning to the picture on the wall of the room. The image of the cat resonated in my mind in ways that I couldn't fully understand. I felt warmth and unease, interest and a confusion of emotions I didn't fully grasp.

There was something about *that* cat. Why? And why was it that cat that was pictured in that room, the room where I was being assessed? Just when my thoughts about the picture seemed to be reaching a fever pitch, the door opened, and Joyla beckoned me inside.

She was about to direct me back into my seat, but before she could say a word, I found I couldn't keep myself from blurting out, "I really have to ask you something."

Arna and Joyla looked at one another and then Arna looked back at me. She nodded, giving me permission to continue.

"I'm sure this may sound out of place to you, however shortly after entering this room I noticed the picture on your wall." I motioned to the picture of the cat, "I was wondering how it is, that the very cat I have programmed in my leisure pod is the very one that adorns your wall?" Although I spoke these words with all the power of the emotions roiling within me, a red blush crept up my cheeks as my face betrayed a feeling that I had somehow spoken out of turn. "I don't mean to sound rude," I added quickly. "But I just can't help but ask…"

I was surprised to see a look of relief wash over Joyla's expression. She leaned towards me. She smiled. "You may not have anticipated it, but we are quite glad that you asked. The determination to question things, whether obvious or not, is essential to scientific inquiry. Scientists are naturally curious when presented with a puzzle.

"We were, of course, aware that you spent much of your time with this pre-programmed animal in your pod. We felt it was an appropriate picture to put on our wall in an attempt to disclose your curiosity."

At this point, Arna also spoke, "Having that image there was in a sense, a final test for you, Ari. We had to find a way to assess your natural curiosity; whether or not you have that curiosity which will animate your inquiry." She smiled. "And it appears that it does."

"Congratulations," they both said. "You will be placed into the Sciences division."

I beamed so wide the muscles in my face hurt. It was all I could do not to clap my hands together in glee. I had been accepted into what would be the foundations of my work in the Sciences.

Although both Joyla and Arna smiled at her reaction, they stayed on point. "Based on the answers selected in your testing your occupational profile will be drawn up. It appears that the system has selected that you would do well in Climatology. Is that an area that interests you," Joyla continued.

"Oh yes, definitely!" I could hardly believe that all my hopes were being fulfilled. Although I was completely excited, a part of my thoughts turned to Jace, wondering if he had made it through as well. Somehow, I knew that my excitement would be lessened if Jace were not able to enjoy this future with me.

Arna rose and extended her hand. "Well then, we are finished here now. Again, congratulations Ari. Good luck with your studies and we look forward to hearing great things about you in the future."

Joyla also rose. She too extended her hand to me. "Congratulations," she said. "Also, for the remainder of your time here, I will be your counselor." She smiled. "My door is open to you anytime."

A moment later, I was ushered through the door and into my awaiting future.

Time seemed to stand still. I sat in the courtyard, letting the warm light hit my skin. I could feel the sensation of the air brushing against the hairs on my arm. I could hear the silence of the courtyard. It was a complete and fulfilling feeling. I was so happy about my result but, of course, I could not be absolutely happy until I knew what Jace's future held. And so, I waited in the courtyard, as we'd planned. Waited for his arrival so we could, no matter what happened, have this moment together.

It seemed the most natural thing in the world, to have been together now. We had been a pair since we arrived at the Academy. Our intelligence, our natures, and our curiosity had matched us. But now, I could not begin to help but worry. Why was it taking so long for him to join me? And just like that, I was no longer fully engaged in the moment. I was antsy. Jittery. As the seconds and minutes ticked by, I began to pace.

"What's taking so long?" I asked out loud, surprised by the sound of my voice.

I had my eyes down, watching my feet as I paced back and forth. Who knows how long he'd been standing there before I finally noticed him?

"Jace!"

I stopped immediately. My excitement at seeing Jace was deadened as soon as I saw his posture and expression. His head was bowed. He had an aura of misery about him.

"Oh no," I sighed as my heart dropped. I ran to him and took his hand in mine. "Oh, Jace," I said softly, gripping his hand.

Suddenly, he burst out in laughter. "I made it, Ari! I've been accepted into the Sciences!"

I let go of his hand and slapped him hard across the shoulder. "Jace! You had me scared!"

He continued to laugh for another couple of seconds. "You should have seen the look on your face," he said.

"Why would you do that to me, Jace?" I snapped, pushing him away from me. "I felt terrible for you…"

"If you could only see the look on your face now," he chortled, teasing me for my earnestness – as always.

The truth was, despite my anger at being teased, I was elated by his news. Only my pride kept a pout on my face, and then for only another couple of moments. "Jace," I said, quickly coming around. "What area?"

Even though it was remarkable that he had been chosen for Science, given his family background, it would still be devastating if he was directed to some area of Science far removed from my own, like Archeology or some other such discipline.

He looked me in the eye and held the gaze for a moment. I felt like I couldn't breathe.

"Well?"

"Climatology," he said finally.

I didn't make a conscious decision to jump on him and hug him but the next thing I knew my arms were wrapped around his neck and my legs around his waist. "Me too!" I shouted.

He returned my hug before setting me down on the ground of the courtyard again. "I take it that you're pleased," he said with remarkable understatement.

Now that there was no suspense, I could afford to play his game. I shrugged my shoulders. "It is one of the outcomes I'd considered," I deadpanned.

He smiled, seeing that I was back to my 'usual self'. "And there I thought you'd be disappointed if we weren't going to be together," he sighed.

"I mean, I suppose it will be all right, having you in the same program," I said, conceding the point.

"Well, for my part," he said, smiling widely, "I am very glad that we will be together still."

I matched his smile, beaming broadly. "Me too, Jace. Oh, me too!"

Knowing that our educational path was now clear, we would still have to devote ourselves to our learning. Having a path was not the same thing as success. The way I saw it, with both of us getting into Climatology we could spend the remainder of our time at the Academy studying or clowning around. Of course, as appealing as clowning around might have been it was sure to lead only to a life in a think tank. My goal – and Jace's too – was much loftier than that. I wanted a position on the Environmental Council.

Only the cream of the crop were given a position on the Council. With such a position came a great deal of prestige and autonomy. A real life, in my opinion.

Neither of us had to say anything. We were of one mind when it came to our desire for excellence. However, curiously, the environmental studies that were part of our course were more challenging to Jace than either of us anticipated. Perhaps it was because of his upbringing outside of Science.

"This is very disheartening," he said, moping about one day after a lecture. He was carrying a study pod.

"What's the matter?"

"I'm just having so much trouble understanding these systems," he said. "I've never had trouble like this before."

It was true. Like me, he had always breezed through his studies, understanding new things easily. I could not understand how he must have felt, but it was disorienting for me as well, to know he was feeling less certain. I took his hand and squeezed it. "Don't worry," I told him. "We'll figure out a way."

He smiled, but there was no real joy behind his smile. He was clearly feeling lost and feeling lost was not a feeling that came easily to him.

I was not going to get this far only to leave Jace behind. So much of the material came easily to me because of my family background. I was not going to allow Jace's different background to hold him back. In our spare time, I devised new and different ways to review the material. We explored. We returned to the museums that Ann had shown us. We moved through the dioramas. We found samples of ancient species. We drilled. We played games. We studied.

One day, as I knew it would, everything simply clicked for Jace. A light came on, and he fully understood everything. It was as if he needed to incorporate a context so that all the disparate lessons of climate studies had a home and logic. When that context was in place, everything became crystal clear.

His test scores immediately reflected his understanding. Soon, he was striding ahead of me, challenging our teachers with his knowledge and insights, and me. It was a wonderful time for both of us. We were able to spend a great deal of time together, learning, studying and growing.

More exciting, we would be spending more and more time together after we graduated from the Academy. For it was then that our studies would become a practical reality. We would be tasked with continuing and improving on the work done by scientists who had come before us, returning the planet to a pristine condition after the 'Parched Earth' disaster.

* * *

On our last day at the Academy, each student was called to a small room to meet with his or her counselor, to receive their final scores and to receive their area of employment. It was a day filled with anticipation, sadness and joy. As we all contemplated our meetings with our counselors, we understood that we stood at the precipice, on the very boundary between our past and our future.

As I walked toward my meeting, I had a heavy feeling of time weighing on my shoulders. The future was exciting indeed. But the past was slipping from me like a skin that had covered me too loosely.

"Hello, Ari," Joyla said, greeting me in the small room. "And congratulations. You have exceeded even our lofty expectations for you here at the Academy."

"Thank you," I said, feeling genuine humility. Regardless of results, I knew that compliments were not handed out recklessly at the Academy.

"Your future is indeed bright. You have been chosen to do lead work at the Environmental Council."

My eyes widened. I felt my heart flutter in my chest. Lead work! I could not have hoped for a better outcome. My parents will be pleased.

"Your dedication and your natural talents have been amply demonstrated by your excellent grades," she went on. "You will be an asset to the team."

"Thank you," I said, extending my hand to her. This time, at this moment, we were equals. I did not have to wait for her gesture. She was sending me off as an individual, not a student.

I strode purposefully toward the courtyard, the very same courtyard where I had met Jace all those many months earlier. I was aware of other students, students who had, like me, also received their "marching orders". Even with the singularity of my purpose and focus on my destination, I was aware of the many bright, resolute faces.

For many of us, our time at the Academy had been rewarding beyond measure, and now we would be tasked with contributing to our world.

I was surprised to find Jace in the courtyard, already waiting for me. He was smiling ear to ear. No games today. Today, his joy was evident from across the courtyard!

"I'm the man," he crowed when I came closer. "Yes, yes, yessiree! I'm the man indeed. Environmental Council, here I come! S.C.I.E.N.Tist!" He was yelling now, at the top of his lungs and happy to have everyone hear him. I was happy to hear him too!

I let out a yelp and ran across the courtyard, flying into his arms. He swooped me up into the air. As my body lowered against him, I could feel every fiber of my womanhood pressed against his strong, masculine body.

We had always been close but our interaction, although not ignorant of the growing attraction, had never felt so powerfully *human*. Suddenly, I felt fully alive not as a student or as a friend but as a woman.

Our lips met in the first kiss we'd ever shared, but it was a kiss that felt as true and comfortable as if we'd been kissing our entire lives. His strong arms tightened around me as my body swooned against his. Even as my body lit in sudden heat, a clear thought became evident in my mind – it would not be long before we were husband and wife.

"Oh Jace, this is the best day of my life!" I exclaimed in between our loving kisses.

"It only gets better," he promised, his eyes aflame with passion.

Of course, our joy would only be short-lived. The task ahead was too dire and too urgent. After a few more moments in the courtyard, we were able to get something to eat and then we were directed into the amphitheater, the very same amphitheater where we had begun our careers at the Academy.

Once again, we were greeted by the Headmaster. Only this time, his greeting was tinged with the somber tones of a man speaking to his peers. He no longer intended to intimidate us or motivate us.

Now, he needed to enjoin us in a call to arms.

He introduced a film showing footage that had been kept from us during our first year at the Academy. Despite the many things we *were* exposed to, this content was deemed too powerful, too evocative, and too oppressive to show us. Until now.

The footage was recorded from inside the ARC using a network of webcams that had been set up around the cities. As we sat in numbed silence, the images showed cities from around the world in various stages of anarchy, sickness and starvation. The faces on the people sent shock waves through us, as did the bodies lying around on the streets. It was all I could do to look at the screen in front of me. I wanted desperately to turn away, but I knew I couldn't, for what I was seeing was the real-time urgency of the task.

Still, I could only hang my head in shame at the barbaric behavior that we humans are capable of when challenged.

Those images framed what should have been one of the happiest days of my life with the darkness I had been trained to combat. With those images, I came thudding back down to reality.

When the images stopped, and the lights came back on, the Headmaster considered us with a serious expression. "So you can see," he said solemnly. "You can never go back. The future is out there, but it is not a gift. You must confront it clear-eyed. It is a challenge that you must overcome."

Our One World Government continued, but it was no longer functioning the way it had been planned to so many centuries ago. It was not the world domination that had been intended. Far from it. The rich, the powerful and the slaves suffered and died in equal measure in the ARC's. Now, we, their descendants, were able to access the knowledge bases and view the footage that had been preserved. In the beginning, ARC's all over the world kept in touch with each other via satellite uplinks. When those failed, there were radios. But even they only lasted a relatively short while.

As a result, a new world order was established, one that has survived throughout the ages; one we follow to this day, one that is independently connected.

Hell is empty, and all the devils are here.
William Shakespeare

CHAPTER EIGHT
THAT DAY, AND WHAT ENSUED

I hazarded a quick glance back to the beach and then again upwards towards the sky. In my life, I had never felt or seen anything like it... I felt a tug, a hesitancy to move but Jace continued to grip my hand tightly.

"Ari, come!"

He was yanking me with him, in the direction of his vehicle.

We had barely spoken since the event. What could we say? What *would* we say? Neither of us could find words to describe what was happening. We could not grasp it. There was no boundary or context to whatever *it* was. We had no idea what was happening, could have no idea. Not then. All we knew, and this thing we knew with the deepest certainty of our souls, was that something was very, very wrong.

Nothing in our studies at the Academy had prepared us to confront the phenomena that was occurring all around us. Nothing I had heard, read about or even imagined came close to giving definition to what was happening. Nowhere in any written history that I had ever read or heard about described anything that even came close to what we were seeing and feeling.

Which only added to the sense of urgency, desperation and foreboding we felt.

"Come on!" Jace screamed.

Together we ran, jumped into Jace's vehicle and started towards home. There was a moment, a very brief moment that seemed to last for an eternity when Jace pressed the ignition point, and nothing responded. During that seeming infinity, my heart leapt to my throat. And then, perhaps in reality only a nanosecond later, the roar of turbos and we were on our way, heading away from the beach and towards home, taking the quickest route possible.

We were not alone in seeking the main road from the beach. Although we had found an isolated area of the beach, there was a great deal of coastline. Thousands of others had taken advantage of the day.

As a result, traffic was at a near standstill over the bridge that linked the city to the beach.

"Hurry!" I cried, my fingers gripping the dash in front of me. "Hurry!"

I looked at Jace and could see the tension in his jaw and his neck. I knew he was determined to go as fast as he could, but I couldn't help myself from yelling for him to do so anyway. He jerked the vehicle one way and then the next, trying to find an edge to the hordes of people who were feeling the exact panic that we were feeling. The only difference? We would be called upon to do something about whatever it was that is happening!

We had to get to the city!

In starts and stops, we crawled over the bridge and onto the broader highway. Once there, the traffic sped up, but not by much.

"I know a way," he said, as much to himself as to me. He jetted to the nearest off ramp and took a convoluted route on a winding, uncertain journey through towns and villages, on country roads and graveled roadways. But at least we were moving, and that fact alone gave me the closest thing to hope that I'd had in what seemed to have been a very long while.

Along every street and road, there were people outside, staring up into the sky and pointing. Their faces were masks of fear and panic. Children were crying, hugging their mothers' legs. Mothers were screaming. Men were grim-faced and clearly confused.

No one knew what to do.

Scenes like this followed us the entire way to my house, and even along my very street. People, neighbors, were in their front yards, their heads tilted heavenward, their expressions united in foreboding.

People I have known all my life were gathered in small groups, their conversations animated and exaggerated, their concerns clear even to me through the glass of the vehicle's windows. I scanned every face. I did not see my mother or my father.

"Hurry," I said, and not for the first time.

Jace screeched to a halt in front of my house. Even before the vehicle was fully secured, I pushed open the door and jumped free, running toward my door. I knew Jace was right behind me.

"Ari!"

My mother pushed open the door and stepped out to greet me, wrapping her arms around me and hugging me tightly.

"Mom, what's happening?" I asked, wrapping my arms around her.

"I don't know," she said.

I released my grip on her and pushed away. "Where's dad? We need to speak with dad!"

Just as I went to go into the house, Jace joined me. Together, we arrived at my father's study to find him pouring over computer printouts, old texts, tables and equations. He seemed overwhelmed in a way I'd never seen before.

"Father!"

He looked up. His eyes took me in, but his expression seemed not to change. His focus was so entirely concentrated on the task at hand that he didn't seem to have time for the most paternal of emotions.

"What have you seen? What do you know?" he asked.

He didn't at that moment want feelings. He needed information. Data.

I couldn't imagine what it must be like for him, for my mother, for our neighbors. Jace and I, as confused and fearful as we were, had seen the event begin to brew. We'd had an inkling that something was coming. But when we'd left my parents earlier in the day, they had been enjoying a leisurely breakfast on the deck, enjoying the warmth of the early sun.

We'd been gone less than an hour!

Jace quickly told my father what we'd seen. Father's eyes widened. He grabbed a phone and called the office. "I'm coming, yes. Right away," he barked into the phone. "I will have Ari and Jace with me. They saw it."

Only a few moments later, we were being hurried into our family's vehicle, Jace and I scrunched alongside one another in the front with dad. Then, without any further delay, we were on the way to the office lab.

Along the way, my father peppered us with questions.

What did we see?

What was the air like?

Could we describe any additional physical phenomena?

Was it warm and then cold? Cool and then warm?

We answered each question as accurately as we could, accounting for the fact that he was asking the next question even as we answered the one before it. He was desperate for information. We didn't know what piece of data might be useful so we told him everything we could think of. We tried to remain organized, as we had been taught at the Academy. But the magnitude of what was happening; the need for information right away... the uncertainty as to which piece of information might prove useful, all this conspired to have us saying anything and everything we could.

The sky was still a slate grey when we arrived at the office and hurriedly piled out of the vehicle. My father ushered us inside, taking an impatient moment to work through the various biometric security measures on the outside and then the inside doorways. Quickly enough, we were walking fast along the smooth, tiled corridor.

"This way, come on," father said impatiently, leading us through a doorway on the left.

How he knew which doorway was beyond me. There were no markings on the walls and none on the doors that I could see. But he knew exactly where he was going.

"Ari, Jace, please meet Noel," he said, nodding in the direction of the wiry gentleman inside the lab we'd entered.

Of course, both of us knew who Noel was. He was quite renowned in the field. Not only was he an Atmospheric Scientist but he also headed the Environmental Council. He would be, in short order, Jace's and my "boss."

The Environmental Council was an umbrella for a number of different fields and disciplines. As climatologists, Jace and I fell into the category of Atmospheric Science even though our roles would differ to a great degree from my father's.

My father's work, some of which had been a mystery from the time I was a little girl and other parts of it were things he shared with me freely, ran the gamut from weather prediction to research aimed at preventing the degradation of the Earth's atmosphere.

I remember even as a little girl him asking me if I thought it would rain on a given evening. I would look up into the sky, which was inevitably bright blue and I would shake my head.

"No, it won't rain."

"Are you sure?" he'd ask with a smile.

"Of course I'm sure. The sun is nice and warm, and the sky is blue. There's not a cloud anywhere."

"That observation is true. But I haven't asked you if you thought it would rain *now*. I think it is quite clear to everyone that it won't rain *now*. But what do you think *will* happen in eight hours? Or tomorrow?"

"How should I know? No one can predict the future," I said with certainty.

He raised his eyebrow in amusement. "No? I'll tell you what," he went on. "I say it will rain tonight. You say it won't. If you're right, I'll buy you a pony..."

"Daddy! Really?"

He laughed. "Yes, really. But what shall I get if I am right?" He took a thoughtful expression. "Hmm, maybe a hug and a kiss."

Even then, that seemed like a safe bet to me, so I took it. That day, I spent most of my time looking out the window. Throughout the afternoon, the sky stayed blue and bright. I was starting to think of names for my pony when, not long before dinner, some clouds began to move in. The breeze picked up. There was an electric feeling to the air.

Even so, I could still see stars through the forming clouds that evening.

However, not long before my bedtime, I heard the first, distant roll of thunder. Then a bolt of lightning shattered the darkness. Within fifteen minutes, raindrops began to fall, soon hitting the roof so hard that it sounded as if we were living under a waterfall.

"Daddy, how did you know?"

"I can see the future," he said smugly. "Shall I collect my hug and kiss now or in the morning?"

I agreed to "pay" him right then. But I still wanted to know how he knew that the weather would change. I pestered him through the evening and then again in the morning until finally, he laid out the rudiments of meteorology.

The more he spoke, the more fascinated I became. When he finally ended by saying, "I think that is enough for your first lesson," I was hooked. From then on, I was devotedly interested in Science and Climatology. I would constantly ask my father about cloud formations, weather patterns and how climate affected just about every aspect of my life.

Although my father spoke expertly about meteorology and answered my questions thoughtfully and completely, meteorology was not my father's area of study or passion. His knowledge of meteorology was secondary to his true focus, the study of the Earth's atmosphere.

It was in this context, the study of the gases that cocoon our planet, that my father's importance and value to our existence was most acute.

So it was that when Noel saw my father come into the room, followed by Jace and me, his expression brightened slightly. "Good, you're here. Everyone is waiting." He stood and led us through another door and into a lab, this one crowded with think tank drones. The drones immediately clustered around my father and all began talking at once.

I immediately felt uncomfortable and reached out to grasp Jace's hand. Unlike the decorum and order that I had come to associate with my father's lab and, honestly, all aspects of scientific research and inquiry, this room was an explosion of noise and movement. It was easily as chaotic as the events unfolding outside. Rather than remaining at their workstations, focusing on their tasks and assiduously pouring over data, each member of the team seemed to have been jolted into motion by the most unpleasant and disturbing shock. They clamored around my father. Several paced nervously. Others tapped their feet, their eyes darting around the room. They all seemed to exhibit behaviors and postures that I associated with someone who had suffered significant emotional trauma.

In rapid fire, they spewed out figures and coordinates, temperatures and atmospheric wind speeds. I listened intently but was only able to understand every third or fourth word. Another was talking so fast and in such a frantic manner that he failed miserably at communicating, successful only in tripping over his own words.

Another member of the team was moving around the room, a stylus behind his ear, and desperately trying to get anyone's attention by shoving papers covered with graphs in their face.

Still, another waited anxiously, a multipad at the ready, desperate to take note of the smallest bit of information my father might provide. As if this scene was not manic enough, even before any sort of order was able to take hold, several other people, equally distressed as the ones already in the lab, came tumbling in, adding to the noise and the confusion.

They crowded around my father and, even as Jace and I were being pushed to the back of the room, I could see that my father managed to maintain his placid and calm demeanor. Even so, I could see that he had just about all that he was interested in taking. He raised his arm into the air and barked at the top of his lungs, "Enough!"

The room fell into a sudden silence.

"Now," he went on, bringing his arm down. "Let us proceed *one at a time.*"

There was a moment of absolute silence, followed by an immediate explosion of noise as everyone tried to be the *first* voice that spoke "one at a time". In disgust, my father shook his head and pushed through the scrum of people and made his way into the conference room. As he made his way, he caught my eye and indicated that he wanted both Jace and me to join him. I reached out and grasped Jace's hand and pulled him in the direction my father was moving.

Jace and I slipped into the conference room, as did five of the top scientists. Father shut the door, keeping the buzzing drones at bay.

Although it is quiet and focused in the conference room, it is clear that everyone there is deeply worried. To this point, father had not received any coherent information about what had happened, and what was continuing to happen. Having known my father my entire life, I knew him to be a man of exquisite reason, reason tempered with awe and appreciation for the world around him.

It was no accident that he and mother met and fell in love. His responsibility kept him from the many adventures that mother took me on as a child, but he was fully supportive of them. What I did not know then was that mother would tell him about our adventures, filling him with longing for the wonderful way I was being allowed to grow up.

My father was a decisive man. It fell to him to make some very vital decisions. Still, he was never rash. He needed information. He needed to know what had happened, and what was happening.

He looked at the scientists in the room. "This is my daughter Ari, and this is her colleague, Jace. They were due to begin with us tomorrow." He sighed and rubbed his face with his strong hand. "It seems that events have conspired to have them begin early."

There were nervous chuckles in the room. The nervousness was shared by Jace and me, but not the chuckles.

"As these events certainly will affect all of us, I have decided to bring them in now on the ground level so they can get up to speed with the rest of us."

With that, he turned to a tall, thin man. "Mitchell," he said, his voice direct and matter-of-fact, "talk."

On cue, he began. "At 9.20 am this morning there was an apparent earthquake…"

"Apparent?" my father asked.

Mitchell nodded. "I am making my assessment based on the fact that the ground shook. At about the time the incident occurred, our machines seemed to go crazy, and no discernable data was gathered.

"Stranger still, there also appears to be no epicenter that we can locate."

My father looked distressed. I could not tell if it was because of what he was hearing or the degree of uncertainty behind the information. "No epicenter or discernable data? Apparently, an earthquake occurred? Damnit, Mitchell, was there or was there not an earthquake? How can your equipment fail to record an earthquake?"

Mitchell shook his head. He raked his fingers through his thinning hair and cleared his throat. "The problem is not the equipment," he said.

"You're certain?"

He nodded. "It was all checked just recently. It just… it just didn't record anything of value. Artifacts, nothing else."

My father brought his hand down against the conference table. "Does anybody have *any* data for me that we can put on the table so we can begin to work out what is happening out there?"

There was a brief moment of quiet when a small voice began. "Yes," Sim piped up. Sim, a short, boyish-looking man who tended toward blushing even when he was not embarrassed and whose shyness made him much more comfortable in the background, was about to have his moment to shine.

He was younger than the others and only joined the Environmental Council a year earlier, after graduating from the Military Academy. He had quickly distinguished himself with the value of his data and insights.

"Thank God," father sighed as he turned to look at the young man. "What can you tell us, Sim," my father queried.

Without looking up from the stylus in his hand Sim began, "This morning Sir, the carbon dioxide levels jumped to almost double their normal level. An astonishing rate of change to pre-purge levels, which would be in keeping with a 3.0c to 4.5c rise in the global climate, Sir."

My father shook his head as if to dismiss the information. "There has to be some mistake," my father said.

The young man was clearly uncomfortable but held his ground. "No, Sir. Definitely not, Sir." Sim might have been shy and timid, but he had absolute faith in his numbers.

I was impressed by him. Clearly, he was shy and just as clearly he was intimidated by my father. The thought quickly went through my mind how odd it was to think of my father as intimidating. As his daughter, I always knew him to be anything but. However, here, in his workplace, I could see how his authority would affect others.

Father seemed to accept what Sim said. "Are there any more facts to be presented?"

Jordan pushed some paperwork across the table to my father. After my father looked down at the papers, Jordan then dealt copies of the packet to the rest of us.

Jordan's area of expertise was Oceanology and Marine Science. She had loved the sea since she was a young girl and always returned to it – whether as a study subject or a place to hold her dreams and hopes.

On the council, it was her task to monitor the ocean for changes and to report those changes back to my father. As the person responsible for the Ocean Carbon and the Biogeochemistry program, she had a great deal of responsibility. She also headed the project on Ocean Acidification.

Her voice was steady as she reported the information in the packet. "Immediately after the event this morning, the acidity of the ocean quickly peaked to its current pH level of 8.7%."

That was the first bit of information that made sense to me. Not how the ocean came to have the sudden rise in pH level – that was still part of the strange events that were occurring and needed to be explained – but why the ocean appeared to have that rust color. The change in pH would equate to a rise in algal blooms. I shook my head, amazed that I had not thought of that myself. But then again, perhaps the best lesson of the morning would turn out to be an appreciation of how much you miss when you are in shock.

Jordan continued in a voice heavy with sadness. "There appears to be little or no plant or marine life left."

A pall descended on the room. Managing marine life had been a significant goal of the Council.

"You're sure?" my father asked.

Jordan nodded. "We cannot detect any. And, quite frankly, no life could survive in such an alkali solution."

"I hate to add to the horrible news," Thomas said, "but atmospheric conditions don't appear to be much better. I haven't had time to crunch the numbers, but carbon levels in the atmosphere are past critical." He paused as if the importance of what he was about to say next just fully occurred to him. "It's only a matter of time before our ability to survive will become untenable."

A 3.0c to 4.5c rise in global climate would be enough to displace those living in tropical populations; would be enough to destroy natural ecosystems, force changes to agriculture and ultimately, to our very way of life.

"My God," my father sighed as he slouched back in his chair and brought his hand over his face. In some ways, seeing my father's posture and hearing his sigh was more unsettling than the events Jace and I had witnessed this morning. After all, environmental calamities were one thing *if* my father and the council could address them. But if my father felt defeated… then we had indeed reached a very dire impasse.

Then, as if speaking to himself, he began to ask questions. "What has caused it? Where has it come from? What happened to the world we woke up in this morning?" Frustration obvious in his voice. I was sure I was not the only one to note how tightly he was gripping his fists.

After a moment, he looked up. His eyes landed on Jace. "Jace, open the door and let the think tank in please."

Jace immediately jumped up and went to the door. When he opened it, it was obvious that a large number of people had been idling just outside. "Think Tank please," Jace said.

In short order, a short line of men and women from the Environmental Council filed into the room. At that moment I found myself looking directly at Jace, and for the first time since we'd gotten to the Council, I looked at him, really looked at him. I had been so wrapped up in my own thoughts and feelings that I had neglected to take into account what he must have been going through. Looking at him now, I felt a wave of sympathy as I saw the concern on his face and tenseness in his body. This all must have been so overwhelming for him. I tried to will him to look at me, to give me the chance to silently express to him that I cared, that I understood. But he was too engrossed in everything that was happening, taking in everything that was being said, and picking up on all the unspoken cues, the frustration, the fear, the sense of foreboding.

"Ideas please?" my father asked in a matter of fact voice that seemed to suggest that his team had already come up with all the answers necessary to address this latest crisis and were just letting the Think Tank weigh in on the situation as a matter of courtesy.

But his question was met with stony silence.

A second passed, then another, and another until finally a thin man softly cleared his throat.

"Yes?" my father asked calmly.

The man, whose sallow complexion gave silent witness to the many hours he spent doing his task, that is, thinking, swallowed hard. I could tell by his posture that he had only defeat to share with us.

"Sir, we have no ideas," he said softly and quickly, lowering his eyes even as he spoke.

Before my father could answer, his pager sounded. He glanced at it and sighed heavily. "I'm sorry," he said, "I need to attend to this."

He stood up, turned and walked from the room. No sooner had he left than the room exploded in a cacophony of noise and voices. I caught Jace's eyes. I could see in them the concern he felt. I nodded. Then I tried to listen to all that was being spoken around me. I could pick out words and sentences, but all I could make out were questions. Not answers.

"Could it be a covert attack?"

"Who though?"

"Have we missed signs?"

Ideas, fears, all expressed in a panicked staccato. Without my father to act as an authority, every voice had equal standing.

The most frightening fear I heard expressed was that all of our systems were failing at once, plunging us back to pre-purge Earth.

Most frightening? As it turned out, the truth would prove to be much, much worse.

Just then, my father returned to the room. As soon as he stepped through the door, there was a sudden silence. Clearly, he was not happy that his presence caused the cessation of conversation.

He raised his hand in apology. "I have been called to a meeting with the Ministry," he said. "I will return as soon as I can. In the meantime, I would like you to continue working on whatever ideas, thoughts, plans you can come up with. However farfetched. We do not yet know what is happening and so we do not yet know what could prove to be successful in addressing it."

He added that a great many tools were available to us and that science had made incredible progress since the purge.

"We should be able to sort all this out fairly quickly, wouldn't you think?" he asked by way of farewell. Then he left once again.

CHAPTER NINE
THE MINISTRY MEETING

"Noel, come in and sit down," the Minister began when my father entered the conference room. "I believe you know everyone."

My father nodded to the various people gathered around the table, then he settled down at a vacant seat. As he did, the Minister began, intoning in his deep, resonate voice, "Based on initial assessment reports, the long and short of the situation is that we have no idea what exactly is happening. As you can imagine, in addition to the threat that might be posed by the events unfolding, we also have the risk of social unrest.

"There is no way to minimize the threat that these events pose to our way of life. Our situation could turn dire. Therefore, I have called you all here today to assist the Ministry to formulate a plan to counteract whatever it is that has happened.

"For those of you with only a partial sense of what has occurred, I need to paint for you a more complete picture. And, to the extent possible, I need to explain everything that we know.

"Does anyone have any questions before I begin?"

Around the table, his question was met with stony silence.

Satisfied that no one had anything to say, he continued, "The Communications Division reported that, at 9.20 a.m. this morning we lost communication with every other country in the world." If possible, his voice grew even grimmer. "We continue to have full communications within Pulchra. However, all signals outside of Pulchra are silent except for some chatter picked up at approximately 9.40 a.m. across radio and satellite signals, using channels that have not been used in centuries."

"Did we attempt to communicate using those signals?"

The Director shook his head. "No contact was attempted at that time. We were, and continue to be concerned enough by the situation, to believe that we must learn more before betraying that we are picking up *any* signals. Our Communications Division continues to monitor the situation and will update me regularly." With that, he paused and turned to my father. "Noel, what is happening in the Science Council?" the Minister requests to know.

He sighed, understanding the depth of the situation. "I'm afraid that we have no real answers at present. Just questions that still demand answers.

"I have just come from a meeting with the heads of departments. I can inform you as to some objective measures that we have been able to acquire. The ocean is currently measuring a pH balance of 8.7%. In such an alkaline environment – as we would expect – marine life has become non-existent. Carbon levels have doubled, which would correspond to a 3.0c to 4.5c rise in global climate." He drew a slow, measured breath. "Although I would like nothing more than to be able to explain to you *why* this is happening, and to help plot a path forward in response to these changes, the fact is that we do not know how this has happened. That said, I would like to get back to my lab as soon as I can so I might be able to sort this matter out."

The Minister tapped his fingers on the table. Although he maintained his dignified posture, it was clear to everyone there that he was less than pleased. "Does anybody here have anything to add to this enigmatic event?" he asked simply.

Once again, his question was met with silence.

"Noel, if I understand you correctly, we are facing an unprecedented crisis."

My father nodded.

"To review then, even a 4c increase in temperature will lead to the certain loss of the Greenland ice sheet and bring about a multi-meter rise in sea level."

"That corresponds with our calculations, yes," my father said.

"People, we are confronting melting glaciers, early snowmelt and severe droughts. The continent will be altered in ways that can only be hinted at.

"These are frightening times," he intoned as if he was already practicing the address he would give to the people.

CHAPTER TEN
WHAT ABOUT THEM?

Come on," Ari said, taking Jace's hand. "No use just sitting around letting ourselves go crazy." She pulled him up and gave him an informal tour of the Science Division, a place she had been visiting since she'd been a little girl. Without a formal responsibility, they had nothing better to do.

As they walked around, there was a kinetic movement all around them. Researchers were peering at computer monitors, doing calculations, receiving various readings from sensors placed throughout the land. Ari tried not to read too much into their worried expressions as they did their work.

"The first time I came here, I was fascinated," Ari said, showing Jace the lab. "I knew right away I wanted to be a scientist."

Jace, as determined as Ari to avoid being drawn into a panic, laughed. "Are you sure that's what did it?" he asked. He knew, as well as she did, that the narratives that we tell one another are not always exactly what happened in our lives. However, there was, in Ari's case, plenty of room to wonder. Ari's mind was very capable of such a thought and such a memory.

For her part, Ari didn't answer Jace directly. Instead, she continued the tour of the lab as she noted all the places she'd seen on that first visit.

"My father brought me in here," she said, noting the crowded ocean monitoring lab. "He explained to me the importance of the tides, the saline content of the ocean, and the ability of the seas to sustain life... but only so long as they were respected. Which, of course, they had not been."

"How old were you during that visit?" Jace asked, leaning forward to gaze at the various monitors showing the quickly changing readings of the seas and oceans.

She shrugged. "Seven. Maybe eight."

He nodded. His own interest in science and the oceans was taking form at the same age. Only his experience was very different than hers. Not coming from a family in the Science caste, his interest was both interesting and frightening to his parents. However, they recognized that in Jace they had given birth to a prodigy whose interests were worth supporting.

Jace's background and experience made his interest and perspective on Science slightly different than Ari's. He did not, for example, have the degree of faith in Science that Ari had. Her belief in Science was intertwined with her faith in her Father. Jace knew that Science had too often fallen short in its ability to change the course of events in the past, and so, could do so again in the future.

He had learned early of the history of the world told in a way without the certainty of science. He knew how the history of people going back millennia was a series of poor, short-sighted and greed-motivated decisions that resulted in mistakes upon mistakes that essentially degraded the planet until it could no longer sustain life as it had since time immemorial.

The elite locked themselves in bunkers to protect themselves from the damages of the planet and the threats posed by overpopulation.

The place where they lived, Pulchra, had risen up from the seabed in a dramatic and devastating earthquake which occurred shortly after the bunkers had become fully functional. Pulchra had remained pristine and ecologically balanced for nearly a thousand years. But now, the events they were seeing called that balance into question.

The same short-sightedness that had been so damaging to the world at large in the past was proving to be a threat to their world. The scientific community, having learned so much from the experiences of the generations, was not being heeded.

To Ari's father and to her and the other scientists, science was the objective and benign force that could allow them to survive and then thrive. But to the political leaders, the advice of the scientists too often conflicted with their other aims.

When the scientific community saw problems, the political elite did not want to spend the money to address the issues when they could be addressed easily. Then, as the problems grew, they began to appear insurmountable. And, of course, the elite's decisions had only their interests in mind. They left the rest of mankind to fend for itself in the hope that it would purge the population of the world and leave them fresh to start again in a powerful and, according to the elite, "natural" and necessary way.

Pulchra had remained a sanctuary, an island continent in the middle of the Pacific Rim. For five centuries it had been a safe haven. On this island continent, the Ministry established its own systems, a self-contained ecology. The Ministry allied itself with other world authorities to form a One World Government.

The Head of the Ministry sat on the OWG – a political organization that the elite had been trying to establish since before the Purge. While the Ministry concerned itself with the day to day process of life – population control, health, housing, science and the Arts – the OWG focused on the more comprehensive rule of the earth.

Although Jace was aware of the systems, he had remained silent about his awareness that the population was taught to believe they enjoyed individual liberty, only to be controlled in virtually every aspect of life and experience.

Only Ari knew of his awareness and to his eternal relief, shared the understanding, as well as the need to never speak of it to another soul.

As a consequence, both Ari and Jace have lived and learned the same as the others, as if they were flesh and blood robots to be controlled by the OWG, but they, alone in their social strata, did understand the truth of individual liberty. As well as its risks.

As they went through the labs, both Ari and Jace understood that they needed to familiarize themselves with their work area and to do so fast. Whatever else the expectations of them had been prior to their graduation, something new and unexpected had happened to their world, and neither of them could know what would be required of them in the coming days.

In addition to being acclimated to the labs and research areas, Ari introduced Jace to those people working there. Over the years, she had become well-known and trusted. At first, as a courtesy to her father but then, as her own brilliance and ability became obvious, for her own ability.

Even Jace, capable of learning so much so effectively, knew he would never remember the names of all the people he met that morning but he knew he would remember what they did, and that would be enough.

Meanwhile, as Noel prepared to leave the Ministry building an extremely large and unsettled crowd began to form. Although they were reasonably orderly, there was a current running through the gathering that was unnerving. They were nervous and skittish. They were scared and wanted news to help them understand the strange and frightening events occurring around them.

To add to the unease, it was clear that the quality of the air was already degrading rapidly. Many in the crowd were coughing and breathing with increasing difficulty.

As he looked through the doors of the Ministry, Noel was grateful to be a Scientist and not responsible for directly addressing the crowd. He made his way to his vehicle. As he opened his door, he heard the voice of the Minister coming through the loudspeakers set up on the steps.

"My friends, let us all calm down," the Minister began, his sonorous voice, serene and in control. "I have just met with all the heads of state and, although we do not yet have anything specific to advise, let me assure you that our best minds are focused on the cause of these recent events.

"We will keep you informed as we find out what is happening. If any of you are suffering any breathing difficulties, eyesight problems, cognitive disturbances, or decreased motor control or if you notice a bluish tinge to your skin, please report to the Medical care unit immediately where you will be taken care of, if they have not already asked you to do so. We all have to work through this together. Meanwhile, if you could stay in your homes, you should be able to remain safe for the foreseeable future. We will issue alerts as information comes to hand. That is all for now."

As Noel started his vehicle, he considered that the advice was well-placed. Most homes were fitted with carbon filters to keep the interior air pure. They were similar to those used in the ARCs but even more efficient.

The Minister's words or perhaps more correctly, his voice, seemed to have assuaged the crowd. At first, one by one and then in larger numbers they turned from the steps of the ministry and began to walk away. Their departure was orderly and quiet. All to the good, Noel thought. But he knew that if the event, whatever it was, continued, the first casualty would be order and quiet. Researchers and statisticians had calculated that it required three days, or nine meals, for anarchy to descend on a society.

A harsh deadline, but one supported by science.

Noel sighed. He hoped the people – the Ministry and the Scientists – were up for the challenge.

* * *

Meanwhile, in another part of Pulchra, a counter culture society had grown into existence. Although the Pulchran Ministry knew of its existence, it could not accurately monitor its actual size or resources. It was, without question, the greatest threat to the Ministry, the OWG and society as it has been conceived and structured to serve the Government.

Entire Ministry committees had been secretly formed, sometimes at cross purposes, with the sole intent of infiltrating and undermining this counterculture. However, they had always come to a dead end. Editorials, articles, broadcasts had been generated, damning the counterculture; making clear the threat that such a culture posed to the dominant culture.

"We must, and we will crush this counter-culture!"

The Ministry was of a single mind when it came to this counterculture. The threat was clear. Even though the counterculture posed no material threat to the Ministry and the Pulchran government, its very existence called into question everything about how the Ministry had structured the OWG.

The counterculture lived outside the reach and the rules laid down by the OWG. Their existence spoke to their refusal to be governed, or even the need *for* the government! They would not allow themselves to be dictated to. Their lives, how and where they lived, what jobs they did and how many children they were "allowed" to have were all decisions that they insisted belonged to them, not the State.

Infuriating to the OWG, the counterculture managed to create a society that was fully self-sufficient and existed beyond its reach. They grew and raised their own food sources. They took care of their own.

It was true, they were not diverted by the many pleasures and enjoyments that the government provided those of us who lived within its parameters. They lived simply. But the simplicity of their lives seemed to enable them and increase their satisfaction rather than the other way around – quite opposed to the expectations of the government.

Paradoxically, their existence was treated both as a fundamental threat and a non-entity so that whenever we heard about them, it was either with an "end of the world" shrillness or a dismissiveness that bordered on the exasperating. As a result, we became numb to messages and reports about them and, by and large, society tended to ignore them.

So, even though the Ministry viewed the counterculture as a "fundamental threat" the truth was, as they well knew, they did not pose a true threat. As a result, other than rhetorical attacks, the Ministry left them alone.

Of course, if the counterculture were to have grown in numbers or influence or to conduct the kinds of raids that could materially undermine the Ministry's authority, or the power of the OWG, then the response would be immediate and ruthless.

Curiously, despite the fact that Noel was completely ingrained in the government and Ministry, he could not help but have some admiration for the counterculture. Their determination and resourcefulness impressed him, as well as the creativity with which they solved many of the challenges that they faced. As such, as he drove back to the Science Division, he found himself feeling troubled for the counterculture. With these strange events degrading the environment at such a rapid rate, he could not imagine how they would survive. Even in the best of times, they lived a most basic existence, depending only on what the land could offer. Scorned by society and shunned, they would never presume to enter the city limits, knowing that if they did, they would be immediately arrested and locked away in punishment.

"Bloody shame," he sighed to himself, feeling the same concern that he would feel when watching a trapped animal struggle valiantly – but futilely – to survive. But, as he drove, he could not afford to worry too much about them. He had more pressing concerns, concerns for which he was solely responsible.

When he arrived back at the lab, his presence seemed to create an explosion of activity and noise. However, when he asked if anyone had any additional hard news to report, no one could tell him anything of worth. The only reading that was able to be absolutely confirmed was that the world had returned to pre-purge levels of carbon in the atmosphere.

"Fine and good," Noel noted, "but it is the level of methane in the atmosphere that I find disturbing – almost as disturbing as not understanding why we are getting these readings! Ladies and gentlemen," he said, eyeing his team, "the question confronting us is, why is all this happening?"

The danger of the methane was clear to everyone. A natural gas, under normal circumstances. A gas emitted into the atmosphere through a number of natural pathways as well as human activities, and often a by-product of the decaying process of organic matter. However, in even the smallest concentrations it could be lethal to humans.

Noel took a deep breath. He did not like the way events were trending, not at all. He knew that this new information needed to be communicated to the Minister immediately. Even as he picked up the phone, he was rehearsing in his mind the last time the atmosphere had this level of methane. It was pre-purge when the permafrost had melted and the oceans warmed. The melting of the icecaps and permafrost released the methane, triggering rapid climate change and resulted in massive destruction and death.

He felt momentarily lightheaded, realizing that unless something was done, very soon they could all be dead.

Meanwhile, the work in the lab had become even more frantic. Despite the frenetic activity, the mood in the lab was solemn. There was a protocol and the machinery to remove the carbon from the air, but for the effort to be successful, there would have to be a united worldwide effort. Unfortunately, along with the other challenges the day had brought, they had found their means of communication with other countries seemingly compromised. Rather than being able to have a united international response, they found themselves isolated, unable to communicate with any other country.

"What does it mean?" the Minister asked.

Noel thought carefully about how to answer. He wished that the problem was with the *mechanics* of communication. Sadly, and frighteningly, he knew their communications equipment was fully operationally. Which left the more devastating probability. "I'm afraid, sir," Noel said, "the most obvious conclusion is that at this time we are the only survivors of whatever it is that has happened. With each passing hour, our hopes of finding anyone else to communicate with diminishes." Thereby eliminating the help we so badly need.

There is silence on the other end of the line. Then, after what sounded like a long, slow sigh, the Minister said, "I will be in touch with you shortly." True to his word, only a few moments later, Noel received a page from the Ministry, "Ministry building. Emergency meeting at 1800 hours. All Heads of Departments to attend."

Noel glanced at his watch. He read the page again. He felt his pulse rate quicken. Scanning the paper again, he then quickly gathered the Heads together. "Come along, everyone now!" he called, moving everyone into the only lab space large enough for them to assemble. As they looked at him anxiously, he considered giving them some background as to what was happening. But he realized he really knew very little so he simply told them, "You must all go over to the Ministry building now." No one moved. There were only looks of confusion and a long, awkward silence. Knowing that inaction was not an option available to them, he raised his voice. "I mean, *right* now!"

Then he looked at Jace and me. "You two will come with me," he said firmly – whether out of protectiveness or the hope of moving forward I couldn't say.

As I followed along after my father, I realized just how much there was to take in. I had listened closely to everything that had been happening. There was the intimation that we were the sole survivors of some cataclysmic event. That alone was overwhelming. But add to that the remaining question of our own continued survival and the weight of the circumstances were nearly unbearable. But, the antidote to hopelessness is youth and hope. Jace and I had those in abundance. I know that in addition to feeling frightened I was feeling awed and privileged that I'd finished the Academy in time to be witness and participant to this history.

When Jace turned and looked at me, I could see in his eyes that he felt the same way. Two weeks earlier, and we would have still been students, on the outside looking in. Now, we were traveling to the Ministry to try and be part of the solution.

I felt positively electric on the way to the Ministry. I didn't know what to expect but, with the stakes so high, I was sure that there would be drama. So I was surprised and disturbed to find that the overall energy at the Ministry was subdued. Despite the obvious gathering dangers, it was not apparent to me that anyone truly grasped or fully understood why the meeting had been called, so they simply continued their business while they waited for the Minister and for the meeting to begin.

Rearranging the deck chairs on the Titanic, it seemed to me!

None of this is to suggest that there wasn't tension in the air. There was. But it was a controlled tension. Perhaps it would have been no different had they have known what was happening. These were professionals, after all. They'd dealt with many emergencies over the years, though none approaching this level of seriousness. That the danger facing them was profound was not in question. Still, it did not occur to them that they would not be able to find a solution. They were professionals, and they had full confidence in their knowledge and ability. For them, it was just a question of when, and how damaging the destruction that might occur to their world would be until they could come up with some practical way to address it.

The lights dimmed. Our attention was directed to the stage where a single light shone on the podium. A moment later, the Minister strode to the podium. He stood erect and proud. There was a tension in his features that I'd never noted before, but even so, he gave the appearance of one who was prepared to weather any storm.

A consummate professional in a room filled with other professionals.

However, whatever faith I had had in his appearance was quickly damaged by his message. His words, however, quickly betrayed his appearance and undermined the basic confidence of those in the audience.

"Ladies and gentlemen," he said, his voice heavy with emotion. "We have had a breakthrough of sorts into the mystery of what has happened. Our Communications Division has been able to ascertain from listening to ever more limited communications from around the globe..." He paused as if gathering the strength to utter what he would say next. "...it seems that we have been thrown back in time."

I turned and looked at my father. He had not moved, but I could see the tension in the muscles of his neck. I reached for his hand. He glanced at me, and there was a real worry in his eyes as he gripped my hand.

With my other hand, I reached for Jace. He held on tightly, to reassure me.

Meanwhile, in the instant after his announcement, there was a discernable hum reverberating around the room.

"Please, please," the Minister said, raising his hands to calm down the noise. "Please." When it was quiet, he continued. "At 1800 hours we ceased attempting to make contact with the systems around the world. Since then, we have, however, kept ears on them. We have picked up some desperate requests for help. We have also managed to pick up a previously unknown military channel emanating from and between the ARCs.

"For background, the only time that the ARCs transmitted messages was during the Purge in 2025 and for the 500 years following." The Minister paused and sighed, an uncharacteristic indication that he felt a bit at a loss. "At this time, we are still unable to contact any of the other Ministries from around the world. It appears that we are on our own."

The Minister scanned the audience. "Any questions?"

"Sir," a man called out as he stood up.

Over the years I had attended many of these sessions with my father. I had watched many more on monitor. I was familiar with just about everyone involved in the Ministry. Some of them felt almost like family. But this man was unknown to me, a fact that was as unnerving as the forcefulness with which he asked his question.

"Sir, the next step seems straightforward enough. Why don't you just communicate with them and ask who they are?"

The Minister nodded as if to demonstrate that he had heard the question clearly. "Yes, that would seem a fairly obvious path to take. However, we are confronting so many unknowns. We have not attempted communication to this point because we have been unsure of what has actually happened. If, in fact, we have been thrown back in time then any action we take could have profound ramifications on our existence. If we were to attempt contact, we might risk upsetting the timeline which could impact heavily on our futures." He cleared his throat. "Could affect us *now*."

"Then why not send a small group of people to investigate?" he asked, insistent. "Surely that would be a cautious and sensible path."

The Minister moved about some papers on the podium. "Yes, that is a reasonable thought. I will take that into consideration, thank you."

The questions and answers were, of course, merely a concession to the sensibilities of those of us in the audience. All of the questions, and many more had already been asked and answered during earlier discussions with Security, a young man known as Ashley.

Ashley knew that sending a small group of people from all ranges of skills to the mainland – if it still existed – would have the best chance of getting the answers that they so desperately needed. He also knew that it was a risky and dangerous enterprise.

The Minister agreed with the assessment but had asked for more time for consideration before giving the go-ahead. Given everything at stake, he didn't want to make a rash or impudent decision.

Meanwhile, there were many more questions about the climate that needed to be asked and answered. What was being done to counteract the levels of carbon in the atmosphere?

What had actually happened? As the meeting evolved, each of the representative heads was given the opportunity to speak on their subject of expertise. By the time the meeting ended, everyone there had a similar sense of what was happening and what could be done. In short, everyone was on the same page.

Before adjourning the meeting, the Minister called Jace and me by name and asked that we remain behind after the meeting was adjourned. Jace and I looked at each other, surprised by the request. Of course we would stay. How could we not? But what was the request about? I looked to my father, but he seemed as surprised by the request as we did. He seemed not to know any more about it than us. He leaned close and whispered to me that he would stay as well, at least until we knew what was going on.

I squeezed his hand. I was grateful for that.

A handful of others were also asked to remain behind. So, when the auditorium emptied, there were only a small number of us remaining.

"Let's make sure those doors are secured," the Minister said into the microphone as he stepped out from behind the podium. Behind us, the doors to the auditorium were locked by people I had not previously noticed. A moment later, when the doors were secured, we were all ushered into the Communication Divisions room where we were joined by the Minister and Ashley.

We all waited, anxious to know what was next, but also demonstrating the discipline that had allowed each of us to succeed in our particular endeavors. Without a word to us, the Minister motioned to one of the communicators. A moment later, one of the speakers came to life.

"Please… please… help me… you must help me…"

It was the voice of a girl, a young girl it seemed to me. As she pleaded, she told the story of her family's demise, how one after the other of her family members had died and now she was the only one left.

"I have a fever… I am sick too… I don't know how much longer I can last… Please come and get me. Please… please…"

Silence.

This was followed by another communication. This one sounded more official and formal. It was a report on numbers of people, food allocations and general conditions within the ARC.

"Oh my God!" I exclaimed, unable to silence myself as I realized what we were hearing. We were listening to the past.

"Yes, Ari," Ashley said, nodding toward me. "It is the past. But not exactly the past. It seems that we are hearing – or experiencing – a distortion of the past. We cannot know unless we respond."

"Then we must respond!"

"Always the impetuous one, ready to rush headlong in," father sighed under his breath.

Ashley, despite the tension of the situation, smiled. "Actually, Ari, we have already made an initial step." Then he frowned. "Unfortunately, it did not go as well as we might have hoped." With that, he nodded toward the communications specialists. A new transmission came over the speakers.

I immediately recognized the voice of our Minister. "Hello. This is Minister Lincoln of Pulchra. I am attempting to make contact with Sergeant Major O'Riley."

No response.

"This is Minister Lincoln of Pulchra, I am attempting to make contact with Sergeant Major O'Riley."

There was crackling over the speaker. "Sir, you are using a military channel, please terminate your transmission immediately."

"Sir, I am the Minister and leader of our country Pulchra, and I would like to speak to someone in charge."

"We have never heard of a country named Pulchra or of a Minister Lincoln. Clear this channel now. You are not to use it."

Silence.

"So, as you can tell, that did not go well," Ashley observed. "It seems that the only option available to us is our second option and that is to actually have eyes out there." He drew a deep breath and raked his fingers through his thinning, gray hair. "The Minister agrees that we simply must know what is happening.

"We cannot do that without placing boots on the ground. We need to send out a team of dedicated professionals…"

His words hung in the air as we each suddenly and fully understood why we'd been asked to remain behind.

"After careful consideration, we believe that those of you in this room are uniquely suited to the task. You have the aptitude, training and dedication to make a field trip into the unknown.

"As a team, as a unit, we feel you are capable of accomplishing the mission."

"Minister!" my father cried out.

The Minister raised his hand, silencing him and turning his attention back to us. "You are the best and brightest."

Hazarding a closer glance around at those in the room, I see the fresh faces of recent Academy graduates. During my studies,

I had read that in the days before the Purge there had been a politician named George McGovern who proclaimed, "I'm fed up to the ears with *old men* dreaming up *wars* for *young men* to die in."

Why did that come to mind now? Maybe because we are young, we are expendable. I needed to rid myself of such thoughts.

I knew that we had to find out what was happening. But I could not keep from feeling that somehow there was a lesson already "*learned*" and that it was about to be learned again – with me as one of the unwitting participants.

We were told only that we were to be ready at 0800 hours the following morning. We were to pack minimal supplies, for we would be gone "for only a few days."

More foolish words had rarely been spoken.

CHAPTER ELEVEN
THE MISSION

Already heady from the events of the day before and feeling slightly ill from the poor air quality and lack of sleep, Jace and I arrived at the flight port earlier than the assigned time. Each of us carried our travel kit, filled with devices to measure and bring back information for the Ministry to examine. I could see in Jace's eyes the same excitement, trepidation and exhaustion that I felt. It was harder to read my father's expression.

He had come to wait with us. I like to think his expression held more pride than fear, but I knew his heart, and I knew that he was worried about what might be out there awaiting us.

Fortunately, I did not have long to ponder my father's fears or feelings. Jace and I were not alone in finding ourselves arriving early. Our small group of eight found itself gathered.

We were familiar with one another, even if we were not close friends or intimates. What we did know was that we were each chosen because the Ministry believed we were capable of expertly accomplishing our part of the mission. We each would have a very specific job to do once we were on the ground in Colorado. Exactly what that job was remained to be defined.

Ashley, our Security Advisor, had chosen Cate as his advocate. No one, certainly not I, would have challenged the choice. Cate was always the top of the class in our combat year at the Academy. In fact, we had a nickname for her, calling her 'Cate the Savage'. Some of us showed our talents early; some late. It was obvious from the beginning that Cate would end up in Security, from demonstrations of her outstanding prowess. Her abilities were always highly valued. Even though we had no need for Armies to protect us, the Security Council had always kept a watchful eye over our country and community.

Although we were not particularly close – Cate was an imposing figure under the most benign circumstances – she and I had spent some time together at the Academy. In a curious way, I'd found her to be quite funny.

She made me laugh.

Not that humor would ever have been the first thing one assumed upon meeting Cate. The first thing people noticed about her was her striking beauty. Long, raven locks. Piercing, emerald green eyes. Honey-colored skin. Standing about five foot six inches, with a lean, fit physique, she moved with feline grace and comfort. It was only when she was in a combat situation that her musculature became defined and her ruthless determination and strength came to the fore.

Not long after meeting her, when I'd expressed astonishment at her strength, she smiled. She stood straight and brought her hands down along the lines of her body, accentuating her shapely charms. "Little ole me?" she asked in a coy voice. Then she laughed a strong, hearty laugh. "My dad always said my body was like camouflage. People see a pretty girl and not a ferocious warrior.

"I like it that way."

"Well, you sure had me fooled," I said.

"Hey, it's not like I mind being pretty," she said, smiling so her eyes twinkled. "I like when boys are nice to me." Then she paused. "I just like to be able to whip them in battle."

I smiled. "I like your style."

If there was anyone I wanted at my side for protection, it was Cate.

Of our group, Cate was the only one besides Jace that I knew at all. There were faces and names I'd seen or heard, but it was their expertise that brought us together, not any social dynamic.

Along with myself, Jace and Cate, a professional communicator, structural engineer, medical doctor, negotiator and a pilot rounded out our group. Each of us, of course, was trained in combat but it was our other expertise that qualified us for the mission.

I wasn't overly concerned about combat skills. From what I'd been given to understand, if we had truly gone back in time and the ARC's had already been locked down, then based on the few communications that had come through, we would not be confronting very much in the way of immediate danger in the form of other people. Combat was not high on my list of concerns.

Each of us was deep into his or her own thoughts when the Minister and Ashley arrived for a final briefing before our departure.

With their arrival, the air in the hanger seemed to thicken. I know I straightened up just a little more, watching as their vehicle approached and came to a slow stop. My eyes never left them as they got out and strode over to where we were gathered.

Whatever excitement we felt in our youthful foolishness was quickly transformed into a vague, but very discernable apprehension. Whatever awaited us was not anything we could have been adequately prepared for, certainly not in the Academy. What awaited us was new and completely unknown.

Although we had received the broadest of outlines about our mission the evening before, the Minister and Ashley had come to fully brief us before we embarked. Of course, "fully briefed" was something of a misnomer in this context. Briefings were designed to truly define the parameters of the dangers and the mission. Such parameters were unavailable to us now.

We were silent as the two men came toward us. Standing in the hanger, we glanced at one another, trying to discern each other's feelings and emotions. I hoped my own expression did not betray the uncertainty that I felt in the pit of my stomach. I did not quite identify it as fear, but it was close.

"Ladies and gentlemen," Ashley said, speaking up as soon as he and the Minister came close. "Thank you again for taking on this very important mission…"

Yes, like we really had a choice! Not that any of us would have opted out of it even if given a real choice in the matter. A mission like this was a once in a lifetime – heck, once in *several* lifetimes – and we were proud and honored to be the ones going on it. Still, it seemed bad form to make it sound as if we'd *invited* the opportunity.

"Nothing that has occurred since yesterday evening has done anything to alter our understanding of the events unfolding." He frowned. "Indeed, if anything, we are learning that the situation is even direr than we might have considered. In short, this is not a mission that we send you on lightly, or happily. It is a matter of life and death, for the future as well as the past. There are some things we can tell you about the mission because there are things that we have learned. However, there are a number of things that we simply do not know. And can't know." Then he added, almost as an offhand remark, "None of us like sending anyone into the unknown, but we have no choice."

At that point, Ashley reminded us that nobody in our timeline had ever been on such an important mission and that the fate of Pulchra and the lives of all Pulchrans rested firmly on our shoulders.

Thanks for taking off the pressure, I thought to myself! I was trying to process what I was hearing with what I already knew. What I was getting was a strange message – there might be "some" as yet undetermined danger to the mission, but it is an absolutely essential mission on which the future and past of our people rests. Okay, got it. Now, why is it again that I wasn't worried about combat?

Ultimately, his advice to us was to remember our training, remain vigilant and return home safely.

Got it.

Almost as an afterthought, he noted that "You may encounter the odd person here and there, but you are *not* to approach them or help in any way!"

"Sir," I asked, unable to help myself, "why not?"

He looked at me for a moment, as if to determine whether my question was sincere or meant to upend his message to us. Seeming to have decided it was a sincere question, he answered, "If indeed you have gone into the past and you do anything to alter the flow of events, you could unwittingly and adversely affect our futures." He straightened the papers in front of him. "Your mission has a great many unknowns. We are not sending you out to do anything other than gather information," he emphasized. "We do not expect, or want, you to engage in any events, situations, or realities that you encounter. Simple information gathering, that's it."

He paused and gazed at each one of us, taking an extra few moments to lock his eyes on mine. "Do you understand?" he asked quietly. Then, again in a voice that rose to an angry roar, "Do you understand?!"

"Yes!" we replied in a single voice. I had never encountered anyone in my lifetime that had spoken in such a way, loud and obnoxious, to drive home a point. It certainly grabbed our attention and made us stand up and take notice.

"Good," he said. Then he vacated the podium, making way for Shaun to come to the podium to announce that, "While you are away, your PAD's will not work."

There was an audible intake of breath from us as a group. Without our PAD's it would be impossible to communicate. We would be isolated. Adrift. Vulnerable.

"The only communication that will be transmitted from them will be your medical information which will be closely monitored by Justin on his portable Electronic Medical Hub, *(EMH)*." He glanced at Justin and gave him a quick nod. "Justin is prepared for just about any medical possibility. He can provide, literally, a medical science lab in the field. You can rely on that." With that, Shaun turned and left the podium.

There was a moment of awkward quiet before the Minister stepped up to each of us individually shook our hand and quietly repeated the same words, one after the other. "Speedy return, do us proud."

And just like that, the formal ceremony was over. I felt as if I could not breathe. The future – my future – was upon me! It was time. When he had shared his words with each of us, I turned to my father. I felt like a little girl again as I wrapped my arms around him. I wanted his strength, his comfort, his protection. I wanted to be his little girl again. But, as I well knew, I was no longer a child. I felt the strength of his embrace. I hugged him as hard as I could. And then, at the same moment, we released one another.

My eyes were moist as I turned away and stepped up onto the platform and into the Fúyún.

These Fúyúns are sturdy and rather large flying machines developed by the Chinese, and more commonly known as the Fú. In design, they are similar to a spacecraft yet able to hover using only air pressure – an astonishingly helpful feature, and magnetic levitation. I felt safe approaching the Fú. I loved and appreciated the forward-thinking Chinese engineers; they seemed to always seek the most elegant engineering solution to any problem or design. Without question, they were the technological leaders of our world. In the Fú they had created a machine which, as the name implies – literally means floating on clouds – and would serve our purposes well.

Not only was the design brilliant but with the development of the Fú's the Chinese came upon an exceptional use for the many tons of chrome rubbish found lying around during the resettlement period. With the ruling that all machinery and transport developed needed to meet strict environmental codes, enforced by the OWG, many thought the real genius of the Fú was its incredible material efficiency.

Behind us, the gathering applauded. But the sound of their clapping faded as we each found our seats and strapped ourselves in.

"Everyone in?" the pilot asked.

One by one, we acknowledged that we were, in fact, securely in place. None of us had time to be emotional or philosophical. Once we were in position, we had practical matters to consider which occupied our attention. Each of us had a sequenced series of tasks that we had to complete before take-off.

"Doors to shut," the pilot said, initiating the take-off sequence.

The doors shut. As they did, I glanced to my left, and caught a last glimpse of my father. His expression no longer showed pride. Rather, his eyes were filled with worry. It would be that look, that look of concern on his face that would remain in my thoughts in the coming hours and days.

"Beginning launch sequence," Tim intoned. Although he was in control of his voice, it was clear to me that he did so only by a Herculean effort. Beneath the smooth tone of his voice, I could hear the strain; his voice was washed with emotion, his fear was obvious.

"Launch sequence."

One by one, we authorized the sequence to go forward, each of us displaying the same effort to maintain our calm vocal tone. The design of the Fú was a "fail-safe" design, one that allowed any one of us to halt the sequence and the take-off. However, with no indication of any mechanical problem, none of us had any mind or reason to do something like that. The launch sequence proceeded smoothly and, in a few moments, the Fú trembled slightly – like the sighing of a large animal – and we all experienced the subtle lift as we rose from the ground. Rising smoothly, Tim adjusted his controls and the machine oriented itself and turned toward our destination.

Having been a frequent passenger on the Fúyún's as I had traveled to the mainland with my mother and father for business, I was familiar with the smoothness and speed of the flights to the mainland. As I attended to my responsibilities, I tried not to think of those other, earlier trips.

In no time, we could spot the coastline below us.

"Leaving ocean space," the pilot announced. "Land beneath us."

And just like that, we were now flying over land, heading toward the Denver International Airport.

As we crossed the coastline, I glanced down and could see the hulls of broken ships and the wreckage of ocean liners scattered along the shore. I shook my head at the hubris of man as I allowed myself to gaze at the once proud and mighty relics of how man sought to tame the ocean. How mighty man once thought of himself! But now look at his relics! Rusting and rotting, awaiting nature's inevitable cleansing as she erases any and every footprint of human society and trespass. The first indication that we were indeed back in the past.

Tim adjusted our flight pattern and, as he spoke into the microphone that connected with our headsets, moved us toward the remains of the great "city of angels" – Los Angeles.

Such a beautiful and evocative name! And yet, to me, I couldn't help but feel deep sadness as I wondered what had become of all those "angels".

"Oh my," Tim sighed under his breath.

Below us, all that remained of what must have once been a magnificent metropolis was a shadow, a mere suggestion. Mighty? No more. All that was left were ruins, crisscrossed by streets and freeways emptied of traffic or people, and crumbling buildings in various stages of disrepair.

The streets and freeways seemed to extend endlessly toward the horizon. The buildings seemed to dot a landscape that rolled out as far as the eye could see. But there were no angels, and no ghosts either. Just the empty hulls of what was once a place millions called home. The extent of the ruins below us was our second indication that we had indeed gone back in time. The thriving metropolis of our own time was nowhere to be seen.

"Note that there are no indications of a modern, rebuilt city," Tim said breaking me out of my deep thought. "And the coastline has changed dramatically."

I shook my head in wonder. Whatever other lesson nature taught, the most basic was that nature should never be trifled with. She always takes back what is hers. We needed no further proof than what was obvious below us. For Jace and me, it seemed that our lessons at the academy truly did no justice at all to what we now saw unfolding before our own eyes, neither of us truly appreciated the extent of damage done to the pre-purge earth. Man had created metropolises that he believed would last for eternity, but, as it turned out, eternity is but the blink of nature's eye. Looking at what had transpired to the world beneath us I felt my breath taken away. Nature was taking back what rightfully belonged to her. Rusted automobiles littered what had once been wide boulevards and tree-lined streets and avenues.

I shudder, imagining what the people – the "angels" – must have suffered in those last horrible months after the doors to the ARC were locked down, leaving them to fend for themselves in the most severe of environments. I imagined that as bad as the physical torment of those times, the worst of it was the sense of being abandoned. Left behind. Alone.

I sighed deeply. Like all others, I had grown up living my life with the presumption of communal good, of an enveloping matrix which allows me to address the world as an individual as well as a member of that communal enterprise. I had the presumption – as I'm sure these poor "angels" had – of a communal structure that ensures many aspects of life – delivering electricity, removing garbage and waste, making food available, clean water – and to have that suddenly snatched away so that each and every aspect of survival became an individual mission… how could that sense of abandonment been anything less than astonishing?

Regardless, the psychosocial torment they experienced must fully have been what is meant by the term, "existential crisis". How interesting that term had been when I studied it in my classes. How horrible to consider now, as I looked down and imagined what it must have been like to actually experience it!

More than the hunger, more than the thirst, the cold, or the brutal heat I could only imagine it would have been that deep and unrelenting fear and aloneness that was most devastating. Each of these angels must have cried out in anguish, and only hearing silence from their community were left to struggle like animals just trying to survive from one day, one moment, to the next.

Horrible. Beyond horrible.

My imaginings left me unsettled and disturbed. I drew a deep breath and turned my attention to the gauges in front of me, trying to focus on the matter at hand.

"Something to think about, no?" Tim asked, glancing in my direction. His expression told me that he might as well have read my thoughts. His voice, still erased of emotion, cut through me. Yes, the scene below us was "something to think about". The devastation on the ground held many secrets about our past that we were yet to discover *if* we were ever to discover them.

I nodded slightly, not trusting myself to speak.

One thing that was obvious from the landscape below us was that whatever else occurred during the evacuation process into the ARCs, whatever had been successful or necessary, there was a great deal that had not been well-thought out or well-executed. Emergency management clearly had not managed the vast evacuation as well or as efficiently as circumstances required.

"Farewell, City of Angels," Tim said, guiding us away from the scene below us.

We might have left the City of Angels behind us for the moment, but we could not escape the evidence of nature's power over man. I looked down as we moved over the landmass. From my studies and from my own visits to the mainland, I knew how so much of the events played out that it seemed to be written into my soul. There had been dozens of dams holding back the Colorado River at any number of points, but with no upkeep from man, the river eventually reclaimed its original path – after all, nature would have her dominance. Man could forestall many things if he had acted prudently and consistently.

After two centuries without maintenance or upkeep, erosion and rust will weaken the spillways, causing them to collapse under surging flood waters created by heavy spring runoffs from the mountain's melting ice. This, in turn, will cause a domino effect on each dam along its path until the waters reach the Hoover Dam. With the growing water pressure from each collapsing dam finally reaching its greatest pressure when the waters surge against the Hoover Dam, the mighty dam will not withstand the rushing water and will give way, allowing it to once again spill out from its man-made limits and find its way back to the ocean.

Despite the damage this will cause to man-made structures, ultimately the destruction of these dams will be a good thing – as all things in nature are – because new estuaries will be created, which will quickly become breeding grounds for hundreds or thousands of species of animals. That it will wash away a large chunk of the human environment in doing so is something that cannot be avoided.

The task, in the face of nature's unrelenting power, is to minimize the harm to man in the process. We were fortunate that anticipating exactly the process that would occur, they had the foresight to shut down all of the nuclear power reactors around the world.

I shudder to think how long our race would have had to remain underground if the flooding had included numerous accidents in which nuclear materials were dispersed into the atmosphere.

"We are approaching the Rockies."

I looked through the window to see the graceful, looming mountains. Still snow-tipped, still beautiful. This is how they have looked for eons. Sometimes, we are given a glimpse of a world unchanged and unchanging. It was a welcome relief from the dramatic changes we'd seen of man's efforts to control the world.

We arrived at Denver Airport. It was only then that I realized that Jace had remained quiet throughout the trip. I had been so lost in my own thoughts that I didn't even realize that others had been as well. Now, I looked over at him and could see him staring out the window at what lay below us. Unlike in the past, our Fú's do not fly high in the sky, they fly quite close to the ground. As a result, we were able to not only see a great deal during the trip, but we could see everything in great detail. Much of what I had seen during our trip was quite disturbing. Even so, the journey had somehow steeled me. I could feel a strengthening within myself. I felt stronger in my belief that nature is resilient. We humans do a great deal to try and "tame" nature and bend her to our will, but what I had seen reinforced my knowledge and faith that even after the folly of human capriciousness, nature does and will regenerate.

Any sadness I felt came from the realization that so many people had to perish to prove that lesson once again. And why? Ego? Power? Greed? Yes, yes and yes. The question that gnawed at me even in the face of the obvious was, can we be fully human without feeling these horrible emotions or be driven by these horrible drives? What would it mean to be a creature that lived in harmony with nature rather than at odds with her?

Even after the lessons of our greed and recklessness became clear, people – and we should make no mistake, governments are just people – refused to clean up our mess, refused to take on the difficult task of making amends with nature. And why not? Money. Economy. We would lose jobs, they claimed. Our standard of living would decline, they opined.

Well, how important are those jobs now? How might you describe the standard of living now?

"Prepare for landing."

The pilot's voice startled me out of my reverie. There were tasks to be attended to. I had my responsibilities in the landing sequence, although they were hardly as essential as those of the pilot. Still, I, along with the others, focused on the task at hand. In another few minutes, we had hovered down, touching down with barely a whisper of sensation.

There was a momentary silence, as we each seemed to draw in the same breath. We had arrived. Up until that point, our experience was one that we had experienced any number of times before. But now, in light of what had happened, we were going to leave the Fú. As confining as it is, it is a safe space. Leaving it would open us to all the dangers and threats that existed on the outside, whatever they may be.

"Let's gear up."

That directive made concrete our task. As much as I wanted to remain fully "present" and to process everything I saw and experienced, I also had a job to do, a job that I was trained well to do. So, my training kicked in. Like the others, I began to gather my equipment and tools. Optimally, we would each have exactly as much as we needed, no more and no less – everything we might need to do our job but not so much as to weigh us down.

In reality, things don't usually work as neatly.

For my part, I wanted to be sure that I had my most important devices. Whether or not it was onerous to carry or move, I needed what I needed. The same, I knew, was true of the others.

One by one, we descend from the Fú. When we are all on solid ground, Tim locked the Fú to ensure that it was secure upon our return. None of us was interested in any surprises upon our return to the craft!

We gathered in a small circle as if to take a check of our status as individuals and as a group. My eyes travel from one to the next, landing finally on Jace. Our eyes held each other's a bit longer than might have been necessary, but just long enough to communicate everything we wanted to be sure to communicate with one another.

"Ready?" Tim asked.

One by one, we nodded. Yes, we were ready. As ready as we would ever be.

"Then let's do this. We have a long, long road ahead of us."

Indeed we did. We had a long trek in front of us. Even so, as soon as we arrived at the tarmac, Jace began to take air quality readings. We were all, of course, outfitted with CO protection. Even so, we had been advised not to take any chances with our health. There would be enough dangers we could not anticipate – CO poisoning was one danger we could anticipate and prepare for.

As Jace took his readings, I raised my head and looked around. The tarmac was littered with aircraft, both small passenger and larger passenger planes. One or two military transports were off to the side of the tarmac. In all, I took in an image of chaos. I had in my imagination an image of multiple planes trying to take off or land in a haphazard and desperate attempt to escape whatever the immediate danger was. There were several planes in such a position that it seemed their wings clipped, adding to whatever kept them on the ground at that time.

All the planes showed emergency exits opened and belts that once held the inflatable slides that allowed passengers to escape the plane. The slides were long gone, as were the people who had desperately fled the planes when it was apparent to them that they would not be taking off, and even if they did, there would be no place for them to go.

"We're good," Jace said, sliding his meter back into its holder.

"Let's move on," Tim said.

We crossed the tarmac in a single-file line. Tim led us into the closest terminal. Based on my review of the Denver Airport, this would have been the International Terminal.

We scaled the terminal and entered through a broken window. We walked through a terminal at which time seemed to have stood still. There was still luggage alongside seats. Still cups of beverages in the seat cupholders. Still magazines and newspapers opened.

"Look at this," Jace said, pointing to a half-finished crossword puzzle.

I don't know if he noticed that a pencil, possibly the one that had been used on the crossword, was still teetering on the chair.

It was an eerie scene indeed. All around us, we could see the evidence of people, but absolutely no sign of people. There were diaper bags, but no babies. It was as if everything stopped all at once, in an instance.

What we were seeing did not comport with what we'd been taught in the Academy. There, our professors and instructors had indicated that a climate change had caused a deadly increase in CO levels, wiping out the populations who could not escape.

But CO poisoning of that degree might have allowed for some planning, some coherent strategy. It was clear that people were *trying* to get away. But from what? I didn't believe it was Carbon.

I felt Jace brush against my shoulder. I appreciated the contact. It brought me back to the present. I could see in his expression the same kind of concern that I felt. Both inside and outside the terminal, the atmosphere felt heavy and dark. Its weightiness was as much psychological as it was physical.

Rusting aircraft remained anchored to the ends of the airport walkways. Some had become covered in moss and vegetation. Small animals seemed to scurry around. But those animals were the only signs of life we could discern.

With each step I took, I felt the strange sensation that I was somehow walking *between time*. I felt as if time had stopped and I was moving at that moment between when one draws one's breath and when one exhales again. I was in a moment of existential pause. Nothing was moving. And yet, *we* were. We were walking through the terminal, pausing to glance at the artifacts of lives once lived, of lives suddenly ended; walking past the artifacts and evidence of some catastrophic and cataclysmic change which was at once devastating and unhurried. Children's sippy cups were still standing upright. Strollers remained alongside chairs once occupied by young parents.

All the signs that people had been here, but there were no people!

Other than the artifacts – the small airport restaurants and sandwich shops – and the thing people had left behind, there was nothing. Not a body. Not a soul. No one.

We pushed open doorways. Restrooms. Looking, looking. Searching. No one. There was ample evidence that people *had* been there, but it seemed they had simply vanished, from one moment to the next.

There was long, long before the remains where a great volcano had overrun the city, entombing an entire population. Clearly, at that time, the noxious gases of the volcano preceded the dust and ash, murdering people in place. Then came the ash and the materials that entombed them, allowing future generations to see them *as they were*. But here, there was none of that. Just an empty set, devoid of actors.

I looked out the giant, plate glass windows still intact. On the tarmac, catering trucks sat next to cargo holds. Refueling trucks remained attached to some of the planes. Personal luggage and suitcases remained on flatbed trays waiting to be put onto aircraft by hands that never reached for them and would never reach for them again.

Some of the luggage was overturned, perhaps rifled through in haste in the last moments or maybe just overturned by people in their haste to escape, but escape what?

But still no *people*.

"Oh my God."

My eyes widened. Jace turned to look at me. Looking into my face, he turned his own eyes in the direction I was looking. As soon as he saw what I saw, he began to walk, then run, toward the airline at the end of the gateway.

Through the windows of the plane, I could see skeletal remains. The group followed after Jace. Walking quickly and then running. We worked as one, turning the rusted door lock and then pushing our way into the plane, we could see a plane filled with the remains of passengers who never left the aircraft. Some were in their seats. Others pushing against the doorway.

Whatever had brought about their demise, had, unlike what had happened inside the terminal we'd been in, caught them unawares.

"Don't touch anything," Justin said as he moved through the plane's cabin, observing. "I have to test everything. Until I have readings, I'd suggest leaving the plane as well, in case there is something here that we cannot filter."

"But then you..." I began.

He waved me away. This was, after all, his job. Besides, if there was a danger better to lose only one rather than all of us. So, realizing the logic of his suggestion, we left him alone in the plane to take his measurements and samples.

As we waited for him, I considered what I knew about life when this cataclysm struck, at a time before the purge.

I knew that pre-purge, humans driving cars pumped an average of ten billion tonnes of carbon dioxide into the atmosphere every year. Ten billion! That worked out to nearly one tonne per person on earth – and that was only half of the dangerous greenhouse gases that impacted global warming. The remainder was the result of industrial activity.

This human contribution – cause – of global warming continued to astonish me. Why hadn't someone recognized and *done* something about it? I knew that there were any number of scientific papers written, even mass movements, calling attention to the coming danger. But the government, the decision makers, had remained remarkably deaf to the evidence and protests.

Job losses.

Inexact science.

Out and out lies.

Economy.

People love their cars.

Whatever the excuse, the government had used it... until it was too late.

After the discovery of the skeletal remains on the airplane, it seemed that we were finding bodies and remains everywhere. For whatever reason, the terminal and area we had first entered had been abruptly abandoned – perhaps in the face of imminent danger. Perhaps an alarm had been sounded. Whatever, that area had been evacuated. That was not true of any other area of the airport.

If nothing else, I made a mental note to never draw absolute conclusions based on an isolated sample. As we walked forward through the walkway connecting terminals, I recalled the folk story my father had once told me about blind men encountering an elephant. Each man, touching a different part of the beast drew wildly different conclusions about what they had encountered.

All were wrong.

"We are all blind," my father told me. "And life is an elephant."

We arrived in the welcoming hall of the terminal. This building, which I could imagine bustling with thousands of people, excited to be flying out or arriving, was deathly quiet except for our footsteps. Instead of the excitement of travel and adventure, we were greeted by lifeless bodies. Some still seated. Most on the floors. Some slumped in chairs. A few piled upon others. Some of the smaller bodies, children, still held in parents' arms. Almost all the bodies had been reduced to skeletons, but some still had toughened, leather-like skin stretched over their bones.

Jace grabbed my hand. "Put your mask on," he said, his eyes glancing in the direction of the bodies.

I nodded. It was a prudent and sensible thing to do. Even if there was no longer any trace of whatever killed these people, there could still be some degrading toxin in their bones and taut skin.

We moved carefully making sure not to disturb any of the bodies. Justin, who had caught up with us after leaving the plane, was particularly interested in those bodies that still had some skin on them. Kneeling beside one after the other of them, he opened his kit, took out a sterile scraper and a vile and scraped a small amount of skin into each vial, making sure to document as much as he could about the source of each sample.

Once he finished, he saw that we'd been standing around, watching him with a variety of astonished expressions on our faces. While he had devoted a good deal of his time at the Academy to biology and had looked forward to experiences of this sort, the rest of us had focused our attention on other matters and found his scraping and pulling off the parchment-like skin somewhere between fascinating and macabre.

"I'm good," he said.

Cate breathed an audible sigh of relief. "Good. Let's keep moving. This place is giving me the heeby-jeebies."

Justin laughed. "They are only bodies," he observed.

Just bodies! Easy for him to say! I wasn't as troubled as Cate was but I couldn't say that I *enjoyed* finding myself surrounded by skeletal corpses.

We continued through the terminal, taking mental note of everything we were seeing – not only the bodies but everything we were seeing. Food courts. ATM machines toppled on their sides. Bins and garbage containers on their sides, their contents were strewn all about. Most likely from small animals, I thought to myself. Surely humans wouldn't have eaten from bins and garbage.

The small shops in the airport were emptied out – nothing remained on their shelves. Not a tee shirt, mug, or magazine. Strange.

"Look at that," I said, pointing to a Gargoyle sitting in a suitcase perched on an outcrop high above the area.

Jace shrugged.

"Seems an odd sort of thing to have in an airport, don't you think?" I said, half to myself. The fact was, I had seen pictures of this airport in texts, and I'd never noticed a Gargoyle in any picture I saw. I did though, think of the photographs of where I had seen gargoyles. Medieval churches. Universities. Places where the architecture felt the symbolic power of a gargoyle was necessary, gothic architecture – whether as a protection from evil or a nod to classical thought. But this, I thought to myself, is an airport. What was this Gargoyle doing here? What symbolic significance could it have? And, perhaps as importantly, *when* was it put up?

The eerie feeling the Gargoyle created in me caused me to tremble slightly. Jace turned to me.

"Are you all right?"

I nodded.

As strange and disturbing as it was to see the Gargoyle, it was even stranger to see the murals that adorned the walls of the long walkways. They were so disturbing that I tried to avert my eyes from them, but they seemed to call to me, forcing me to look at their scenes of apocalypse and rebirth.

I reached out and held Jace's hand. I could not keep a tremor from going through my body.

There were, in total, four murals. Related but distinct. In the first, three women, dead, lay in coffins. By their looks and attire, they are an African, an Indian and a young Jewish girl. Beyond the coffins, in the distance, there seems to be the destruction of cities and forests. All around, there are images of extinct animals.

In the second mural, a man in a gas mask is carrying a sword and a gun. The technique and image reminded me of a depiction of a German soldier from my studies. In the mural, the man is walking down a street through a devastated city. It appears that the buildings are on fire. His sword is piercing a dove, which is the symbol of peace.

The message was not subtle. Peace will be destroyed.

Dead children and babies lay on broken bricks. Weeping women surround the children, raising their eyes and arms to the darkened sky. On the floor in front of this second mural, there was a plate on which the symbols "AUAG" were clearly etched.

"Gold and silver?" I asked aloud, looking at the plate.

"Maybe," Justin agreed. "But that is also the symbol for Australia Antigen, one of the more lethal strains of hepatitis ever known."

I narrowed my brow. Here we were, surrounded by evidence and clues of some cataclysmic event and even the most straightforward 'clue' could easily mean multiple things. It seemed overwhelming. Still, whatever its meaning, the floor plate had been placed before a mural that depicted a genocide. Perhaps that suggested that Justin's suggestion was more apt.

The third mural showed children of all nations taking weapons from their countries and giving them to a boy. He looked to be taking the weapons and molding them into something else. In this third mural, the soldier from the second mural lies on the ground, appearing dead, with two doves perched on the butt of his gun which is still in his hands.

In the final mural, people are running towards a figure that seems to be of some significance to them who is standing over a plant.

"Symbol of rebirth?" Jace asked aloud.

"Makes sense," I thought, but I no longer trusted my presumptions about symbols and meanings.

The people in this last mural all seemed to be happy. The simple meaning and message seemed to be that all the nations were going to live together in a world of peace. In the mural, animals are roaming free. There is, in the mural, a curious suggestion that everything was in perfect harmony.

It depicted a new, brave and safe world. Our world?

In the pictorial story the murals told, I interpreted a story, not unlike our own story. The final mural spoke to a hopeful and uplifting conclusion to the troubles the people endured – very much as I'd been taught in the Academy. Still, despite the hopeful conclusion to the series of murals, they left me feeling uneasy. Even when they were behind us, they were still present in my mind.

Walking along the underground terminal, I felt tired and overwhelmed. Even when we'd made our way to the middle of the building and Jason instructed us that it was safe to remove our masks, I couldn't shake the heaviness of my emotions.

It was not so long before that we were at the Academy, studying history. Though it was not long ago, it seemed like a lifetime! Rather than being youthful and full of promise, I felt heavy and burdened. I could not have imagined anything more exciting than a mission like the one I found myself on and yet, now that I found myself staring history right in the eye I had the unsettling feeling that we had not been presented with the entire story! It was difficult and upsetting then when I was only studying it, looking at images and reading descriptions of what had happened. But now, staring directly at the reality of those events... it was shocking, unnerving. Confusing.

There was no way to cope with the destruction, the pain, the agony... and all of it so unnecessary!

"Come along," I told myself. "Get a grip of yourself." I knew I needed to clear my head of these thoughts. I had a task to focus on. I couldn't allow my performance to be clouded by emotion.

Emotion, as I'd been taught, is the enemy of accomplishment.

And yet, here I was, caught up in emotion! I knew that my vital signs were reflecting my emotions. I could feel my pulse pounding and sweat forming under my arms and in the center of my back. Under normal circumstances, I would already have been notified by the medical centre that my stats were no longer within the normal range and that it was necessary for me to adjust my bearing. But here, with only Justin and his EMH device to monitor our well-being, there was less oversight. My vital signs went unmonitored, as did those of the rest of the group. Never before in our lives had we been so untethered to monitoring!

In order for the EMH device to pick up on changes in our bodies, it needed to be on and operating. But, unless we showed obvious signs of illness or distress, Justin had made it clear by his actions that he had little interest in starting it up. We were not his primary focus. The corpses around us were.

"We need to pick up the pace," Tim said. "There is only a short amount of daylight left. We need to make it into the tunnels and at least halfway towards our destination before we can rest."

If we were able to reach the ARC by the morning, Leon could try to determine the frequency of the communications device that was being used within the ARC. The plan was that, with that information, he could make contact with whoever was sending out the messages, and then hopefully, Bella would be able to enter into some kind of negotiation with them.

The operative word being 'hopefully."

CHAPTER TWELVE
THE TRUTH

We moved quickly through the quiet and dark pathways underneath the airport. The tiles were damp, and our footsteps echoed as we hurried along.

As we moved, Tim continually referenced his guidance screen, following its instructions as it told us when to turn and when to ignore turn offs as we worked our way through the labyrinthine pathways the below-ground station presented to us. "Here!" Tim called out when we'd finally arrived at a tunnel which, to my eyes looked no different than any of the ones we'd passed before it, though it would allow us to begin our descent toward one of the known entrances to the ARC.

Despite finding the correct entrance, there were still miles of tunnels ahead of us and less and less time for us to cover the distance before us. But we were all young and strong, just one of the reasons that we had been chosen for this mission. Tim kept increasing the pace until, before we knew it, we were moving forward at an easy jog. Whatever equipment we carried presenting no problem at all. We were, as I've noted, young and strong.

The lighting in the tunnels was dim, casting almost as much shadow as illumination. Still, that there was light at all was the amazing thing. In truth, we were astonished that there was *any* existing lighting. Despite the years of presumed disuse, I could not help but note that the tunnels were in good repair and extremely clean. Almost as if they'd been used on a regular basis.

This reality – of an existence of a lighting system and the status of the tunnel – stood in stark contrast from our presumptions based on what we were able to view from above ground. There seemed to have passed a great many years since the closure of the ARCs. But here we have found ourselves in illuminated tunnels, illumination which not only suggested but indicated that there was a working power source.

I glanced at Jace. Jace glanced at me. We were both astonished by what we were seeing and the obvious statement it was making. There should be *no* power source save for the ARCs themselves. But here we found ourselves miles – many miles – from our destination and yet there is clearly power being provided to these lights.

"It makes no sense," Tim said, clearly as troubled by this obvious – and seeming – contradiction between what we were led to expect and what we were finding.

I don't think anyone was troubled by what we'd come upon. Confused, perhaps. We certainly did not take it for evidence of anything being amiss. It was, I think more appropriately, something of an enigma to us, a puzzle that we would undoubtedly be able to solve as we learned more.

We did not, at that point, consider the existence of power, of well-maintained tunnels, of any of the things we'd seen as evidence of something of concern.

As we jogged along, I wracked my brain, trying to remember anything in my studies that would give me insight into what I was encountering. But I could come up with nothing. Everything I was seeing was contrary to what had been taught in the Academy and in my classes.

I did not yet make any connection that would have caused me to doubt the knowledge, expertise or opinions of my instructors.

I wondered what was going through everyone else's mind. We were moving through something that was contrary to all we'd been taught to expect. What else had our teaching gotten wrong?

The first indication of anything that could be considered "troubling" was when we encountered the first of many "viewing devices" established along the tunnels. As we moved forward, small red lights blinked on and off and the head of the device, swiveling on a mount, seemed to follow us as we moved along.

"Ever feel you're being watched?" I whispered to Jace.

He chuckled. "Just... every single step I'm taking."

"Yeh, me too," I agreed.

The "eyes" on us and the long miles began to wear on me after we had traveled what seemed like hours. So, after we had managed to put many miles beneath our feet, I suggested that we rest for the night.

"I'd like to get to the ARC as soon as possible," Tim said, clearly not taking kindly to my suggestion.

"But we don't know how much further it is," I protested. "It could be another mile, it could be another twenty."

Bella groaned at the thought of it being another twenty miles. Looking at Tim and then at me, she tossed her pack to the ground and then sat down on it. "I thought we'd never stop."

Justin, for his part, might have been sympathetic to my desire to stop but he was also thinking about the need to make progress. "I think we should go a bit further before stopping," he advised. "We may not make it to the ARC itself, but the more distance we cover now, the less we have to cover later."

"No!" Bella snapped. "I won't go another step."

"Justin, relax," Jace said. "We will make it in good time. It does us no good to be exhausted. We've walked miles and miles. Let's just rest."

Justin might have been willing to argue against Bella. He might even have been willing to push back against both Bella and me. But he clearly was not interested in fighting with Jace. Instead, he rested his pack on the ground and pulled out his EMH device. "Then let's see what everyone's vitals are and how everyone's doing," he said, the tone in his voice registering his displeasure with the decision.

Breaking into what quickly resembled a small camp away from the prying eyes of the devices that had followed our every move, we spoke with candor about some of the things we'd seen and experienced.

"Those murals…" Bella began but simply shook her head. She didn't seem to need to complete the thought. We were all able to complete it for her. They had filled us with a strange sense of foreboding – and a hint of optimism.

"How do you think those lights are powered?" I asked.

Justin, who was concentrating on his equipment and what looked like a small sample of dried skin he'd collected earlier, piped in. "There is clearly an energy source. The question is, are they powered by some solar device that we didn't note, or is there some other source deeper underground, perhaps a nuclear source?" From what we knew the power in our Arc had been geothermal.

"I trust Jace and I were not the only ones who noted the cameras," I said softly.

I could feel a small tremor run through our group. "I think it's fair to say we all were aware of them," Tim said.

"What do you think they mean?"

"I think the obvious is the truest answer, we are being watched."

"But by who?"

"Ah, the million dollar question," Tim replied. "I would imagine that the answer to that question would go a long way toward answering the questions about the ARC that we've come to sort out. And, the most likely answer to the question about the power source for the lights as well."

We all nodded in agreement. But we were chilled by the thought of who – or what – could be watching and tracking our progress.

"It is not impossible that the lights and the tracking cameras are simply remains," Bella suggested. "After all, if they were working then…"

"Possible," Tim agreed, seeming anxious not to allow for that kind of reasoning.

"But not probable?" I asked, taking my lead from the tone of his voice.

He shrugged. "Assuming effective solar power, these systems could theoretically continue forever." He paused, choosing his words carefully. "I just don't know that our success should be premised on 'best case scenarios.'"

There was a murmur of assent. We would always like to have the best possible outcome, however, accomplishing positive outcomes almost always means not presuming them.

"Natural selection."

I heard the words and turned my head toward Justin, who had whispered them seemingly under his breath.

"What do you mean?" I asked him, immediately realizing that he had given voice to a thought that had yet to take form in my own mind.

"Positive outcomes. There are no positive or negative outcomes, just the ones that are supposed to occur. Natural selection, Ari," he said. He looked back toward the path we'd taken to get to where we were, and then he looked ahead. "It's plain what happened. They released an airborne pathogen and killed everyone." He shook his head. "Of course we are looking for a carbon pollution, but carbon pollution was not the culprit, not for what we're seeing here. Carbon pollution would not have resulted in the kind of situation we saw in the airport."

"What do you think happened then?"

He drew a deep breath, as though he wanted to weigh the advisability of putting his thoughts into words. "In 2014 scientists from the University of Wisconsin-Madison created a life-threatening virus that resembled the Spanish flu."

"Spanish flu?" I asked, never having heard of it.

"Yes, that was a flu variant which essentially wiped out about 50 million people in 1918."

I felt an ache in the pit of my stomach. "I have never learned about the Spanish flu," I confessed. "Or, if I did, I didn't remember it."

He nodded. "I know. I wasn't taught about it either."

"Then how do you...?"

"Research. One thing I did learn how to do at the Academy was to research, to dig deep. There is a great deal of control over research that is done online and can be tracked. But in the basement of the library complex, there are many, many paper volumes."

"So that's why you never had a tan?" I said lightly.

He smiled ruefully. "One of the reasons," he conceded.

Any lightheartedness in our conversation was unsustainable, given the subject matter of our conversation. I tried a quick smile to match his, but it had no joy or mirth. I thought back to our Academy training. "Why would they lie to us," I asked.

"I don't know," Justin mumbled under his breath, "I don't know if that's what they did. Maybe they didn't know. Or they were fearful of the truth. Whatever, it sure seems that they did."

Everyone quieted down. Everyone had clearly been listening to our conversation and had taken their own measure of what we'd been saying. This new information would take a long while to reflect upon. Meanwhile, we had an immediate task ahead of us, one that we had to accomplish, regardless of what it uncovered.

"Let's just eat and get some sleep," Tim advised. "No matter what has happened, we need to be ready for whatever we encounter."

None of us could argue with his logic, and so we turned our attention to our meal. For myself, I chewed my food with less enthusiasm and joy than any meal I'd ever had. The meal, designed to be nutritious more than tasty, was bland and uninspiring.

Cate looked at each of us when she'd finished her meal. "It's a big day for us physically tomorrow, so we should probably try to get some rest," she said. "I'll stand watch first, just in case." She turned to Jace, "You can take the next watch. I'll wake you in a couple of hours."

"Okay," Jace replied. Then he leaned over to where I'd laid my head on one of our packs. He smiled as reassuringly as he could manage. "Sleep tight won't you, Ari." He reached out and rested his hand on my shoulder.

I smiled back at him. No matter what was going on, if Jace was with me, I felt safer. Of course, knowing that Cate would be standing watch made me feel good too. I couldn't imagine any physical threat that she couldn't turn away.

"Don't worry. We are going to be okay," he whispered. There was an urgency in his voice as if he could hear the chattering worry in my head. Maybe he didn't need to be that insightful. Maybe it was the look in my eyes that told him how worried I was.

I smiled at Jace then I propped myself up on my elbow and looked over at Justin. "Justin, do we have a cure for the disease?"

Justin, who was packing his gear into his pack before going to sleep looked over at me. "Yes, Ari. We do. We have for a while. But don't worry, you won't need it."

"No?"

He shook his head. "You have a natural immunity," he stated with certainty. Then his eyes scanned the group. "All of us do. We are the descendants of the previous generations of ARC dwellers. They had immunity. That was how they survived. At the same time, a vaccine was developed to strengthen that immunity. Everyone who entered the ARC was vaccinated to ensure that any known viruses didn't enter the ARC community."

That was comforting news. I had tried not to think too much about it, but there was no way to avoid the concern about exposure. Knowing that I was immune to the virus that had decimated this community was more than a little relief. "That's good news," I said softly.

He nodded. "Yes, it is. Everyone was vaccinated against all the viruses that were known threats. The immunity in the ARCs was as complete as could be."

With that news, I let out a slow, controlled breath and tried to allow my exhaustion to lead the way to sleep. I was certain that as soon as I put my head down and closed my eyes, I would be sound asleep. My body was so exhausted. But, as it turned out, I would not enjoy anything resembling a comforting, deep sleep that night. My body was surely exhausted, but perhaps my worry was too entrenched. Or I was *too* exhausted. I couldn't say. Sleep had never been a problem for me in my entire life. I could not recall a single night when I struggled to sleep except, perhaps when I was a small girl, and I had a fever. Other than that, I slept the sleep of the dead, peaceful and complete. Not this night. This night I tossed and turned, moved restlessly from side to side, never settling into anything restful. I was surprised to find I was still awake when Cate's guard shift was over.

"Ari," Jace whispered into my ear, resting his hand on my shoulder. "You need to get some sleep, you really do."

I opened my eyes and nodded. I knew he was right. If I didn't sleep, I would only be ill prepared for whatever we confronted the next day, and none of us could afford to be anything but sharp.

"What time is it?"

"Time for my watch," he said.

"Really?" I couldn't believe I'd tossed and turned through one whole watch.

"Do you want to take something to help you sleep?"

I shook my head. The last thing I wanted was something that would make me feel drugged. That would be even worse than being tired in the morning. No, I thought the best thing to do was to stop fighting sleep and just give in to my restlessness. I sat up and rubbed my eyes. "No, I think I'll just keep you company for a bit," I said. "If that's all right."

"You're sure?" he asked, looking at me with a concerned expression.

I nodded. "If I start getting sleepy, I'll put my head down," I promised him.

For a short time, we sat in silence, just being close to one another. Nearby, we could hear the breathing of our colleagues as they slept, except for Justin who sat fascinated by his tubes which contained the pieces of skin he had removed from the corpses. For a time, it was simply comforting to share the space with Jace, it soon felt surreal as I kept thinking about where we were and why we were there.

"It's so disturbing," I said quietly.

Jace, who was eying the darkness beyond our small, informal camp, looked at me. "What's that?"

"We'd always been taught that it was carbon pollution that choked the world. CO concentrations from the greenhouse gases that finally killed those who had not made it to the ARCs. But now..."

He nodded sadly. "I know. I can't get it out of my mind either."

This airborne pathogen, whatever it was – poison, virus, whatever – had killed all the people we'd seen in the terminal. "There must have been *some* warning," I said, trying to sort out the images in my mind. "They ran, they tried to get away... that's the only reason I can think of, for why the first terminal was abandoned the way it was."

"Yes, but the next," he said, focusing on the many, many corpses we'd come upon. "They certainly didn't get far."

"No." No, they hadn't gotten far at all.

Rather than finding answers, it seemed that we had more and more questions. Even the things we *thought* we knew, we clearly did not understand. Was the pathogen naturally occurring? Was it developed in a lab? Was it weaponized or was there simply a terrible, terrible accident...? What happened? I couldn't stop myself from asking that question. I could actually see the words of the question forming in my mind. WHAT...WHAT...WHAT HAPPENED? It was unnerving and certainly not conducive to sleep. If anything, I was becoming more awake, more alert.

There was a time when there was a thriving population here. What happened?

I could only hope that by the time we finished our mission tomorrow we would have some answers. The key was, of course, to get to the people in the ARC. That was the goal and our hope.

I do not know when I fell asleep, but I clearly fell into a fitful sleep because the next thing I knew, I was startled awake by a screeching sound in my ears.

"Shh. It's okay," Jace whispered into my ear. "It's okay. You were having a nightmare."

My eyes opened wide. Jace was rocking me in his arms.

"What happened?"

He gave a half-hearted smile. "Nothing happened. You've been having terrible dreams. Nightmares."

Jace was nearing the end of his watch. When my disturbed sleep became too much for Jace to watch he'd taken me into his arms to gently rock me. His expression told me that he was glad that I was awake and was no longer tormented by my dreams and visions.

Not long after I'd awakened, the others began to stir. Tim sat up and looked around, blinking.

"I'll be glad to be away from here," he said to no one in particular.

Clearly, I was not the only one who had struggled with nightmare visions. Only Cate seemed fully rested – a true warrior through and through!

"It was Sarin gas that killed them all," Justin announced with a sad nuance in his voice to everyone. "After performing many investigations last night it is conclusive, they executed them all, what were they thinking?"

What could we say, what was there to say?

We silently gathered ourselves, getting our gear packed and getting ready to march on. Which, after a very light breakfast, we did.

At first, I seemed unaffected by my lack of restful sleep the night before. But it wasn't long before my feet began to tire and my legs started to feel like jelly. Jace must have noticed me wobbling because he quickly stepped close to me and put his hand on the shoulder strap of my pack.

"Let me carry this for a way," he said, starting to lift it from my shoulders.

I shook my head. "No," I said firmly. You can't do that," I insisted. "You've had so little sleep yourself. I'm a big girl, and I can cope with this. You worry about your own pack," I said firmly.

Jace smiled and even chuckled a bit. "Always Miss Independent, aren't you?" He shook his head, looking amused. "That's what I love about you Ari."

Then we fell into a slow, easier walk, it seemed that none of us was too enthusiastic about contacting those in the ARC after hearing Justin's findings. But then our mission was our mission, and that was what we were here to do, enthused or not. Every once in a while, I looked over at Jace. I could hear his footsteps landing in rhythm with mine. But something wasn't right.

"Did you hear that?" I asked him after a time.

He nodded. "I've heard it for a while. But I wasn't sure..."

So, we'd both heard it. Footsteps. Behind us. I looked at Jace with fear in my heart. "We're being followed."

And then we all heard it. Footsteps, stealth footsteps behind us.

We stopped and looked around as the truth of our realization sank in. We were being followed.

CHAPTER THIRTEEN
SURVIVORS

All we could hear was our own breathing as we listened and then forced ourselves to listen even harder. I was certain I could hear my heart pounding in my chest as adrenalin coursed through my body, paralyzing me between fight and flight. A sensation I was *NOT* used to.

I looked at Jace. He looked at me. Tim. Cate. Justin. Bella. Our eyes darted back and forth as we silently communicated with one another. Do we turn and fight? Do we continue on?

Was it all our imagination?

Was it a feint being perpetrated by whoever was watching us?

Our instructions could not have been clearer: 'Do not engage with any members of the remaining population!' If we were to encounter them, shun them! But here, a very long way from those who had given us those instructions, we might not have the luxury of honoring them. Our choice might only come down to the nature of our engagement.

We were certainly highly armed and prepared for any kind of combat confrontation. Not only were we each trained in combat – with Cate the exemplar of those skills – we each carried with us arms that were capable of stunning a man into unconsciousness as easily as they were able to leave a wound the size of a tea saucer in his flesh. Or, if used in their most lethal ways, cut a man in half.

As a group, we were as proficient in the use of our weaponry as possible. That said, it was also true that *all* citizens of Pulchra were trained in, and expected to be ready to use, these weapons.

There was a time, not long before I went into the Academy when it confused me that every citizen of Pulchra was trained so thoroughly in battle and war. After all, the world we lived in was such a peaceful place. We were "enlightened." We no longer swore allegiance to a country or a people; we swore allegiance to humanity.

I had not had time to think about the apparent disconnect in a long time. However, in the coming hours and days, I would have more than enough time – and reason – to revisit that issue and that disconnect.

Cate was naturally, the first among us to take an aggressive and "attack" posture. She drew her weapon and turned to face the person or persons who were tracking us.

"Cate," I whispered, holding my hand up in caution. "Make sure your weapon is set to 'stun'. We do not want to kill anyone."

She narrowed her eyes. Trained as a warrior, she hewed to the credo that the only good enemy was a dead enemy.

"Cate, either it is an ARC sponsor that has been sent out to greet us – and it would not serve our purpose to be overly aggressive with such a person – or a civilian who has wandered into the tunnel looking for respite."

Of course, I had no sooner spoken than I understood the weakness of my words. How would anyone have been able to get out of the ARC? And, as for a civilian... hadn't Justin only just explained to us the lethal nature of the gas that had killed so many? How would anyone have survived?

Despite the obvious weakness of my caution, she nodded. As a group, we waited.

"I can't stand this," Cate seethed through clenched teeth. "If they will not come to us, then we should take the battle to them..."

"Let us not be hasty," I said, trying to speak reasonably. "Let's consider our situation and our options. Rash thought, and even rasher actions can never lead to any worthwhile outcome."

We waited another few moments. Whoever was tracking us did not show themselves so, rather than actively engage – which was against our instructions – we decided to move forward. It was clear, at least, that whoever it was wasn't from the ARC. Such a person would have identified himself.

"Let's move forward," I said. "We have our orders and our mission. It's important that we fulfill that mission if we are to make any sense of what has happened to us."

Everyone agreed. Although Cate was more reluctant, fearing danger at our heels.

"Cate," I said, "you need to bring up the rear."

She nodded, recognizing the wisdom of my instruction. When she took up her position, we lifted our packs and started forward, single-file further into the dimly-lit tunnel. "Let's go," I said, curiously finding myself in command.

We'd gone forward another couple of miles, still certain that we were being trailed when I raised my hand to stop the group.

"What is it?" Jace asked.

I pointed ahead. In the dim light, we could see the end of the tunnel – a large, steel door. I nodded and then indicated that we should go on. We were all still aware of the person or persons behind us, but our focus was on what was before us, our objective.

The more we traveled, the less ominous whoever trailed us seemed to be. They were curious, perhaps. But apparently meant no harm to us.

There was discomfort, of course, in being watched. But I no longer felt fear. My thoughts were more and more concentrated on the mission, and the mission was before us, not behind us.

When we stood before the ARC, Leon and Bella quickly set up the communications equipment that they had been carrying. Leon sat cross-legged on the ground and began to adjust a tuner knob, searching for a frequency that would allow us to communicate with those inside the ARC.

As Leon adjusted the knobs on the small console, I looked up and studied the massive, steel structure in front of me. I motioned to Jace and pointed to the four small cameras above the door, monitoring our every move.

Other than the sound of Leon preparing the communications, there was no sound among us – although it was still possible to hear something, someone, lurking in the shadows behind us, just beyond sight.

"Go," Leon said softly, gesturing toward to Bella.

Bella nodded. She brought the microphone to her lips. "Hello? Hello? We come in peace. My name is Bella Formacheck. I have come, along with these others, at the direction of the Pulchran Ministry on behalf of Minister Lincoln. Can anyone hear me?"

I was impressed with how clearly she spoke. I could not help but think she must have been nervous, to be speaking to the past! But she spoke with such purpose!

We were all taken aback by the response she received.

"You are communicating on an official channel. Clear the channel immediately."

Bella's brow creased in confusion. She drew a breath and continued. "Sir, perhaps you did not understand. We have been sent in peace. We are on a mission to make contact..."

Suddenly, the communication link was ended.

Leon quickly adjusted the transmitter to find another channel that was operational. He nodded to Bella to continue.

"Sir, I implore you to listen. We have been sent on a mission to make contact with you..."

"You are communicating on an official channel. Clear this channel immediately."

"No," Bella snapped. "I will not! Sir, or sirs, you do not understand the urgency of this communication..." Once again, the communication was cut off. Once again, Leon found an alternative channel.

"Is there a superior with whom I can speak?" Bella asked sharply.

"You *must* clear this channel. It is for official business only."

"This *is* official business…"

The communication was cut off again. Once again, Leon located a channel for her to use.

"We have come from the future!" Bella said firmly. "We are here to help you! I must speak with someone in authority."

"The future? We have no time for foolishness. You are on an official channel. Cease and desist with your communications immediately."

This, apparently, was all too much for Bella. Despite her training in delicate negotiations, her inability to at least speak with someone of authority frustrated her more than she was able to deal with. "Or what?" she snapped, accepting the implicit challenge. "What are you going to do if I speak on your frequency? Will you come out of your safe ARC and threaten us?"

"Bella," I barked under my breath, astonished by her tone.

But she was too incensed to listen. "Change your frequencies all you want. Our instruments are far more superior to those that you are using. We *will* negotiate with you. Now, I expect to speak with someone in charge …"

There was silence in response. Three seconds. Ten. Thirty. A minute. Several minutes.

Bella leaned close to me. "I'm sorry. I got frustrated, Ari. I'm really sorry. I should never have lost it like that. It won't happen again." She sighed deeply. "I don't know why I just thought this would be easy. I thought they'd be *glad* we were here." She shook her head. "They never prepared me for any of this at the Academy."

I would learn soon enough just how ill-prepared the Academy left us! But, at the moment, my concerns were more concrete. "Don't worry about it, Bella. You're doing a great job. I don't know how you've kept it together this well."

At that moment, the radio crackled back to life. There was some static, which had to come from the ARC because all our equipment was digital and clean. There was another moment of silence, and then a deep, clear voice came over the radio.

"This is John Dawson, I am the Minister of Communications within the ARC. What is this I hear that you refuse to clear this official channel?"

Bella steeled herself and then spoke. "That is correct, sir. We will not clear the channel. We have traveled quite some way to speak with you, as you have refused to speak with our counterparts previously.

"I represent Minister Lincoln and the Pulchran people..."

"We know nothing of this Minister Lincoln or Pulchra. We had a President Lincoln a long time ago but I doubt that he is relevant to your being here."

"Mr. Dawson, through a phenomenon which we have not yet been able to isolate or understand, we have been dragged back from the future to this point in time." Bella paused, realizing how that must have sounded to Mr. Dawson. "There are some things we do know, but there is much we do not. We are trying to establish precisely where we are in time – the year, in particular – so that we can begin trying to understand why this has happened.

"We know the events which have forced you into the ARCs. We respect your caution and distrust. But the simple fact is that your current predicament affects not only you but now it affects us, your descendants. The danger is no longer only in the present but also in the future.

"Sir, we are your living descendants. If we fail to do something to get the earth into better form in the very near future, the future may be choked off before it happens. In short, we may very well all starve to death.

"Sir, please. I understand how this must sound to you, but I assure you that we have the necessary tools to right things in this world. We do need your help though."

We could hear a snort over the radio.

"Sir, we are familiar with your communication systems. We know how you are linked to the other ARCs positioned around the world…"

"How could you possibly know such a thing?" Mr. Dawson demanded.

Bella paused. "Our history teaches us…"

"Your *history*? How dare you mock us with your foolishness?"

"But, sir, it is precisely that truth that has brought us here. We know the linkage that exists between your ARC and all the others. We are determined to be successful in our mission. Our own families depend upon it. But we cannot do it alone. We need your help and, more than that, your support in order to be successful. This effort must be a collaborative one involving all the other ARCs around the globe."

A long silence greeted Bella's heartfelt plea. Then, astonished though we were, we heard a snicker followed by growing laughter. "You say you come from the future?"

"Yes, sir. Three days ago, some phenomenon dragged Pulchra and its people back in time…"

The laughter died down. "I am sorry for whatever difficulty you and your friends have experienced. However, you are currently engaged in a very serious breach of our communications laws. This conversation is over. Do not attempt to contact us again."

"But…"

"Do not. We have your frequency now, and we will block any attempt you make to reach us."

The communication link ended. We stood, looking at one another in stunned silence. No matter what we had been expecting, no matter how dangerous, far-fetched, or troubling, I believed that to be, we were stunned by the response we got. That we were not even allowed to communicate with the ARC, not invited in, nor able to engage with those inside… we never expected that.

Bella spoke first, expressing a most obvious truth. "They didn't believe us." Tears started to stream down her cheeks. She took the failure as a personal one.

"Bella, don't…" I said. "They wouldn't have listened to anyone. They would not hear the truth."

"But it was *my* task to get them to believe us, and I failed…"

Just then, six figures stepped forward from the shadowy darkness. I noticed them first and gestured toward Cate. She immediately reached for a weapon. In no time, we were all facing the small group, who approached with hands up in a gesture indicating they were not seeking a fight.

"Cate," I said, indicating she should put down her weapon.

The six all wore hoodie sweatshirts. As soon as they were standing close enough for us to see them clearly in the dim light of the hallway, I focused on one of them, he was taller than the others. He reached up and swept the hoodie from his head.

He was ruggedly handsome, with sharp features and a day's growth of stubble on his strong chin. His lips were full, and his piercing blue eyes focused on mine. I felt a rush of heat surge through my body momentarily and could feel my cheeks as the heat settled on them.

Cate, not trusting the situation at all, once again raised her weapon. I reached out and grabbed her hand. "No," I said firmly. "Let them talk. I want to hear what they have to say... and why they've been following us."

Jace, appreciating my position was not throwing caution to the wind. He positioned himself alongside Cate in case anything went awry.

"We do," the handsome one said.

"We do what?" I demanded.

"We believe you," he said. Then he stepped closer. Both Jace and Cate tensed. But I felt no fear. I took a step toward him and extended my hand. "I'm Ari," I said.

He took my hand and held it for a brief second. "Tyrion," he said simply. Then he glanced up at the security cameras on the ARC. "Please step away from the security cameras," he said. "We cannot come any further into the light."

"Why should we trust you?" Cate demanded.

He shrugged. "Because we believe you," he said simply. "And we might be able to help." Then he smiled. "And, because you have no choice."

I smiled too. Even Cate couldn't argue with that. Still, I had not forgotten the Minister's words about engaging with anyone we met. However, we had found ourselves with few other options. We had arrived at the ARC, and had been thoroughly rebuffed. Either we engaged, or our mission would be an abject failure, something that I found intolerable.

"Come out of the light, everyone," I said, taking charge.

Bella and Leon quickly packed up their communications equipment and then joined the rest of us in the shadows just beyond the ARC's lights and monitors.

Once we had all gathered in the shadows, I faced Tyrion. "So, what year is this?"

"2040," he said simply, as if the information was insignificant – certainly nothing that seemed as guarded as suggested by our failed communication with the ARC.

"Fifteen years since the purge," I sighed, quickly doing the calculation.

"The purge?" Tyrion asked.

"Yes, the purge. That was the moment when, according to our reckoning, the Earth became completely uninhabitable." I gestured with my head toward the ARC. "That is when our ancestors locked themselves in the ARCs, abandoning the remaining population to certain death."

Tyrion eyed me curiously, not suspiciously, but curiously as one might view a peculiarity he'd come across in a gift shop. "Where do you come from?"

"A place called Pulchra. It is a small island continent off the coast..." I was hushed by Jace pulling on my wrist.

"Not too much information, Ari," he cautioned.

Although my heart told me that I could trust Tyrion, my head told me that Jace was right. I had to proceed cautiously.

Tyrion took in our interaction without any display of emotion or concern. "We saw you fly over our camp in your spacecraft," he said. "We…" he paused and gestured to the others near him, "…were sent to follow you." He glanced back toward the ARC. "We didn't know what they were up to this time."

I looked back at the ARC. "Them? You thought we had something to do with the inhabitants of the ARC? I don't understand, Tyrion. What do you mean, up to? What have the survivors in the ARC been up to?"

"I've said too much," Tyrion said simply, pulling the hood of his jumper back over his head so that his face was hidden. "We need to go."

Cate and Jace stiffened. Tim did too.

"It could be a trap," Jace said.

"It could be," I conceded. "But I don't think it is. Besides, as Tyrion said, we really don't have any choice. Our mission has changed."

There was some hesitation but no disagreement. It was clear that the ARC would not be the source of the information we needed. So, we had to change our strategy.

I caught a brief smile beneath Tyrion's hoodie. It was not a sly or mean smile. It was warm and caring.

We began to follow after them.

"Why do you wear those hoodies?" Tim asked. "Why do you hide your faces?"

"So we are not recognized by the cameras," a voice, not Tyrion's, replied.

Curiously, though we had no reason to be held in suspicion, each of us understood intuitively what he was saying. We had felt the vulnerability of being watched throughout the hall.

Tyrion and his group walked quickly and without rest. It was not easy for us to keep pace with them. Certainly, it was not easy for me. After my sleepless night, I was tired, and my muscles were sore and fatigued. I did not realize how much the disappointment at the ARC had sapped me of energy.

But my own feeling was irrelevant. We had no choice but to follow them and struggled to keep up. We covered a great deal of ground quicker than we had getting to the ARC. Tyrion and his friends knew every turn, every hallway, and every shortcut. We soon arrived at the underground railway station where we'd first entered the tunnel.

Tyrion and his friends paused at the sight of the corpses, almost as a gesture of respect.

"Tyrion…" I started.

He held his hand to his hoody to silence me. "A moment," he said.

Then, we moved on. Not a word was spoken about the corpses, the wall murals, anything that we passed. When we approached the airport, we came to a halt.

"What is going on?" Tim demanded.

In front of us, we could see that our Fú was heavily guarded.

"How are we supposed to trust you Tyrion?" Jace demanded. "You didn't tell us that you had claimed our Fú as your own!"

"We have not claimed it as our own. Yes, your spacecraft is being guarded but only until we were able to talk to you. We did not know your intent. We did not know whether you were friend or foe, whether you could help us, and us you.

"And, truth be known, we are not only guarding it from you."

"I don't see how there could be anything you could do to help us," Jace stated firmly, with the arrogance of a colonizer from the future.

"I think they could be helpful," I said. And it was true. I was not only hoping to defuse a potentially explosive situation. Tyrion and his friends were clearly survivors. Whether through natural immunity or some other means they had resisted whatever had taken so many others. If so, then they could be enormously helpful.

Not for the first time, it occurred to me that we would not be able to return to the future. If that proved to be the case, then it would be vital to understand how these people had managed to survive so many years after the purge.

CHAPTER FOURTEEN
THE NEGOTIATIONS

Tyrion led us to a fenced-off campus a short walk from the grounds of the airport.

As we left the airport, we all noticed a very large blue horse reared on its back legs as if in an aggressive stance. Its eyes glowed red in the growing darkness. I questioned Tyrion about the strange object. Tyrion hesitated at first and then said that the horse had commonly been known as Blucifer. It stood 32 feet tall and was noted to have killed the artist while being moved into place. Most people recognized it as the fourth horseman of the apocalypse, in other words '*death*', and said it was indicative of the demise of the earth. It was as if it was heralding in what would become of us.

He seemed saddened. After seeing the murals adorning the walls of the airport I couldn't help but secretly agree with Tyrion, a chill traveled down my spine. All in all, it seemed there was a message being delivered to humanity through art.

I couldn't speak for the others, but I was exhausted when we finally realized we could put down our packs. Still, I was tense with nervous energy. I could see the same in the eyes of the others.

As I looked around, I felt a certain easing of my tension. Unlike other areas around the city, the grounds of the campus were guarded by others, all wearing hoodies, although some had their hoodies drawn back. The grounds were in excellent condition, clean and pristine. I was fascinated by how beautiful the grounds were, in particular when compared to the dystopian landscapes we had seen earlier.

I would learn that Tyrion's group had taken over the Anschutz Inpatient Pavilion of the Colorado Hospital Group. Of course, none of this was familiar to me or anyone else in my group. I would also come to learn that Tyrion was not just any scout. He was the son of the person in charge of this entire facility.

As we would all come to understand – and appreciate – Tyrion's father was a hard-nosed ex-military man, someone who would have been comfortable running the Academy. He expected the complex to run with the efficiency of an army camp. He was at the entrance to the camp when Tyrion led us to the gate.

The older man stood at the gate, his stature firm, yet welcoming. As soon as Tyrion was within arm's length of the older man, he reached to grab his son and gave him a fist pump to the back in a gesture of welcoming him back home.

Tyrion's eyes were bright with pride as he turned and brought his father's attention to us.

"So this is them," he said, nodding in my direction.

"Yes, sir. This is all of them."

His father nodded. Then he reached out and put his arm around Tyrion's shoulders. Before turning and leading him towards the front room, he barked an order. "Take them to holding."

Jace stiffened. Cate reached for a weapon.

"I thought we were supposed to work in collaboration! We are not prisoners!" Jace yelled.

Tyrion turned back, causing his father to come to a halt. He said something to his father and then he walked back toward us. "You are not prisoners," he said, directing his words to me. "You will be okay and well cared for. No one will harm you in any way. Just please go with these soldiers.

"You'll be called for shortly." As he spoke, he searched my eyes, begging for trust and understanding. I had no problem letting him know that he could find it.

He smiled quickly and then turned to go back to his father. As they retreated from us, the guards came closer.

"Like we're supposed to trust someone we just met," Jace muttered in disgust. "They are holding our craft hostage, and now they are taking us prisoner. At gunpoint!" he added, making sure he yelled it loud enough for Tyrion to hear.

In truth, Jace was not the only one worried. Bella's brow was furrowed with concern. Cate was rigid and tense.

"Cate," I said under my breath, "stand down."

She looked at me as if I'd lost my mind.

"They have not taken our weapons or made any move to do so. Would they behave that way if they really meant us harm?"

Cate looked at the weapon in her hand. She glanced at the gun in Jace's holster. Her eyes met mine and she shrugged, acknowledging my point. It was now clear to everyone who had come from Pulchra, I was in charge. They were taking their cues from me, and I was willing to trust these people – at least for now.

We were led to a building that could only be a medical clinic. It was clean and well-maintained. There were examination bays that were populated by people in white, medical garb.

"Strange place to make camp," I noted to one of the guards, trying to make conversation while learning more about our situation.

"Not at all, ma'am," the guard said, showing me a good deal more respect and consideration than I'd expected. "It's actually a very practical place to set up camp."

I studied the guard closely. Like the others, he was a stern-faced man of indeterminate age, maybe in his forties, maybe his fifties. His face was lined with certainty – the face of a man who had seen a good deal of hardship but who had come out of it stronger and more determined. He wore military fatigues that hugged his body, showing his muscles.

He was, in every respect, a man with a warrior's bearing. And yet, when he spoke to me, he showed me a gentle tone and a respect I had never before associated with a man of battle. It was really quite fascinating. And telling.

As he led us into a room, I could sense that Jace felt foolish about his earlier outburst. It was clear that we were not to be made prisoners at all. Rather, we were treated like guests. The room we were brought to was light and airy. There were soft chairs and sofas arranged in a lazy, comfortable manner. Jace had pre-judged that the people from this era were more barbarian. In truth, that was not far from how we'd been taught in the Academy.

Still, I was disappointed that he had failed to intuit that there was a disconnect between the truth and what we'd been taught. As we would learn, that would prove to be the case more often than not.

"Please make yourselves comfortable," the guards instructed. "If there's anything you want, we'll try and get it for you."

Even as they were offering us these courtesies, three young girls came into the room carrying trays. On the tray were glasses and pitchers of clear, cold water along with fresh fruit, bread and cheese.

"This isn't prison," Tim laughed. "This is heaven!"

We all chuckled, even Jace. But, after eating some fruit, Jace motioned me to a corner of the room, away from everyone else. When we were alone, he scanned the area for any kind of listening device. Satisfied that we could speak, he leaned closer to me. "What are you going to tell them, Ari?"

I thought for a moment. "The truth Jace." "The truth."

He looked alarmed. "Be careful, Ari. You can't tell them everything. We don't know what they want. We don't know anything about them. This room is certainly nice enough but what if this is all a trick? We don't know their plans. What if they take us prisoner and force us to fly them to Pulchra?"

I looked at him as if he'd lost his mind. "Jace, listen to yourself. You are not thinking logically. How many could possibly fit on the Fú? Surely not enough to bring about a revolution." I leaned closer to him, feeling some sympathy for his concern, but no patience for his read of these people, a read that I felt was terribly off the mark. "Anyway, we haven't been asked anything yet so let's just see what happens.

"The truth is, we have so far gotten nowhere with our own kind. Maybe we need these people." Then I lowered my voice even more. "What if we never go back to the future, Jace? Have you considered that? What if we find ourselves unable to leave this time? I, for one, do not want to leave our situation up to fate, I would rather discover if we have allies. What about you?"

He shrugged, essentially conceding my point. "Okay, but remember, we were told not to interact with any survivors. The Minister will not be pleased with this, Ari," he noted, disapproval in his voice.

I couldn't counter that. There was no question that we were on unsettled ground in terms of our instructions. "Well," I noted, not for the first time, "the Minister is not here, so we have to make adjustments. We are not robots, you know. We have to use our judgment and our intelligence…"

Before we could continue our discussion, Tyrion came to the door of the room. "Ari, my father would like to talk to you now."

I looked up, but I didn't move.

"If it would be all right and you wouldn't mind coming with me."

Jace moved before I did, stepping in front of me. "She goes nowhere without me," he stated firmly.

Tyrion seemed to accept Jace's words at face value and without malice. "That's fine," he said. "I should have considered how you would feel about Ari's safety. Please feel free to come along," he said. Then he looked at the others. "Please make yourselves comfortable now. If there's anything you need, please don't hesitate to ask.

"Food will be brought out shortly."

Tim and Leon had amused facial expressions. This was quickly turning into a very positive situation. Not only could we finally rest, but we were also being well cared for.

I chuckled looking at them. It was good to see them so relieved. The pressure of our mission was hard to overstate, and it had been wearing on all of us. This was the closest we'd come to relaxing in what felt like a very long time.

Jace and I followed along with Tyrion. At first, we didn't speak as we made our way along the deserted but very clean and bright corridor.

"I would have thought everything would have been in much worse condition than it is, Tyrion," I said. "I'm surprised – pleasantly – to find this compound in such good order."

"We're very careful to maintain the compound," Tyrion said. "But the truth is, out there most things are in worse condition." He shrugged sadly. "We can't save everything after all.

"When the purge, as you call it, happened, my father had the wisdom to come to the hospital, not to seek medical care as he didn't feel that sick but to assist in the care of those who were ill and to help bury the dead to stop the spread of infection and disease. Having been a Major General in the Marine Corps, he was quite competent to take charge and to put in place a procedure that allowed for success – limited though it may have been.

"Many people headed to the hospital, as he expected. Sadly, most died before arriving here, and many more were so sick that nothing could be done to help them. However, a good number did survive.

"Of that number, there were many with diverse knowledge and skills. Fortunately, many had medical backgrounds. But even more than the doctors and nurses, we learned that no skill and no knowledge base was too modest to be of help. Maintenance. Mechanical. Agricultural. Sewing. Everything needed to be done and, fortunately, we were able to find someone who could do it.

"Our compound started out with a relatively small group, but it has been growing consistently over the years. We have continued to expand the land we control. In exchange for skills, we offer protection and safety.

"Even now, we will have random survivors arrive at the gate. Not as many anymore. But some.

"Perhaps most importantly, a number of men who my father had commanded and who survived heard about his command here and sought him out. They are really the ones we can thank for our survival. Warriors and fighters.

"No matter what our other skills or knowledge, they have taught everyone in the compound to fight and to survive. We have an active and powerful militia capable of fighting those within the ARC..."

"What? You fight those in the ARC? We would have thought that they would have been your natural allies..."

Tyrion laughed softly, but before he could say anything more, he announced that we had arrived at our destination. "Welcome," he said, guiding Jace and me into a large, columned room. As I walked along the long, central aisle, I had the image of a cathedral like I'd studied in the Academy when I studied about medieval Europe. On either side of us, there were long benches of shining, oiled wood. But rather than an altar before us, there was a large table surrounded by chairs, occupied by both men and women in earnest conversation. In the center chair sat Tyrion's father.

Seeing that we had arrived, Tyrion's father rose to his feet and walked closer to greet us. "I'm glad I can more personally welcome you, ma'am," he said in a firm yet kindly voice.

I smiled. I had never before been treated with such respect and kindness. These accomplished survivors were showing me the respect they would show a peer. I was humbled by their consideration.

He reached out to shake my hand. My own hand was nearly lost in the grip of his large hand. Still, like his voice, his grip was firm yet kind.

"My name is George," he said simply as if we were to be friends and we were meeting at a dinner party.

"Ari," I said easily.

He turned to Jace. "How are you, sir?"

Jace nodded. He was disarmed by the kind of welcome we'd been accorded. He clearly understood that his role was subservient to mine, but he was still being shown a great deal of respect.

"Please," George said, gesturing me to take a seat at the table in front of us.

After I had settled in the chair and George took his place at the head of the table again, the other voices died down. There was a gentle tension, a waiting of anticipation. It didn't last long.

"My son tells me that you claim to be from the future. I don't mind telling you that that strikes us as very unusual. That said, a lot that wouldn't have made sense once seems to be the case now, so, we are very interested to hear your version of events."

I could see that there was some skepticism in the expressions of those seated at the table. "Yes, we are from the future. The year 3014. Several days ago an anomaly occurred that for reasons we cannot understand yet, has thrown us, and our country of Pulchra, back in time. From what we now understand, to the year 2040.

"We had been sent on a mission to make contact with the ARC in Colorado and to enlist the assistance of those inside to bring the world back from the brink, so that we all might survive, now and in the future." I paused. "As you are aware, things did not work out as smoothly as we'd presumed."

"What made you think that those within the ARC could, or would, assist you to change the current state of the world?" George asked.

"Had they listened, we could have explained that we carry with us the technology to clean up the distress on the global system, but the process demands worldwide co-operation. It is no use trying to clean only one country at a time."

"And just how would you accomplish your aims?"

"The 'how' is far too technical to address in one sitting. I hope it will suffice to say that in the centuries going into the future there were a number of advances in science and technology that would allow us to reverse the carbon and methane issues that decimated the population during the purge. If that is what purged the population. But again, we need the collaboration of those in the ARC if we are to be successful."

George listened with a serious, intent expression. When I had finished, he cleared his throat. "You are aware that what you propose will never happen," he said.

I was stunned by the certainty in his voice. "Surely they would see common sense," I said.

"Wouldn't they help if they realized that it was possible?" Jace added.

George smiled, but his smile showed no joy, only a bemused sadness. "Jace, I understand that you have a great deal more knowledge than we have, coming from the future. But there is one area in which I am much more knowledgeable than you. I know who we are talking about. You don't.

"I am not sure what you have been told or taught where you come from, but those within the ARC have no interest in helping anyone but themselves."

"That can't be so…"

George cut him off. "Shortly before my retirement, I was transferred here to Colorado to assist with the final preparations for the closure of the ARC. I was promised a spot for myself and my family in return for my discretion in the task.

"Well, I was discreet, as I was asked to be. I kept their secrets, but on the day when the call went out to close the ARC, I was left behind, as was my wife and child, Tyrion, who was born a few years before all of this happened.

"My wife passed away as did billions of others across the globe when the pathogen and Sarin gas was released." He looked at me as if to emphasize what he'd said. "Pathogen, *not* carbon. Not methane. A pathogen. So not just one thing, but both together exterminated the population. Where there were larger populations of people Sarin was used, such as airports, train stations, buildings etc., then the pathogen was released into the general populace to ensure that there were '*no*' survivors. It didn't take very long at all, weeks at best before the earth itself went quiet."

"It happened that I had a natural immunity to the pathogen which thankfully had been passed on to my son. But those bastards looked on as billions died. They lied to those of us who they had promised to help. No, you will get no help from them."

"Quite the opposite. Even now they want us dead. The leaders in the ARC send kill squads nightly. To be frank, I am surprised that you were able to traverse those tunnels and still be alive when you reached the door of the ARC..."

Jace and I listened in stunned silence to what George was saying. It just didn't seem possible. And yet, in my heart, I did not doubt his words for a moment.

"They had their reasons, of course. They had their goal, and they would not be deterred. They wanted a One World Government. One Government to rule the world, One Government to dictate everything, a ruling class of the elite. When you have nothing more that you need, power is the only thing you can take."

"They were willing to establish their government for all the people... only they learned that the people were not interested. They faced so much opposition that they ended up imprisoning detractors in camps. But even as they built more and more camps, they could not keep up with the resistance."

"They tried to sterilize the population, thinking that that would end the resistance but that too was unsuccessful. Then they introduced a deadly virus, to the children first. And even then, they weren't satisfied."

"That was when they decided that they would have to destroy the environment itself if they were to get their way. That wasn't quick enough though, so then came the Sarin and the pathogen."

"They left us all to die," George's head dropped as if recalling the very moment that he realized what had been done. "I have nothing but pain in my heart for my part in what took place and the many lives that were lost."

I felt a tightness in my chest and could not for the moment catch my breath. "We have a One World Government, the OWG," I said, my voice barely above a whisper. "They are everything you describe. They dictate everything that we do. Who we can marry, where we will live, how many children that we can have."

"But certainly there is wisdom in their rule. We live in a peaceful world that does not have the conflicts that your world had. We will never be over-populated and starved of resources. We work for the good of all humanity."

George chuckled. "Is that what you think, Ari?"

"But it works George! It does. We live in harmony. The world lives in harmony," I insisted.

"So tell me, what is the version of events you have been told about this point in history, Ari? Jace?"

The others sit quietly, expectantly.

Jace looked at me, then at those around the table. It took him a moment, but then he found his voice. "We were taught that the world had become overpopulated, resources were dwindling, and people were starving. Climate change had taken its toll on the ability to grow food and provide for the masses, so the governments of the world built ARCs to save humanity. The ARCs were locked down for 500 years. Nobody could leave until the doors opened."

"Were you also told that they caused the climate to change? Were you ever told why they did that?"

Jace shook his head.

"No. I didn't think so. Your view of the past is flawed." George rose to his feet and began to pace. It was clear that he felt very taken by the conversation.

"I'm sorry," he said. "Our conversation is very upsetting. What they did to us… what they did to the billions of innocents who depended on them. And why? To squander the world's riches among a few wealthy families.

"Ari, Jace, they left us all for dead." He laughed out loud with anger and pride. "Well, the joke was on them. We didn't die. We are here, and we are still fighting. We will survive. They are not going to kill us off, not if I have any say in the matter!" He slammed his large fist down on the table. "I can picture them even now, sitting in the ARC counting out their money."

He leaned toward me. "They came after us. Even safe in the ARC they couldn't stand that we still lived. They sprayed us with chemicals day in, day out. They changed weather patterns.

They allowed mining companies to dig up carbon that had been buried safely in the ground for centuries. The more carbon they pumped into the air, the hotter it got."

"Industry was allowed to remain operating unfettered. They were warned by the experts that their actions and decisions were unsustainable. But they ignored them. They had their plan, and they were going to realize it no matter what."

"They confused a very gullible public into believing that climate change was a load of hogwash, made up by conspiracy theorists to bring down governments. To damage the economy!"

"Their strategy had a certain genius, I'll grant them that. Increasing global temperatures melted the ice caps in Antarctica, releasing previously untappable oil, gas and mineral resources."

"They gained access to untapped reserves of oil, buried beneath the Russian permafrost."

"Of course, with the melting of the permafrost came a new crisis, the release of vast amounts of methane gas that had previously been trapped below the surface. We are talking billions of tonnes of methane. They were not interested in survivors.

"And so here we are now. They are not interested in having anyone who remembers what they have done."

I listened to everything George said. But for the life of me, I could not follow one aspect of his narrative. "George, can I ask you something?"

"Of course."

"What is money?"

Despite the seriousness of our conversation, the whole room burst into laughter. George had an astonished expression on his face. "You don't know what money is? My God, they did all this for what then?"

"May God strike them down dead."

I tilted my head to the side and engaged the courage to ask, "God? What is God?"

George, who had let his gaze turn to the courtyard visible through the large windows behind the desk, turned suddenly and stared at me. "You're serious? You can't be…" But he could see by my expression that I was. "You really are asking me what God is…"

"I am."

George lowered his head. A tear streamed down his leathery cheek. "Then they've won. They succeeded." He shook his head but did not bother to wipe away his tear. "Those bastards inside the ARC are guided by a Luciferian Ideology. They intend to turn the world into their concept of a Luciferian authoritarian communist state. They want to offer our earth up to the very Devil himself as their gift to him. They have demonstrated that they will eradicate all those who oppose them."

"Based on your question, Ari, it seems their most wicked goals have been realized."

I felt frustrated by my ignorance and how emotional George had become. "I truly hate to be tedious but what is this Devil?"

George stared at me with confused astonishment. "Ari, there is so much more I need tell you, but now I need to find out a bit about you." With that, he returned to his seat.

I remained quiet, trying to make sense of everything I'd just heard. Could it all really be true? For now, I knew that something about George rang true in my heart.

Even so, sitting here, I could hear the Minister's voice in my head, and I wondered if I hadn't overstepped – by a lot. I looked at Jace. The expression on his face told me he was thinking much as I was.

"Well?" George asked, neither pleased nor displeased by Ari's hesitance. Perhaps he understood the reason for it, perhaps he did not. That did not seem to matter much to him. What did seem to matter was that they move forward, if only in fits and starts.

As much as this conversation was a leap of faith for Ari, it was at least that for George. As vulnerable as Ari felt, the risk to George and the others was greater. For it was obvious that they had risked a great deal, and continued to risk a great deal, just to survive. Now, they were showing a willingness to share information with Ari and the others.

But for that, they needed a sign, a show, something to demonstrate to them that their willingness to trust was not ill-placed.

Ari thought hard about how best to go forward. She knew that she should have been thinking rationally, going through a logical strategy for the discussion. At the Academy, the various games they'd played – chess, in any number of dimensions, as well as that a game called 'Dingo' – had trained them in the rhetorical skills necessary for negotiations.

However, Ari didn't feel like this was a negotiation. This was something powerfully different. This was not transactional. She found herself not so much thinking with her head as responding with her heart.

CHAPTER FIFTEEN
TALKING WITH HER HEART

Ari drew a long breath and tried to still the butterflies in her stomach. "Butterflies in her stomach" – what an odd expression! She tried to think the first time she'd heard it. She must have been a young girl. She could remember that it was when she was young enough to ask her father, "How do the butterflies get *into* your stomach?"

He had laughed, that strong, glorious laugh that made her feel that all was right in the world. Then he had hugged her tight. "My little warrior, they are not real butterflies. It is an expression to describe the flittering feeling one gets in her stomach when she is nervous, or excited, or filled with anticipation."

Ari had scrunched her face. "That seems silly. And why wouldn't someone know if one feels nervous or excited? They are not the same thing then, are they Father?"

"No, indeed they are not. And it is important to be able to tell the difference between the two."

"But then, what do the butterflies have to do with anything? And what kinds of butterflies?"

He hugged her even tighter then. "You will see, my precious warrior. One day, you will know, and when that day comes, I hope you will be able to tell me exactly what kinds of butterflies."

"Okay," she said.

"Promise?"

"I promise."

He smiled, and then he rubbed his nose against hers like he had often done then – a warm, special demonstration of his love and affection for her.

She had thought about the butterflies through the years since. Often at odd moments and always when she saw butterflies flitting in the wind, or in a bush. But she had never really put together the old saying and the actual *feeling* before. Not during the Academy or any other time. She had simply never felt that wonderful, confusing, unsettling and glorious combination of nervousness, excitement, and anticipation before.

Until now.

She felt a momentary loss. An unsettling confusion. Her stomach seemed to be doing backflips.

"So *that's* it," she whispered aloud.

"I'm sorry," George said, leaning forward to catch her words. "What is it?"

She laughed softly, the first genuine laugh she'd laughed in… she could hardly remember how long it had been. Be she felt a lightness and delightful joy at realizing that her father was spot on with his description of the butterflies. She shook her head. How she wished to be able to tell him right then about her experience of the butterflies.

It was all unsettling but curiously exhilarating. Ari felt nervous but somehow more fully alive than she had in a very long while.

"I was just thinking of something my Father had told me many years ago," she said.

George smiled. "Well, judging by the curious light in your eyes, it must have been a very good thing."

"I think it was," she conceded. "I think it really was." Then she looked directly into his eyes. She could see a deep desire to understand in his eyes. She could see that he was convinced that he knew that she had something incredibly valuable to give to him if he could only make her comfortable enough to do so.

"What would you like to know George," Ari said, holding her emotions at bay and putting the onus on him to guide her.

"What do *I* want?" he asked. He smiled a quick, guarded smile. "I want to live free. I want to live in safety and dignity. I want the people I am responsible for to be safe." He narrowed his eyes at her, not in an accusing manner but in a pleading, beseeching way.

"I think… I *believe* you can help me do that. You know things, Ari. I can see that you do. You know things that could save us all…"

"No," she said quickly, rebelling against that awesome responsibility. "I cannot save everyone. That is not for me…"

He waved away her protest. "You have the knowledge. I know you do. I can sense it. Talk to me."

She felt such a strong desire to tell George everything she could but, despite what her heart was telling her, her head urged caution. Her years in the Academy had done more than teach her content; they had instilled in her an ethos and a way of thinking that, at this moment, urged caution.

Her instructions too had been explicit.

But her heart… she was certain that George could be trusted. She felt in her deepest self that she had to give him something, *anything* that would help him to understand. But what could she give him really?

The risk was profound. This was not merely a situation where she was helping someone she trusted. She understood deeply that if she said too much, or if she said the wrong thing or even the *right* thing, she could very well change the future! By doing something she thought might be "right", she could ensure that she would cease to exist when her moment in time actually arrived.

The burden of her decision weighed heavily on her.

"I know this is not easy for you," George said. "I can see it in your eyes and in your body language. But this is not easy for me, or for us, either. This is a dangerous and frightening time.

"You have answers. I believe you do. Can't you lend a hand to help us?"

It was a direct, honest and heartfelt plea and it resounded in her heart. This then, was what she weighed; her heart said to help. Her head said to move forward with caution. Still, her intellect saw merit in either position.

Everything she had ever learned about ethics and morality suggested she help George. Her political science classes leaned toward caution. And yet, she could not help but wonder if they even had a future to return to. After all, they had already remained in the past longer than they'd anticipated. They'd been here, in 2040 for days now. What had transpired in the time span between now and the future?

She shuddered. Indeed, did she even exist any longer in the future? Did her family? Was anything still the way it had been a mere few days earlier?

She bowed her head. So much was in the balance. So much was riding on this budding alliance between them and George and his Organization. She drew a deep, shuddering breath. When she lifted her head and looked at George, she saw him looking at her with earnest and questioning eyes.

She nodded.

"Let me begin slowly then," she said finally. "Where shall I begin?" She drew another breath as she pondered how to proceed.

George reached out and took her hand. It was a simple, kind gesture but it meant the world to Ari. She knew how desperately George wanted information, but he seemed to be as concerned for her and her well-being. He didn't want to rush her. Didn't want to force her to do anything she didn't feel comfortable doing.

He wanted her help, but he wanted her to give it freely.

"Maybe if I tell you what we are ruled by and then… well then maybe we can go forward there."

George squeezed her hand gently and then released it. "That would be a great place to start," he agreed.

"Okay then," she said, realizing that she had decided to go forward. "So, not long after the opening of the ARC in the year 2525, communities headed out in organized groups to various parts of the USA with the simple goal of rebuilding. They were like the early pioneers. They were guided by only a very small number of rules. The first was that the population had to be maintained under 500,000,000 people if humanity was to maintain a healthy balance with nature. This number was divided between the eight ARCs.

"History and experience had made clear the danger of losing that balance.

"Consequently, those in charge were to guide reproduction wisely…" She paused and lowered her eyes. Suddenly, discussing reproduction felt very intimate. She felt her cheeks burn. She controlled her breathing and continued. "Because the total number of people was so closely regulated, it was important that those who were alive were the best and brightest possible. Fitness, intelligence and diversity were the watchwords. Studies had made clear that if those three factors were respected and adhered to, the population would thrive in quality. Genetic engineering plays a large part in sustaining a healthy, smart and thriving population.

"Of course, just having a lot of healthy and smart people wouldn't be enough to maintain a viable planet. Communication was vital. Experience had taught that a failure to effectively communicate often resulted in disaster. So each community was charged with uniting humanity by engaging in formulating a new, living language that would enable everyone to communicate directly and without confusion.

"All things essential to human experience – passion and traditions – would continue but they would be tempered by reason. So much of human history had been marked by tragedy simply because reason was ignored. If humanity were to continue to survive, even more, to thrive, then reason would have to dominate.

"From reason, laws would be formulated that would protect individuals and nations fairly and truly. Because diversity respects differences, the rule was that each nation should have control over their internal matters. However, when it came to resolving any international conflict, there would be a world court whose decisions would be honored.

"Of course, the advice was for each nation to avoid petty laws and useless officials. Nothing dampens the light of human experience so much as a bureaucratic weight over each and every aspect of living. The goal was to find the balance between personal rights and social duties and communal obligations. We sought to value truth – beauty – love – all the while seeking harmony with the infinite.

"Be not a cancer on the earth – leave room for nature – leave room for nature. These are the precepts that had been handed down through the generations, from elder to elder."

George listened attentively to everything that Ari said. Some of what she said made perfect sense to him; other things seemed to be little more than words when weighed against the truth of human experience.

Still, he wanted to listen to everything she had to say before reacting.

Ari studied George's eyes and expression, trying to assess how her words were being understood by him. In the past, she had been able to recite these "laws" easily, with absolute faith in their rightness. However, now she spoke them at the same time she was trying to "hear" them through George's ear. How did they sound to him? Were they sound? Were they just words spoken or did they carry the weight of truth?

For the first time in her young life, she was not sure. She had always accepted the wisdom of the laws and customs taught to her but considering them through another's perspective made her wonder if she had missed something.

Or, perhaps more importantly, if those very sound and important rules had been used to cow a population rather than lift it up.

"What are you thinking?" she asked, giving voice to her genuine curiosity but also to her uncertainty.

George understood her sense of vulnerability even as he knew that it was really he and his organization that was vulnerable. Even so, both because he had a larger heart than just about anyone else Ari had ever come across and because he needed her to continue to share information with him, he sought to reassure her. "I think those are incredible guidelines. I don't know that they were adhered to as well as they should have been – and even if they were adhered to by the letter, I think that they might not have been adhered to in spirit.

"That said, clearly the leadership in the ARC was being forward thinking."

"Oh yes, they were," Ari agreed. "They tried to make sure everything worked out successfully. Establishing the world language had actually been completed during the time in the ARC worldwide.

"A census had been taken and specific rules determining who could have children, and how, were codified…"

"How?" George asked, raising his eyebrow in a teasing fashion.

Ari's cheeks reddened again. "Well… uh… um… *you know* what they meant," she said, in an exasperated voice.

He chuckled. "I supposed I do," he conceded. "Please go on."

"For example, if Jace and I were to marry, the Ministry would advise us exactly how many children that we would be allowed to have. No mistakes are tolerated, and additional children are not allowed, so each mother is sterilized after the birth of the allowable number of babies."

For the first time, Ari glanced over at Jace and noticed that he too had a look of embarrassment on his face.

"I don't see how that makes sense," George said, ignoring the glance between Ari and Jace. "In fact, it seems shortsighted to have such a drastic action in place."

"What do you mean?"

"Well, for example, what would happen if a baby became ill and died? Or a young child was in an accident? Those parents would no longer be able to have their 'quota' of children, would they?"

For the first time, Ari felt almost smug in her answer. "Well, such an eventuality would be highly unlikely. Certainly in the case of illness. Not only are the parents screened to exacting standards, but each child is genetically perfect when it is placed into the mother's womb..."

"Ah… I guess that explains the 'how'," George said with a smirk.

Ari paused and then let out a soft snort. "Yes, well, I guess it does then. In any case, the fetus is perfect. The womb is sound. The mother is healthy and extremely fit. And the medical care is exceptional.

"The chances of an adverse outcome are practically nil."

George shrugged. It was a point well taken.

"As for injury or some exposure to disease, for example, anything beyond that can almost certainly be taken care of with the help of our PADS."

George straightened slightly. Ari had referenced something that was new to him. He wanted to know more, but he didn't want to betray his desire. "PADS?"

Ari paused. She realized that she had already said a bit more than even she had intended. She also realized that there was no going back now. She glanced over at Jace again, but his expression was impossible to read. She nodded to herself and decided to go on. "P-A-D, or PAD, stands for a Personal Assistance Device. It is a device that allows us to be monitored around the clock, twenty-four hours a day, seven days a week, three hundred and sixty five days a year for all the years of our lives."

George shuddered. Whereas Ari only thought of the benefit of the PADS, he immediately recognized the potential dangers as well.

Ari, however, did not note his reaction and continued. "At birth, each child has a small microchip embedded in them.

This chip holds all of their information – personal, financial, educational, health, *everything* functions from your PAD." She smiled to herself, remembering the cat. "Even personal entertainment." She felt pleased with herself as she concluded her explanation, absolutely convinced that hearing about the PADS would only elicit the greatest respect.

She was wrong of course.

George listened and then looked to the others. Person to person, they shared a worried expression. Ari followed his gaze and, seeing their expression, looked back to George for some kind of explanation.

He frowned, cleared his throat and then explained the reaction to her. "RFID Chip," he stated simply, calling the PAD by a different name. "It exists for a number of reasons, but the primary one is that when and if someone gets out of line, it can simply be powered down, shut off." He lifted his fingers into the air and made a sweet, silent motion. "Poof. You are no more. You cease to exist. You see, your miraculous chip does a great deal more than store information or provide content so that any so-called errors in your being can be fixed. Its design and existence is for one reason and for that one reason alone – to be able to erase your existence if the powers that be deem it necessary to do so."

As bridled against his words, she felt an anger rise up in her. "No!" she cried out passionately. "You don't understand."

George sighed. "Oh, I'm afraid I do. My friend, it is you who does not understand," he said.

"But, but… the PAD is good. It is necessary." She shook her head. She looked to Jace for support. She felt lost and suddenly sad. It was as if she was falling through the air and she knew that there was nothing there to catch her. "Don't you *see*? They would never do such a thing. How would one function without a PAD?"

She felt lost and confused. The PAD was so essential to her understanding of existence that having it questioned or challenged was as if her very existence was being challenged as well.

"You are exactly right," George said. "I could not have made the point any better." He eyed her closely. "So you know of no one who has ever had their chip turned off?"

"No, of course not," Jace chimed in. "That would be horrible. What exactly do you think of us? Do you think we are barbarians?"

George considered Jace for a moment, deciding how to respond. "It was only a question," he noted. "Only a question."

Ari, who felt that the conversation was reeling away from her, stepped in to regain control. She felt it was necessary to reestablish that what they had done was good. "To continue then," she said, cutting off any thought either Jace or George had of continuing their stand-off, "We are very mindful of the need to keep nature in balance. Jace and I both work in an area that takes care of that."

"And everyone is taught as they grow how to be mindful of what is around them, all living creatures and plants. There were many new types of creatures, some friendly, some not so friendly when our descendants exited the ARCs."

Just at that moment, Ari caught sight of movement from the corner of her eye. She glanced over to see a small, ginger colored cat pad into the room. Her eyes widened, recognizing the creature. True, this particular cat had clearly seen better days. It was not soft and "kitten-y" at all. It was scrawny and had a hungry look to it. What's more, its fur was patchy, and one eye was missing, closed over by the eyelid.

The cat turned and looked at Ari, focusing its one good eye on her.

"A cat," she said unconsciously. "It's really a cat," she went on, looking at George with astonishment.

"Well yes, it's a cat," Tyrion acknowledged, not finding the appearance of the cat nearly as remarkable as Ari clearly did.

"Can I... may I pick it up?"

Tyrion shrugged.

"Of course you can," Tyrion said. Then he turned and faced the cat. "Tipcat. Here, Tipcat..." The cat darted toward him, and Tyrion bent down and took up the scrawny ball of fluff in his muscular arms.

"Tipcat? That sounds a funny name. What made you call it Tipcat?" Ari asked as George lifted the cat towards her.

He chuckled. "Not for any interesting reason. Someone found it at the local tip when they were scrounging and thought that she might lighten the heavy atmosphere that we had around here. And she's certainly done that. The children love her."

"Tipcat owns the premises I'd say. The locals all chip in and feed her." He looked at Ari closely as she reached out and snatched the cat. "Why are you so excited to see a cat?" he asked.

Even before she could answer, the feel of the cat in her arms transported Ari back to her POD and her wonderful memories of holding the cat she had conjured up all those years earlier. "Oh my," she sighed, bringing the cat against her cheek. "Tipcat, you feel so ever much better than the one from my POD."

Tyrion leaned his head to the side, "POD?"

"It's a leisure device, Tyrion," Jace stated. "It allows one to experience all manner of sensory perception without ever leaving the comfort of a safe space."

George raised his eyebrows in astonishment. "Really? Don't know if that sounds good or not but I'd be willing to give it a go one day then," he said.

Ari smiled as she stroked the cat's fur.

"Hmmph," Jace snorted under his breath. In truth, he did not like the way this whole conversation and meeting was going. He was feeling more than a bit miffed by the attention Tyrion was showering on Ari. Even more, he found himself feeling jealous of Ari's reaction to the attention.

His thoughts and feelings, however, were interrupted by a sudden scream from Ari.

"Ouch!" she cried out, throwing the cat to the ground.

"What's wrong?" Tyrion asked worriedly as he darted quickly to her side.

"It attacked me," Ari cried out, pointing to Tipcat.

Meanwhile, Tipcat had rolled along the ground and come to a gentle stop and sat looking perfectly angelic. Or at least as angelic as a one-eyed scruff of a cat could look.

Tyrion laughed when he realized what had happened. "No Ari, Tipcat didn't attack you. He was only puddling. Didn't you have that in your POD?"

"No, what is puddling?" Ari asked, suddenly feeling very sheepish. "I feel like there is so much I do not know. I don't like this feeling. Where we come from, we know everything. Here everything seems new."

The realization of how limited her experience and knowledge was, both disheartened and excited her. Here, she realized, there was so much to know and do.

"So Tipcat does not mean to harm me?"

"Not at all."

She put her hand down and gently picked up Tipcat again. She took her seat and allowed Tipcat to resume her puddling, wincing every once in a while through the pain caused by Tipcat's skillful claws.

George observed all this and waited until she seemed comfortable again. "So, tell me more," George urged her.

"Of course," Ari said, ready to begin again even as she was distracted by Tipcat's purring. "What would you like to know?"

George was quiet for a moment. "Where is Pulchra and how big is it?

Ari drew a quick breath. Still cautious, she knew she had to give George an answer but still was unsure if he and these people were friends or foe. She wanted to be forthcoming but not too forthcoming.

She wanted to trust them, but even if she did, she didn't feel she had the authority to decide how much to tell them. Before she could answer, they were interrupted by a knock on the door. A young man in camouflage clothing stood silently waiting.

George nodded to him.

"Sir, it is time for colors," he stated.

"Carry on then," George said.

"If you would just mind waiting for a few minutes and then I think we will withdraw for tonight and you can head off for something to eat and Tyrion can get you squared away. We must prepare for tonight's onslaught."

Ari was just about to ask what he meant when the sound of a single pipe sounded throughout the complex. Everyone in the room stood at attention, except of course for Jace and Ari who remained in their seats. A short time later, another pipe sounded, and everyone went back to what they were doing.

"Come with me please," George said, beckoning Ari and Jace.

"Can I bring Tipcat with me?" Ari questions.

"Of course," Tyrion smiles shyly in Ari's direction.

Ari didn't question the ritual that had just occurred. It seemed to her to be innocuous, a cultural thing. However, she had taken note of George's mention of an onslaught that night and was curious as to what that meant.

"Tyrion, what did your father mean when he said that you needed to prepare for tonight's onslaught?"

His expression darkened. "I believe I told you earlier that every night we face the ARC's kill squads. To date, they have failed to penetrate our defenses, but we fear it is only a matter of time. My father is aware of the arsenal of weapons that lie below the surface, and if they chose to use them, we would not last very long.

"Many who were unprotected by these walls have perished already. That is the reason for the steady stream of refugees we see, seeking assistance to survive.

"Here we are," George directed Jace and Ari towards a scarcely furnished ward that had private rooms.

They were comfortable enough, more comfortable than when they had slept in the tunnels anyway. The rest of the group had already showered and were well rested when they met up again. They were greeted warmly as they walked in.

"I'll be back in a short while to take you to eat," Tyrion said before turning and walking away.

Meanwhile, George was in his office documenting the discussion that had taken place that day, noting anything that could be of use to them in the future. Not that Ari had really given them anything to digest yet. One thing had impressed George; the collection of laws that Ari had shared with them all. She had stated that these were the laws of her land, the laws that governed her and others like her. Something about what she had shared bothered him. The message of the laws was one thing, but it was the words themselves… Suddenly, he thought of something. He got up from his chair and headed to his small library. He found a book titled, 'Common Sense Renewed' by Robert Christian.

He remembered that the author described a 'New Rational World Order,' where an extreme form of eugenics would be enforced. The rational sounded reasonable, something about trying to improve the gene pool of the human race but it had always struck him as cruel. However, it certainly corresponded with what Ari had said.

This book had been written to discuss the ideologies of the author and as a tome to accompany and clarify the Georgia Guidestones. Which were chiseled and placed on a hilltop in Elbert County, Georgia. Masonia and Rosicrucian are the Governing Stones' likely constructors. Although it stated that the sponsors were 'A small group of Americans who sought the Age of Reason.'

The stones read as follow:

1. Maintain humanity under 500,000,000 in perpetual balance with nature.
2. Guide reproduction wisely — improving fitness and diversity.
3. Unite humanity with a living new language.
4. Rule passion — faith — tradition — and all things with tempered reason.
5. Protect people and nations with fair laws and just courts.
6. Let all nations rule internally resolving external disputes in a world court.
7. Avoid petty laws and useless officials.
8. Balance personal rights with social duties.
9. Prize truth — beauty — love — seeking harmony with the infinite.
10. Be not a cancer on the earth — Leave room for nature — Leave room for nature.

George closed the book on his desk and looked forward to their meeting in the morning, armed with this new information.

CHAPTER SIXTEEN
IMPORTANT EVENTS

What were you thinking?" Jace challenged Ari when they were safely in the room.

"What do you mean?"

"You said too much. You should have been more careful. Did you see their reaction to learning about the ARCs?"

Ari shrugged. "They are realities of our world. Whatever I said could not have helped them much." She looked closely at Jace. "I don't think they're the enemy. I think we can trust them."

He frowned. "I'm not so sure." When he said that, he was not thinking of George. He was thinking of Tyrion."

"You're tired. I'm tired. I think we should get some sleep and deal with everything in the morning."

Although both Ari and Jace were certain that their thoughts and feelings about the day would keep them awake, they fell fast asleep and woke up only when bright light streamed in through windows high on the walls.

The next three days followed what became a familiar and disturbing pattern. In the morning and throughout the early part of the day, George would call them to his office. There, he would question them about aspects of the future, often – as he did the first morning – showing them texts and writings from his library that seemed at first glance to form the foundation of much of what they had been taught.

"You understand," he emphasized, "that these teachings and doctrines were all articulated to cow people, don't you?"

Ari was astonished that first morning when George showed them the Georgia Guidestones. She could not fathom why their true origin had not been taught to them.

"Because," George pointed out, "your leaders are using them not to raise up the world but to subjugate it."

Jace reacted angrily to the statement. "That's not true!"

"Prove it not to be," George said simply.

Jace fell into a sullen silence, for he could not. For her part, Ari was troubled by the revelations that George continued to make. They were inspiring, confusing, unnerving and unsettling. They seemed to call into question everything she had assumed about her life.

The mornings left her troubled. The afternoons, however, were more enjoyable as they were spent in Tyrion's company.

Walking, riding, being introduced to new flowers and plant life. She felt herself warming to him.

"They are brainwashing us," Jace whispered urgently to her.

And Ari might have been sympathetic to that warning if not for what happened each and every evening. Like clockwork, the compound was attacked by kills squads sent from the ARC.

The repetition of these patterns caused George to become more and more insistent on information. Finally, on the third day, he slammed his hand down on his desk. "You *must* help us! We cannot withstand the attacks much longer. You *must*!"

He had reached his breaking point at exactly the same moment that Ari had reached hers. Although Jace bristled at George's impatience, the look in Ari's eyes told George that she was willing to help them.

He sent Jace from his office, leaving Ari alone with him.

"Ari!" Jace cried out. "Beware!"

When the door closed, George shook his head. "I'm afraid your friend is more dramatic than necessary," he said, his tone a mixture of anger and resignation. He was too concerned with his people to be overly concerned with people he thought made their existence more tenuous.

"He means well," she said, a bit too earnestly. "He's a good person. None of us knows what to make of the things we are learning here."

"You either?"

She shrugged. "I trust more than the others. I don't know if that's good or not," she conceded.

His posture and his voice changed. "Ari, no one here wants to hurt you. But we are desperate. The killers come each night. I fear we will not be able to hold them off very much longer. They have the armaments to destroy us." He sighed. "Sometimes I think they are only toying with us. Although I do not understand why."

"I'm sure that if the Minister could only speak with you things would be different..." she said.

George eyed her closely. "Do you think so? Honestly?"

"I... I can't be sure of course. But I can't see how they wouldn't be. The things you've shown us... the things we've learned. I'm sure that the problem is a communication problem."

"Ari, you are kind and innocent. For all your education, you are somewhat naïve. But you have a good heart. I will trust that for the moment."

Ari didn't know whether to be flattered or not by George's words. She did feel comforted. There was something in his words and tone that reminded her of her father. She couldn't imagine that this man would harm her. He had been teaching her to see more clearly. Yes, some of what he'd shown her called many lessons she'd learned into question; called much of what she'd presumed into question. But she could not help but sense the truth behind everything he had said to her. She had experienced the nightly raids. She knew the pressure he was under. And yet he showed her patience and consideration.

He took the time to teach her.

The things she'd experienced in the past three days had affected her profoundly. "Yes," she said out loud. "The Minister will be convinced. He *must* be convinced."

George chuckled softly. "That's a very strong statement, Ari. You do not understand power. You understand a great deal, more than any other person I've ever met. But power, bald, unadulterated power, is beyond you.

"I do not think your Minister will be as amenable to our plight as you think he might be…"

"He *must* be," she said again. "I will prove to you that he will listen and learn. I will take you to Pulchra."

George raised his eyebrow. "You will?"

She nodded her head.

"I have to tell you, Ari. From everything you've said to me, everything you've shared with me, I think there is something amiss with your Minister. I think he has been tainted by too much power."

"No, there are protections…"

George shook his head. "Protections are meaningless once one has grabbed the reins of power. When that happens, it is only the soul of the one in power that limits what is done. It takes a very special person to wield real power honestly and for the good of others…"

"You'll see," Ari said.

She was determined to bring George and a small party to Pulchra, to parlay with the Ministry and the Minister so that the Independent groups could find some peace and protection.

Ari told Jace her intention.

He shook his head. "I don't think that is wise."

She thought for a moment. She considered everything she knew about Jace – and her long relationship with him. She thought of all the times they'd been paired together. She thought of her own dreams – and assumptions – of how her life would unfold, and Jace's place in that unfolding. She wanted nothing more than for the two of them to be of one mind about this.

But she could not agree with him. Her heart would not let her. She hoped that when they moved forward, Jace would come to agree with her.

"I am decided," she said firmly.

Jace thought to argue, but he could see that arguing would be futile. "Then we will do as you say," he agreed. "We will take precautions, but we will do as you say." He sighed deeply. "I hope you are right, Ari. I hope you are not being blinded by some spell this man and Tyrion have put on your heart."

"I am not blinded," she countered. "In fact, I believe it is only now, for the first time, that I truly can see."

So it was, they made their plans. Ari looked forward to the journey with both excitement and trepidation. George, using some of the tools Ari brought, was able to discern and see through the cloaking technology which kept the ARC safe from attack and where the soldiers come from to attack.

On the night they were to go to Pulchra, a small unit of fighters from the compound surrounded George, Tyrion and the three others who would make the journey. The air was electric with anticipation. Ari and Jace led the way to the Fùyùn.

When they came close enough, they deployed the technology that allowed them to see through the cloaking mechanism.

"Run," Ari yelled, indicating that they needed to board the Fùyùn quickly.

However, the group had been spotted, and a number of soldiers emerged from the ARC and began rapidly firing at the group.

Ari and Jace stood up straight, with their arms in the air, as they had seen in the many programs they had been shown at the academy, they wanted to show that they were friendly.

Ari turned to directly face the squad "I am Ari," she declared, staring directly into the eyes of one soldier.

There was a brief moment, a lull, in which silence took over the sound of fighting. And then a single crack, and a whining sound cut through the air. There was a bright flash. Ari turned sideways to see a soldier from the ARC, camouflaged and ready for battle laying on the ground with a bullet wound to his chest. She turned to find some solace in Jace, but he vaporized before her eyes. He was gone. Absolutely and wholly in every respect. He just disappeared.

Her eyes widened in disbelief.

Whatever happened next, there was no chance that she could go back, and nothing would ever be the same. Not now. Not ever. Time had been changed. Ari knew the consequences and her mind was rapidly assessing everything when Tyrion rushed to her side and wrapped his muscular arms around her, both guarding her against any further onslaught and comforting her as they rushed towards the Fùyùn to fly far away from the place that she had last seen Jace, the love of her life.

END OF BOOK ONE.

TO DISCOVER MORE BOOKS BY
SANDI GAMBLE
AND BE NOTIFIED OF
NEW RELEASES, DEALS
AND SPECIALS VISIT:

http://www.sandigambleauthor.com

OTHER BOOKS BY SANDI GAMBLE

'BROKEN'

An Extraordinary Story of Survival by One
of Australia's Forgotten Children.

Be prepared to be shocked. Broken is candid and raw.

When Sandi Gamble heard the Australian Prime Minister on
TV apologizing to 500,000 Forgotten Australians for the abuse
and neglect they had endured as children in "care" in the post-
World War II era, something within her cracked and she began
to cry. The former Magdalene laundry orphanage inmate, who
never felt she fitted in, realized she was a Forgotten Australian.

Thus, began Sandi's journey back to her broken past.

She had to reacquaint herself with Beverley, the girl she had
left behind when she changed her name to Sandi. The painful
memories started flooding in; the memories that held the key
to her life-long struggles with depression, alienation, anxiety,
suicidal tendency, obsessive compulsiveness, and passivity when
dealing with manipulative or authoritative people.

Broken began as a diary to process the memories of the little
girl who was abandoned by her gambling, spendthrift father, and

then her mother. Left at home for hours unattended while her mother worked and drank her misery away, little Beverley was left to her own devices to survive.

This is the story of how one woman faced her shattered past, looking it squarely in the eye. Sandi Gamble shares her story for all Forgotten Australians, their families, and those seeking to be inspired by an extraordinary story.

Australian author Sandi Gamble reveals the struggles and triumphs as one of the many forgotten Australian stories in Australian history.

MORE ABOUT SANDI GAMBLE

*How did you come up with the storyline for Survival Instinct –
Forces of Change.*

For many years the bones of a story floated around my head. You
see I'm great at coming up with ideas for stories, but I'm also
wonderful at procrastinating when it comes to putting pen to
paper. Then one Saturday afternoon I got serious. While sitting
at my computer I decided there was no time like the present,
and I started to lay down the foundations for my novel. The one
that had been rambling around in my head for years was not the
story that appeared on the page in front of me though. However,
that will also be written… 'one day'! The story, the plot and the
characters came to life on the page right there in front of me,
and while I was a little shocked, I loved the concept of this story.
If you had the knowledge to save the world and to save people
from themselves would you do it, and at what cost?

So why write about something like this?

I have always been an avid reader and sometimes believer in
conspiracy theories, and I truly believe that this trilogy will be
a conspiracy theorists dream. Seriously though, why not write
about something like this? Every day our population grows out
of control, we are poisoning the planet and acting like we have
another one to go to. It is horrific, and I hope that by writing it

in a story such as this, that I may be able to pass that message along… if not make the consequences of what is happening, and what our part in that is, just a little clearer for some.

Is this the end of the story or is there more? Survival Instinct – Forces of Change

Yes, it is a trilogy. The story has many components that couldn't possibly be dealt with in one book. Ari is a headstrong, extremely intelligent girl who meets her equal, Jace. Together they question their world and entrust that each other will keep secret what would otherwise be taboo to speak of in their society. To question the Government or any of the rules that they live by, would mean expulsion from their community. However, later in the book when things get out of hand, Ari will be put into a situation that will see her do just that. This will be a journey not only for Ari and Jace but for the reader. I hope you enjoy it.